Copyright © 2025 by Amanda M. Lee

All rights reserved.

No part of this book may be reproduced in any form or by any electronic or mechanical means, including information storage and retrieval systems, without written permission from the author, except for the use of brief quotations in a book review.

FREAKY FESTIVALS
A MYSTIC CARAVAN MYSTERY BOOK 20

AMANDA M. LEE

WINCHESTERSHAW PUBLICATIONS

1
ONE

"What are you doing?"

My husband Kade Denton gave me side eye from the driver's seat of his truck as I contorted to look into the truck in the next lane.

I could've lied, but I, Poet Parker, was a truth teller.

At least with my husband. I had no problem lying to other people if the situation warranted.

Still, I didn't want to own up to my busybody ways.

"It feels like we've been in this truck forever." I stretched my arms over my head and groaned. "Who knew eight hours could feel so long?"

Kade went back to watching traffic. He was a bit high strung behind the wheel—okay, he was massively high strung even when he wasn't driving—and the California traffic wasn't helping.

Normally, when we had two sites in one state, the travel time was a blessing. California was not a normal state. It was big, and even though the distance between San Diego and San Francisco didn't look that great on a map, the hours had started to stretch.

"That's not going to work on me," he said, his eyes drifting down to the dashboard. "Also, we're going to need gas before we get there."

I glanced over to see for myself. "We can make it. We're only an hour out."

"It's better to get gas now."

I grumbled under my breath.

"I heard that," he challenged. "I'm not a mother hen."

"I was just thinking how great it is to have a husband who thinks so far ahead."

"That's not what you were thinking."

Grinning because I'd masterfully redirected him, I asked the obvious question. "What am I thinking?"

"That if you keep talking I'll forget my original question."

My smile disappeared. "I don't know what you're talking about."

"You're trying to distract me. I want to know who you were looking at."

I scowled. How had he managed to read me so well? "I was just..." I broke off, considering, then sighed. "I was trying to see inside Dolph's truck. Now that he and Nixie are a couple, I'm curious."

Dolph was Mystic Caravan's resident strongman. He had a mixture of magic at his disposal, none of it very powerful. His girlfriend—had he ever had a girlfriend before Nixie?—was a powerful pixie from another plane. She looked young but had been around for centuries.

Nixie and Dolph had been nothing but friends for years. Dolph had acted like an overprotective brother as Mystic Caravan—the circus I was in charge of—traveled the country. Now they were together. I had to know more because I had trouble picturing tiny Nixie and huge Dolph doing, well, anything. Gossip and innuendo had been swirling for months, but now it was confirmed.

"What do you think they're doing in there?" Kade asked. "Is she sitting on his lap? Can you see her hands? Are they getting frisky on the highway?"

"No!" That was ludicrous. "I just ... they've been friends forever."

"I remember when we were first dating and got frisky on the highway." Kade almost sounded sad. "Once, we pulled over between Nevada and California and spent a full hour in a rest area." He sent me a flirty wink. "There wasn't much resting taking place if I remember correctly."

He was too cute for his own good sometimes. "I don't recall the incident you're referring to," I offered, embracing the lie when his smile disappeared. I liked messing with him as much as he liked messing with me. I was convinced that was a sign of a healthy marriage. "When did this occur?"

"Don't." Kade shook his head. "That's one of my happiest memories. I won't have you ruining it."

I had to hold back a laugh. "I might need a reminder."

His eyes darted back to me. "What sort of reminder?"

"See what you come up with."

That seemed to excite him. The only rest area we passed after that was closed. He never ran out of gas, so when he found a truck stop to fill up thirty minutes later, the mood had dissipated.

"Tell me your concerns about Dolph and Nixie," he instructed as he rested his elbows on the driver's door, the gas pump steadily churning.

I had gotten out of the truck to stretch. As I grew older, the long rides caused more discomfort than they used to. That was only one of the reasons I was looking forward to moving to Moonstone Bay in a few months. Once there, we wouldn't be traveling between locations. We would have a permanent spot to call our own.

That meant a house—eventually—and a garden. It meant building a sense of community with the locals, who were mostly paranormals. As much as I'd enjoyed our time on the road, I was ready to put down roots. Kade hadn't spent nearly as much time traveling with the circus as I had, but he was ready too. This was a farewell tour of sorts.

"I didn't say I was concerned," I replied as I bent over to stretch my back. "I said I was curious about what they're doing."

"And your mind went to a dirty place."

"I didn't say that."

"You didn't have to. I know how your mind works." He winked to let me know he was joking. "You might look sweet and innocent on the outside but you're a bit of a freak between the sheets."

My mouth dropped open. "That is neither here nor there! I didn't think they were doing *that*." Honestly, that wasn't what I was thinking. Not even a little. "I thought they were holding hands or something."

Kade's eyebrow hiked. "What a bunch of deviants," he teased. "Not hand holding. The horror!"

I rolled my eyes. "I wasn't spying because I thought they were doing something wrong. I was just curious."

He didn't respond.

"I was wondering if they were sweet together," I admitted. "Like, does he send her adoring looks when they're driving? Does he whisper sweet nothings in her ear before they go to bed?" Something weird—or was it frightening?—occurred to me. "Are they wild behind closed doors?"

Kade burst out laughing. "Why do you care?"

I shrugged. "I just do. They're a weird couple."

"People probably thought that about us."

"Why would they think that?"

"Because you're the worldly loa who knows everything about the paranormal world and I'm the inept mage who knows nothing. Because my life until joining Mystic Caravan was completely sheltered. I was always coddled and protected. You jumped from foster home to foster home until you finally lived on the streets. On paper, we shouldn't work."

I didn't know if I believed that. "I think we work great."

"So do I. That wasn't my point. People find each other. Maybe Dolph and Nixie were always meant to find each other."

"Then why didn't they find each other sooner?"

He shrugged. "Do you really think we would've worked if we'd found each other sooner?"

"Why wouldn't we?"

"You needed to soften from being on the streets and I needed to toughen up emotionally. I was a wreck my first tour, adjusting and learning. I think we worked because we found each other at the exact right time."

He had a point. "It's not that I don't want them to work," I said. "They're just so different."

"Maybe that's what works for them. It works for Raven and Percival," he added, referring to the resident lamia and her chaps-wearing clown boyfriend. "It works for Cole and Luke."

My best friend Luke Bishop and his boyfriend Cole Ryan were definitely an example of opposites attracting. Cole was down to earth. Luke had his head in the clouds. Despite their very different personalities, they loved one another without reservation.

"I get it," I said, "but Dolph and Nixie are still weird."

"Because you know them separately. Give it a chance to know them together. They might surprise you."

"They've already surprised me."

He laughed. "This is just the control freak in you."

"I'm not a control freak."

His expression said, "Don't even try that on me."

"I'm not," I insisted. "I'm a control ... minimalist." Was that the right word? "You know what?" I changed course quickly. "I'm perfect. Stop giving me grief."

His grin was the stuff sin was made of. "You are perfect," he agreed. "For me. You need to let Nixie and Dolph decide if they're perfect for each other."

"Yeah, yeah, yeah."

Back on the road, I was determined to change the subject. "We're staying in Golden Gate Park," I said. "Have you ever been there?"

"I was in San Francisco once when I was in the military," he replied, "but not that park." He seemed happy to change the subject, which was a relief. "Tell me what to expect."

"The park is huge. I mean absolutely huge. It has a polo field."

"Get out!" His eyes went wide. "Polo?"

I nodded, amused at how animated he'd grown. "It has a bison paddock."

"With actual bison?"

"No, fake ones."

He wrinkled his nose. "Nobody needs the snark."

Mystic Caravan dealt in paranormals, food, and fun. It also dealt in snark. "Right, because you've never heard me be snarky before." I snorted. "It also has a golf course, an archery range, and a couple of windmills."

"Windmills?"

"They're kind of neat," I acknowledged.

"What about water for Naida?"

Naida, Nixie's sister, was addicted to swimming naked in any body of water we happened to land next to. The smaller the body of water, the more unhappy Naida grew. Luckily for her—and us—she had multiple options in San Francisco.

"There are a few lakes, like North Lake and the water by the angling club at the west end of the park." I warmed to my topic. "It's been years since we've been here, but the beach is on the other side of the highway, and the water is right there, with a great view of the Golden Gate Bridge."

Kade nodded his approval. "She'll have plenty of places to swim."

"She likes to hang out by Alcatraz Island for some reason."

Kade perked up. "Are we going to be close?"

"We'll have to drive to a better vantage point, but it's worth seeing."

"Tell me more." Kade was getting excited. "Tell me about the food."

"Well, we're within a few miles of Chinatown, Nob Hill, and Fisherman's Wharf."

As far as I was concerned, this was the best way to finish our ride to San Francisco. "There's a sea lion viewing area in Fisherman's Wharf. Oh, and this ridiculous mirror maze. As for food, there's the Fog Harbor Fish House and a crab house. There's a pier market and a crepe cafe."

"Which is your favorite?"

I didn't even have to think. "Fog Harbor. It's on the water, and they have a crab menu. Like, they have crab and tomato bruschetta and crab clam chowder."

"Isn't that crab chowder?"

"Not when it has both. They have crab fries and Cajun crab. And garlic-roasted crab." I was getting hungry just thinking about it.

Kade's lips quirked. "Your stomach is already growling."

"Yup. There are the obvious offerings in Chinatown. They're all good. There's this unbelievable steak house in Nob Hill."

"So we'll be going out for every meal." His eyes danced with mischief. "I'm fine with that. There's nothing I love more than watching you ooh and aah over food."

"Nothing?" I challenged.

"Maybe one or two things." He gave me a lascivious wink.

"We'll still hit the grocery store for lunch meat and some breakfast items. In general, if you don't take advantage of the food in San Francisco, you're an idiot."

"Good to know." His smile remained, but he grew more serious. "Tell me about the paranormals."

"There are a lot in San Francisco," I acknowledged. "The merrow population is off the charts. A lot of ghosts too."

"Why ghosts?"

I shrugged. "Depends on who you ask. Some claim it's because of Alcatraz Island and the people who died trying to escape."

"Don't you believe that?"

"Every area has heartbreak," I said. "San Francisco has a rich history of disasters, including three big earthquakes and several big fires. That's on top of the landslides and floods. There was even a tsunami."

"What should we worry about while we're here?"

"In recent years, vampires have taken over portions of SoMa."

"And that is?"

"It's an area south of Market Street. It includes South Beach."

"You wouldn't think vampires would want to hang out in such a sunny area."

"Then there's the Mission District, the Hispanic area in San Francisco. It's one of the oldest neighborhoods in the city. It was built in 1776, and the culture there is out of this world. I head over to check out the markets at least once.

"I remember the first time I visited," I continued. "They had this outdoor market in a park. I spent hours looking at all the crafts and sampling the food. It wasn't long after I joined Mystic Caravan. Everything felt so ... free."

"But?" he prodded.

"There are specific paranormals associated with Latino populations," I replied. "It's not all chupacabras and La Llorona legends."

"So what's the biggest worry while we're here?"

"There are plenty. As great as San Francisco is, it's a hotbed of paranormal activity. We have to keep our eyes open."

He smiled. "I'm excited to explore the city with you. When I was here before, I was with a few guys from my unit. We had fun, but it was all bars and hitting on women."

"Hitting on women, huh?" I wasn't jealous. We'd both had lives before finding each other. Giving him a hard time was fun. "What sorts of women?"

Kade's chuckle was warm. "I can't even remember. You've ruined all memories of other women for me."

That was a load of crap. "You don't expect me to fall for that, do you?"

"Baby, when I was in the military, the whole point of leave was to get my rocks off a few times, cut loose with a few beers, and take a mental break."

"So you were just in it for the sex."

"Pretty much." He looked embarrassed. "It wasn't until you that I realized I wanted more. I had no idea what I was doing back then. I just knew I wasn't in a settling mood. Now, that's all I want.

"I can't tell you how much I'm looking forward to having a house with you," he continued. "I want to be able to sit outside at night and look at the stars. Those things wouldn't have even entered my mind back then."

I recognized the truth because I felt the same way. "I guess we're back to people finding each other at the right time."

"I will always be grateful that I found you when I did. You're what I needed, but I wouldn't have been open to it until then."

"It's kind of nice that it worked out the way it did."

"It's perfect," he agreed. "Just like you."

2
TWO

My best friend Luke was practically dancing when we pulled in front of the trailer Kade and I shared. He grabbed me by the shoulders as I got out of the truck.

"Where have you been?" he demanded.

"What are you talking about?" I pulled away from him and leaned over to stretch. Popping filled the air as my joints cracked. "Man, I am getting old," I complained to Kade.

"You look young and hot to me, baby."

"She has become old and boring since marrying you," Luke complained. "I'm trying to make her fresh and young again. That's why San Francisco is one of my favorite cities."

"It is," I said. "I forgot how much you love this place."

"It's awesome," Luke agreed. "When we move to Moonstone Bay, you and I are going to have to take a few trips here so the city doesn't forget me."

I found I was smiling despite my irritation with him. "I'm sure something can be arranged."

"We can come as a group," Kade said. He was unloading the patio dinette set that we kept between our trailer and the one Luke and Cole shared.

"I don't remember inviting you," Luke fired back, jutting out his chin. "I'll need alone time with Poet."

Kade glared at Luke's back. "Maybe Poet won't want to travel without me. Our goal is to have kids in a few years. She won't want to leave our kids." He looked to me for confirmation. "Right?"

I shrugged one shoulder. "Everything I've learned from television and movies suggests I'll want a break at some point. Leaving them home with Daddy while I go out and have a grand week with Luke sounds fun."

Kade moved his dark gaze to me. "That's hurtful."

Cole chuckled at Kade's hangdog expression. "Imagine a quiet week with just us when they're out of town," he said. "No Luke to irritate everybody. It will be glorious."

"Oh, I see how it is," Luke drawled. "Don't think I'll forget this."

Cole gave his boyfriend a friendly swat on the rear end. Then he turned serious. "There's a liaison from the city here," he said to me. "He was waiting when we arrived. That's why Luke asked what took you so long. He's making everybody nervous."

I followed Cole's finger as he pointed to a thirty-something man in a very expensive suit. He stood off to the side of the action, focused on his phone. As if sensing me staring, he looked up and directly into my eyes.

I smiled and waved. "I'll talk to him." I looked at Kade, who was already arguing with Luke about where the table and chairs belonged. He'd forgotten all about me. I turned to Cole. "Why don't you come with me?"

"Sure." Cole amiably fell into step with me. He waited until we were clear of Luke and Kade to ask the obvious question. "Is there something about this guy we should be worried about?"

"Not that I'm aware of. Some cities occasionally send liaisons. But, as much as Luke loves this city—I do as well—I've found the politicians here to be utter pains in the ass. They're excitable to the extreme and like to follow rules."

"Ah." Cole knowingly bobbed his head. "We're not always great with the rules."

I kept my smile firmly in place as we approached the man. "Hello." I extended my hand. "I'm Poet Parker. I was told you're here from the city."

"From the festival committee actually," he replied. His hand was warm as we greeted each other. "I'm Josh Britton, and I'm in charge of the festival. You've been made aware of it?"

"The basics," I replied, forcing myself to relax. This guy probably just wanted to remind us that we weren't the main attraction. "It's a music festival if I remember correctly. I don't have my file right this second. We just finished the drive from San Diego."

"That is quite a hike." Josh's expression was serious.

"I planned to go through the folder again tonight," I assured him. "We have a few hours of setup to get through, then we'll grab dinner. After that, studying for the festival." That was an out and out lie. I only looked at destination agreements on Mondays.

"Oh, it's fine." Josh waved off my apology. "I'm not here to be a thorn in your side. I just wanted to give you the rundown."

"Of course." I clasped my hands in front of me and waited.

"This is the first year for this particular festival," he explained. "It's the Rock Around the Clock Music and Arts Festival. It's a competition between bands from all over the country. Guests will vote on the best performance and the winner will get a recording contract."

"Nice." I didn't really care who got what, I just wanted this guy to tell me why he was here so I could start plotting with Luke about which restaurant we would grace with our magnificent presence this evening.

"There will be a craft fair," Josh continued. "There will be things for the kids like face painting and rides. No one will be directly on top of you." He smiled, but it was flat. "Are you familiar with our park?"

"Yes," I replied. "We've been here before. Not in this exact location, but we know the general logistics."

"I'll run you through things anyway." Josh's tone was brisk. We were nothing more than a check mark on his to-do list. "The ocean is obviously that way." He pointed west. "If you go to the end of the park, you'll have a nice view."

I nodded because it was expected.

"The closest body of water is Metson Lake. No swimming." He was deadly serious. Now was probably not the time to tell him about Naida's penchant for skinny dipping. It didn't matter anyway. Naida wouldn't choose a tiny lake when she had the ocean at her fingertips.

"The polo field is right over there. You should be able to see it. Just beyond that is the angler's lodge."

"Okay."

"The festival kicks off Thursday, the day you open.

I nodded. He didn't really seem to need me to contribute to the conversation.

"You will see people around the park setting up starting tomorrow. If you have any questions, here's my card." He handed me a business card and smiled expectantly.

I took it, made sure to look at it because that was what anyone else would've done, and then slipped it into my pocket. "We've worked during festivals before," I said. "We know what we're doing."

"Yes, you have quite a reputation," he said, his lips quirking in an odd way.

For the first time since meeting him, he seemed different. What did he mean by the reputation comment? Did he know what we were? I couldn't sense anything magical about him, but if he were, there were ways to shroud himself.

"I hope our reputation is good."

"For the most part," Josh said. "You have a few complaints online. Nothing major. My understanding is that this is your last year on the road."

As far as transitions went, it was jolting. "Um ... yes."

"Someone from a different festival committee wanted to book you for the spring but were informed you will cease traveling in November."

Understanding dawned, and I nodded. "That's true. We're moving to a permanent location at the first of the year. We have a few more stops—Portland, Kansas, another swing through Michigan—and then our life on the road will be over."

"Is that really what you want?"

It felt odd to be having this conversation with a stranger. "As much as we like traveling, it's a changing landscape out there. It's not really cost effective to have so many teams moving us from place to place. In a designated area, we can set up our tents permanently, get rid of the trailers, and purchase homes."

"And have children, I'm sure."

I froze next to Cole. Had he heard the conversation about children? He'd been too far away. Luke was a shifter and even his hearing wasn't that good.

"You look like someone who might want children." Josh pointed to the rings on my finger. He sent Cole a friendly smile. "Your husband is a lucky man."

Cole returned his smile, but it wasn't friendly. "I'm not her husband. I'm head of the midway."

"Oh." Josh didn't look embarrassed despite pretending he was. "I'm sorry. I just assumed. You're a very handsome couple."

"I am married to somebody with the circus," I offered. Why I said the next part, I wasn't sure. "My husband is head of security."

Josh glanced at the trailers, where Kade and Luke were busy shoving one another. "Well ... that seems convenient."

Cole and I exchanged amused looks. Josh was awkward. I couldn't put my finger on exactly what bothered me about him, but there was something. When I tried to get a look inside his head, all I found was anxiety. Apparently, this was the first festival he'd been put in charge of, and he wasn't certain everything was going to come together.

So, maybe there was nothing wrong with him, I told myself as I eased out of his head. Maybe he was just eaten up by anxiety. "I promise we know what we're doing," I volunteered. "You don't have to worry."

"And your animals?" He pointed to the tent at the far corner of our space. People thought we kept live animals there, a tiger, a bear, a wolf. In reality our animals were shifters.

"They won't get loose," I promised him. "I guarantee it. We've never had an animal issue."

Josh blew out a breath. "I did read that about you guys. I'm sorry if I'm being obnoxious. I just want everything to go perfectly. This is a big deal for me."

"It's fine." I meant it. "Everything will go off without a hitch. We're experts."

"Good. Good." He nodded in quick succession. "Well, if you don't need anything else..."

"We're good," I assured him.

"No recommendations for dinner or anything?"

"We've performed here before. We're familiar with the dining options. That's one of the reasons San Francisco is near and dear to our hearts."

"Then I hope you have a lovely time in our fair city."

IT TOOK US MORE THAN TWO HOURS TO UNPACK. Everybody was exhausted and annoyed with one another by the time we finished. Then we had to wait for the sun to set before we could erect the dreamcatcher, a magical device of our own making that protected us from evil while also drawing it to us.

We were monster hunters. Whatever evil happened to be roaming a particular city during our visit, that evil almost always seemed to disappear by the time we were scheduled to leave.

"You're not really going on vacation with Luke and leaving me alone with three kids?" Kade asked as I pulled tight on a dreamcatcher line. Raven had the other end and was pulling just as tight.

"Three kids?" I gave Kade an incredulous look but managed to refrain from tripping as I readjusted. "Who said anything about three kids?"

He shrugged. "I've always imagined us with three kids."

This was the first I was hearing of that. "I thought we agreed on one."

"I never agreed to that."

I emphatically bobbed my head. "One kid and if it's really well behaved, maybe a second."

"Three sounds fun."

He was being unrealistic. "I'm in my thirties."

His forehead creased. "So?"

"We're going to spend at least two years getting settled on Moonstone Bay. I'll be creeping up on thirty-five even if I get pregnant right away."

His expression remained confused, and I was starting to get exasperated with him. "It's harder to get pregnant when you're over the age of thirty-five."

He waved off the statement. "We'll be fine."

"I still want two kids max. If we have too many we won't have time for each other. Is that what you want?"

He gave me a sidelong look. "Not especially. You could have triplets out of the gate."

Now I did trip, but managed to catch myself. "We couldn't handle triplets."

"I'm sure people feel that way all the time."

He was being too much this evening. Way too much. "We'll have one and see how it goes."

"Fine." He scuffed his shoe and sighed.

"Do you want a boy or a girl?" I asked. We'd talked about children before, joked about him being the indulgent father and me being the house rules enforcer.

"Picking is too hard," Kade said. "I can't choose."

"Just tell me."

"Well, on one hand I'd like a son because I imagine us going fishing and camping together. Moonstone Bay will probably have great camping."

As far as I was concerned, our nomadic trailer life was as close to camping as I wanted to get. "You realize a daughter can do those things."

"I'm not being sexist. I want a little girl. I want her to have long dark hair and big blue eyes. I want her to invite me to tea parties."

I made another face. "A boy can have tea parties."

That one seemed to throw him. "Now you're just messing with me," he complained as I snapped the dreamcatcher in place. It briefly flared to life, the magic coalescing, and then disappeared. The scent of pixie dust and loa power was evident in the ether.

I dusted off my hands. "I don't want you getting your heart set on something I can't control."

"Poet, I'm going to love whoever we get. It's just fun to dream."

"What's fun to dream about?" Luke asked as he appeared out of the darkness. "Talking about getting kinky?"

"Kade was making his opinion known about future children."

"Oh, really?" Cole slung his arm around my shoulders as he joined us. "How many kids are we talking about?"

"Three," Kade replied.

"One," I countered. "Maybe two if I don't hate the process with the first one. But there won't be three."

Cole chuckled. "One sounds good to me."

Kade shook his head. "I was an only child, and I was lonely."

"I was an only child and was never lonely," I said. "One is fine."

"Don't argue," Cole chided. "Luke is going to burst if we don't go to dinner now. Besides, even if you have one child, he or she won't be an only child. Luke and I have talked about adopting or maybe getting a surrogate. Our child would essentially be a sibling to yours."

I perked up. "That's a really good idea. We could arrange things so we have the kids for one weekend, and you guys have them the next weekend. That would allow for adult time every other weekend."

"You're really not embracing the idea of parenthood like I was hoping," Kade complained. He looked morose. "I'm going to keep working on you. Eventually you'll see things my way."

"Yeah, good luck with that."

"Food," Luke barked. "Make a decision. I'll die—literally fall down and never get back up—if you don't feed me within the hour."

That was all the motivation I needed to push the children conversation out of the way. "What did you have in mind?"

3
THREE

Luke picked the first place for dinner. It only seemed fair since we'd made him wait so long. Plus, if he didn't get his way, he would turn into a monster, and nobody was in the mood for warring with that particular beast after such a long day.

It was San Francisco, so there was no worry about getting a bad meal. There were too many good places to eat.

We ended up at Fisherman's Wharf—something I was secretly glad about—and settled at Franciscan Crab Restaurant.

"Nice," Cole said as we walked from the parking lot to the restaurant. It resembled a 1950s diner. Blue and red neon strips offset the front, and inside the tables were situated to provide a beautiful view of the water.

"Have you ever been to San Francisco before?" I asked him as we got comfortable at our window table.

He shook his head. "I made it out to the West Coast only once before joining your group. I was always assigned to East Coast and Midwest locations. A few times I went south to Florida and Georgia, but it was mostly New York, Pennsylvania, and Washington D.C."

We'd picked him up in Cleveland of all places and it still made me laugh to think about.

"The menu looks good," Kade noted as he absently rubbed my back. "You love seafood, so I can see why this place was on Luke's list."

The server arrived, a blonde in a high ponytail who smacked her gum as she smiled between us. One look told me she was perky, which sometimes irritated me, but I was determined to be in a good mood tonight.

"Can I start you with drinks?"

I bobbed my head. We'd agreed to drive to dinner, then return to the park so we could walk to a bar for drinks. "I'll have the Upscale Mermarita."

"Fun names," Cole chuckled as he looked at the cocktail list. "I'll have the Arlie's Allure Martini."

Since he was driving, Kade opted for a single beer. That left Luke, who normally made his choices based on names rather than ingredients.

"I'll have the Tattletale Mule," he said finally.

"Any appetizers?" the server asked. "I can get those in while I'm waiting for your drinks."

"Give us the shrimp cocktail, crab and spinach fondue, and calamari," Kade said.

"You got it." The server winked at him—then, for good measure—she winked at Cole as well before taking off.

"Hey." Luke whined. "Why didn't I get a wink?"

"Maybe she thought she'd be wasting her time flirting with you," I suggested as I looked over the menu. "She's not your type, so why go through the extra effort?"

"She's not Cole's type but she flirted with him."

"Maybe she was unsure about Cole." I didn't realize what I'd said until it was too late.

Luke turned huffy in an instant. "Are you saying he could pass for straight better than I can?"

That seemed like a trick question. "What am I supposed to say here?" I asked Cole, legitimately thrown.

His laugh was warm. "It doesn't matter. He's already decided to be offended." Cole gave Luke's shoulder a warm rub. "Women everywhere would assume you were straight if they saw you without me."

It was too late. Luke had no intention of being placated. "Oh, you'll see tonight. We'll pick a bar, then I will wow all the women. They'll be shocked and disappointed when they realize they don't have a chance with me."

"Sounds fun." Cole was unruffled. "I'm getting the World Famous Killer Crab."

I nodded in agreement. "Same here. It's the only thing I've ever ordered here, and I've never been disappointed."

Cole gave me a fist bump, then risked a glance at Luke. "You're going to turn this into a thing, aren't you?" he said when it became apparent Luke continued sulking. "It wasn't an insult. She probably didn't have three winks in her."

"I'm the best looking one here," Luke complained. "You're a close second, but if we were on a runway no one would even notice Kade. How could she not wink at me?"

I cast a sidelong look at Kade to see his reaction. When he'd first joined our group, Luke always aggravated him. Now he seemed to accept my best friend and never let the little things in a life shared with Luke bother him.

"You're the most handsome man at the table," I whispered to him.

"Oh, I know." He grinned. Then he pressed a quick kiss to my cheek. "I'm getting the steak."

"You're getting steak at a seafood restaurant? That's sacrilegious."

He laughed. "While I don't hate seafood, it's not my favorite. Plus, something tells me we'll be eating at a seafood place every night while we're here. I'll get seafood eventually. I'm in the mood for red meat. That drive was long, and I want the protein boost."

"What about you?" Cole asked Luke before he could resume ranting. "What are you getting?"

"A wink," Luke replied. "Before the night is out, I'm going to get eight winks and they're going to be way more glorious than the winks you guys got."

Cole shook his head. "Are these winks going to keep you fortified for drinking later?"

Luke's sigh was long-suffering. "No. The sea bass will do that."

WE WERE STUFFED AFTER DINNER, AND even though Fisherman's Wharf was only six miles from the park it took us almost twenty minutes to get back to our designated lot because of traffic.

"That is one thing I don't like about San Francisco," I admitted as I stretched my arms over my head. "Traffic is a nightmare. I don't think I could live in a city this big because of the traffic."

"I guess it's good we're moving to an island where we won't have vehicles," Kade noted.

"I've been thinking about that," I said. "We'll need golf carts. At least four or five."

"I talked to Galen about that," Kade said as he pocketed his keys. "He said there's no problem getting carts. They're treated like cars on the island. You need a license plate and registration, but that's it."

"Well, when the time comes, we'll figure out how long the wait is and order some, so they'll be there when we arrive."

"We're going to need our own ship to transport everything as it is," Cole said. "We could buy the carts on the mainland—figure out whatever we need to register them from Galen—then transport them with the other equipment. They'll probably be less expensive in Florida."

"Good idea." I slid my hand into Kade's as we started across the street. "Since Luke picked the spot for dinner, Cole can pick tonight's bar."

"Oh, no," Luke complained, adopting a downtrodden expression. "He's going to pick something sporty."

"Why is that a problem?" Cole challenged. "You like sports. In fact, you like boring sports."

"What boring sport does he like?" Kade asked.

"Soccer." Cole made a face. "There's like zero scoring, and it's just people running around on the field."

"I like the shorts," Luke shot back. "I don't like the sport. I like the shorts."

"Yeah, yeah, yeah." Cole waved him off and pulled out his phone. "What's close to the park?" He hummed to himself as he looked. "How does everybody feel about the Little Shamrock?"

I nodded right away. Irish pubs appealed to me.

Kade said he was fine with anything.

Luke pouted. "There won't be a lot of women to flirt with. Find a dance club. Women in dance clubs love me."

"I'll wink at you if it will shut you up," Cole groused.

"You don't count."

"Well, I'm not in the mood for a dance club." Cole was firm. "We spent a lot of time on the road today."

"Ugh." Luke rested the back of his hand against his forehead. "Whatever you want. I live to serve."

I snickered as Cole rolled his eyes. "Let's go to the Irish pub," I said. "Luke, we can find a dance club tomorrow. Everybody is tired."

Luke muttered under his breath. Kade led me toward Lincoln Way. We had to wait to cross, but once we were on the other side of the road, I suggested a quick jaunt around the block to explore other restaurant menus.

Luke perked up—perhaps he thought we'd find a different bar—but I was mostly interested in the restaurants.

"Korean barbecue," Kade noted. "We could do that once the circus opens. It would be quick."

I nodded. He was never picky about food. If he wanted Korean barbecue, I would make it happen. "That sounds good."

"It sounds boring," Luke complained.

Now all three of us ignored him. Cole had even increased his pace to walk with Kade and me. "More seafood," Cole said. "Tartine Inner Sunset is quite the mouthful." He stopped to look at the menu. "Omelets, egg sandwiches, and potatoes if we're in a hurry. Doesn't look like our normal fare, though."

"The Italian place looks good," Kade noted, pointing to Fiorella Sunset.

We walked past a Japanese restaurant, an ice cream shop, and a Mexican place before finding something called The Posh Bagel. Luke seemed to have forgotten he was sulking and was all smiles when he saw it.

"We have to get coffee here at least one morning for the name alone," he insisted.

The sign boasted a cartoon of a butler holding a bagel almost as big as his head, and it made me laugh. "That can be arranged."

"There's another breakfast place," Cole noted, "Art's Cafe." He started across Irving Street without waiting to see if we wanted to turn around and looked at the menu. "Now this looks like our type of breakfast place."

The menu was definitely our style. I nodded, then turned quickly when I heard a scream. I was familiar with city life—I'd spent years on the streets in Detroit after all—and was prepared for whatever San Francisco had to throw at us. I figured it would be a mugger, or a group of younger people having a good time.

Ever since joining Mystic Caravan, my life had been work, friends, and monster hunting. I'd seen every type of paranormal there was. Okay, not *every* type, but I'd heard of most of them. What I saw across 9th Avenue was something straight out of a horror movie.

On the sidewalk in front of a sports bar—Luke would've been appalled if we'd chosen the Mucky Duck for drinking this evening despite the fun name—stood a skeleton in tattered clothes. It followed the screams to the woman emitting them. She was young and dressed for a night out. With her long legs, she looked like a clubbing dream in her sequin shorts and low-cut top. She froze as the skeleton lurched toward her.

We started for the street. Kade grabbed the skeleton by the clavicle just as it cornered the woman in an alcove. He spun the creature until it faced him, then landed a cracking punch.

The skeleton did not respond.

"Go!" Cole barked at the girl as he moved closer to Kade. "*Uro*," he hissed, conjuring blue fire I'd never seen from him. The fire burned hot as it engulfed the skeleton, and the creature went ramrod straight. It exploded and ash flew everywhere.

Caught in a coughing fit, I briefly closed my eyes. When I opened them again, some of the fine ash particles had dissipated, but the air remained hazy. I felt something move in behind me. Expecting Kade, I almost came out of my skin when I found another skeleton going for my neck with its broken teeth.

I called on my loa magic and forced the skeleton to go rigid. A brief glance over my shoulder told me I wasn't in imminent danger, so I took a few seconds to study it.

"What the hell is this thing?" Cole demanded as he leaned close. "Is it a real skeleton that clawed its way out of a grave and decided to go walking around town?"

That was ludicrous, right? And yet just as with the first skeleton, tattered clothing hung from this one. It wore nothing below the waist. If the skeleton had once been a full body and buried, when it started walking there would be no flesh to hold up pants. There was what looked to be the remains of a patterned shirt. The fabric looked like 1970s disco chic.

"It's weird," I murmured.

Kade gave me an incredulous look. "What was your first clue?" He lowered his voice. "Get rid of it. People are starting to come out of the bars."

I detonated the skeleton with magic. Just like the first, ash flew everywhere. There was no shrapnel from which to protect my face.

After another glance to make sure there weren't more, I dropped to one knee to look for a bit of skeleton to take back to the circus grounds. I figured we could use it to run magical tests. There was nothing. Not even a lone finger bone.

Cole must have realized what I was looking for because he was already shaking his head. "How can they explode and leave nothing but ash behind?"

Voices were becoming apparent. More people had been drawn out to look. "We can't talk about it here."

Cole glanced toward the looky-loos, then nodded.

"I haven't found anyone to wink at me yet," Luke complained. "What about our drink?"

"We'll drink with the others at the park," I replied, refusing to let him pout his way into a bad decision. "There are too many people watching us."

"Ugh." Luke rolled his eyes. "I just knew we weren't going to get though a trip to San Francisco without something big happening."

"Just hold it together until we get back to the park." I turned, prepared to cross the road and head back in the direction we'd come from, but the street was being overtaken by official-looking men with flashlights and weapons.

"Oh, crap," Cole said.

"Law enforcement," Kade said grimly.

Cole bobbed his head. "I don't know what department they're with, but that's exactly who they are."

"Well, this isn't good," was all I could manage.

"Not at all," Cole agreed. "In fact, it's very, very bad."

4
FOUR

Dealing with law enforcement was part of the game. Weird things happened around us on a regular basis, and we were constantly questioned in every city we found ourselves in. This group of law enforcement felt different.

"Be careful," Cole warned as the individual in charge—he was barking orders—started walking in our direction.

I nodded. "I know." I didn't have a smile at the ready. A normal person who had come up against skeleton creatures wouldn't be smiling. Instead, I allowed my features to fall into an expression of concern. "Are you the police?" I asked. "Please tell me you're the police." I wanted these officers to see me as a frightened tourist.

"Detective James Jackson," he announced, extending his hand. "I'm with the San Francisco Police Department."

I had no reason to doubt him, and yet that didn't feel like the full story. "I'm so glad you're here," I lied. I would've much preferred we'd escaped before they appeared. "The weirdest thing just happened."

"I saw." Jackson nodded. "You handled it nicely."

Mentioning magic was never a good idea. Strangely, I had the feeling this man would've accepted a magical explanation. "I just hit it. I didn't know what else to do."

"You hit it and it exploded?"

I nodded, allowing my eyes to go wide. "I've never seen anything like it."

Cole stepped in. "I thought it was performance art—you hear about those things in San Francisco—but the one I hit exploded too."

"What was that?" I demanded, my voice bordering on shrill. It was time to put on the performance of a lifetime. "Was it actors? A special effects performance?"

"It wasn't a special effects performance," Jackson replied evenly. "We're not sure what it was. You were close, and we need some information." He pulled out a small notebook and clicked a pen. "First, I need to know who you are."

"Poet Parker," I replied. I didn't offer up any other information. He would have to drag it out of me.

"Are you local?"

I shook my head.

Frustration had Jackson's forehead wrinkling. "Are you a tourist? Here for business?"

"We're with Mystic Caravan Circus," I replied. "We just got in this afternoon. We're at Golden Gate Park all week."

"We're part of the festival," Kade added.

"Right." Jackson bobbed his head. "I didn't realize a circus was going to be involved." He considered it a moment. "In fact, I didn't know there were still circuses in operation. I thought they were all obsolete."

"Not all of them," I replied.

"Where did you come from?" Jackson's tone wasn't accusatory, but he was fishing for information.

"San Diego," Kade replied.

"I was asking your friend." Jackson inclined his head toward me. "I should get all your names if this is going to be a group interview."

"I'm Kade Denton. Poet is my wife."

Jackson continued down the line. "Okay. And you?" He looked at Cole.

"Cole Ryan," Cole replied. "Before joining the circus, I was attached to a special police task force in Cleveland." He volunteered the information as if commenting on the weather. There was a warning attached to the words, though. *We're not going to let you railroad us.*

"Really?" Genuine surprise showed in Jackson's face. "You left law enforcement to travel with the circus?" The judgement regarding that decision was obvious. "Why would you do that?"

Cole gestured to Luke. "You can't help who you fall in love with." That was also a pointed comment. Cole didn't like Jackson. Did he know him? I couldn't ask until we got away from the detective.

"I guess not." Jackson turned to Luke. "And you are?"

"Luke Bishop." Luke extended his hand. He was flamboyant and theatrical most days. When the police got involved, he became the picture of calmness.

"What do you all do with the circus?" Jackson acted as if he was just doing his job, but genuine curiosity bubbled beneath the surface.

"I'm head of security," Kade replied. "Poet is in charge. Cole runs the midway. Luke is something of a jack-of-all trades."

"I'm also the secondary ringmaster," Luke volunteered proudly. "I wear a top hat and tails."

"Awesome." Jackson smiled, but it was flat. I wasn't surprised when his gaze landed on me. "You're in charge of the whole circus?"

"Basically," I replied. "Technically Max Anderson is in charge, but he's partly retired. I handle all day-to-day operations."

"Okay." Jackson licked his lips. "Tell me about your day."

"We left San Diego at six o'clock this morning," Kade started.

"Do you have a bus or something?"

Kade shook his head. "Multiple vehicles. I have a truck. Poet rides with me. Luke has a truck. Cole rides with him. We haul things between locations. Everybody else with the circus has a similar setup."

"What time did you get to San Francisco?"

"About four o'clock," Kade replied. "We made a couple stops along the way, lunch and to get gas. Then we handled our initial setup, which is mostly personal stuff. We have a moving crew that handles the trailers, tents, and midway booths. They unload in our location and we spend the next few days setting up."

"What day does the circus open?"

"Thursday."

"So, three days of setup?"

These didn't seem the type of questions I expected him to ask given the circumstances, but I let Kade take the lead.

"Basically," Kade confirmed. "It's not nonstop setup. We do a decent amount of work every day, but Monday through Wednesday is our weekend. We decompress and get nice meals, relax and enjoy nights on the town. Once Thursday rolls around, we don't have as much time to burn."

Jackson jotted something in his notebook. I couldn't read it, but he acted as if he was marking items off a list. "What happened after you unpacked?"

"I can't speak for the rest of our group, but when we were finished, we headed to Fisherman's Wharf for dinner."

"Where?"

He was going to chase the information. He didn't trust us.

"The Franciscan Crab Restaurant."

"Nice choice. What about after?"

"We parked in the lot next to the circus and walked here," Kade replied. "We wanted to see our options for breakfast and other meals once the circus opened. We were going to get a drink at the Irish pub but decided to look around first."

"You were out for an evening stroll when all of this occurred?" Jackson looked dubious.

"We were just looking around," Kade confirmed.

"What drew your attention to this specific area?"

"Screaming," Cole replied. "There was a woman, she was sort of backed in the corner right here. She screamed, and we thought she was being mugged or something. We ran over to help and found a..." He trailed off.

"You found what?" Jackson prodded.

Cole held out his hands. "I don't know how to describe it," he replied. "It was a skeleton."

"It was like something straight out of a horror movie," Luke added. "I can't speak for everybody else, but I was convinced it wasn't real. Like it was a robot, or some sort of visual trick."

"So you decided to punch the skeleton?"

Luke shrugged. "I didn't punch anything. I would've if I'd been closer. What else were we supposed to do?"

"I have military training," Kade volunteered. "Cole has extensive law enforcement training. Throwing punches seemed the way to go."

Jackson smiled, his gaze bouncing between us, looking for something. Ultimately, he clicked the pen again to hide the tip. "Okay. Thank you for your time."

That was it?

He turned to walk away. "Wait." I touched his wrist, freezing him in place as he turned. I didn't have time to dig as deep as I wanted with the other officers so near. I dove into his mind. There was so much I wanted to explore—was that a chupacabra hiding in the corner of his memory space?—but I couldn't drag it out. I unfroze him quickly and took a step back.

"Do you need something?" Jackson asked, his expression quizzical.

I shook my head. "No. Sorry. I just ... I was hoping you could tell me about those skeletons."

"I don't know." He shrugged. "We might need to follow up. We know where to find you." With that, he headed off to where the other officers were questioning witnesses.

"What do you think?" Cole asked.

"Let's head back," I replied. I couldn't talk freely until we were away from the crowd. We crossed together and headed down 9th Avenue. We remained silent until we were a block away.

"What did you see?" Kade asked.

"They're a paranormal unit," I replied, turning to Cole. "They know a lot about the paranormal world."

"Do they know we're paranormal?" Cole asked.

"He didn't seem to. He's a little suspicious of us, but not because he thinks we're magical. He seems to have some deep-seated prejudice regarding the circus. He thinks we're all grifters and thieves."

"I kind of thought that before I learned the truth," Cole admitted. "Circuses don't have the best reputations."

"I wish I'd had more time to look through his head, but I couldn't risk it."

"What did you see?" Luke asked. "Did you see more skeletons?"

"They've heard reports, but he hasn't interacted with any of them."

Luke pressed further. "Does he know about shifters? What about vampires?"

"He knows. There was also a really weird chupacabra."

"Interesting," Cole mused.

"What do we do?" Kade asked.

"We warn the others to be careful. I have a feeling Jackson isn't done with us. As for the skeletons, I don't know." I glanced around. The Irish bar was in sight. "I'm still up for that drink if you guys are. I might not sleep if I don't relax a bit."

"I'm definitely up for that," Cole agreed. "Let's drink."

"I still need to get my winks," Luke added.

TWO HOURS LATER I WAS A BIT tipsy. Not so much I would have a hangover the next day, but I giggled as Kade chased me from the bathroom to the bed. He was feeling romantic—which shouldn't have been possible given the things we'd seen—but our lives were not normal.

"Are you ready to be romanced?" he asked as he pulled me to him.

"In a minute," I replied.

He cuddled me against his side. "Do you want to talk about it first?"

"About having sex? I'm not in the mood for that conversation."

He made a face. "That's not what I mean and you know it."

I sighed. "It's weird, right?" I asked after the silence had stretched.

"The skeletons? Yeah. You're more worldly in that department than I am."

"I wasn't actually talking about the skeletons. I was talking about the paranormal unit."

Kade scratched the stubble on his cheek. "I know you didn't get a chance to look around long when you tried to read him. What else did you see?"

"I don't think he's paranormal. I can't be certain, but I didn't see anything in there to suggest he was. But he could've realized I was paranormal and hidden the good stuff. Maybe he didn't want me to see the truth."

I traced my fingers over his chest. "I saw flashes of memory. They were fast, and I didn't have time to dwell on them. I saw him with a vampire. He staked it like a scene straight out of *Buffy the Vampire Slayer*."

Kade's eyebrows hiked. "Seriously?"

"I saw some shifters in there. He didn't kill them. They're informants. Is that the word?"

"You mean when a police officer arrests someone and instead of charging them makes them hand over information?"

"Yes."

"That's the correct word."

"There are several shifters under his thumb. They share information with him. What I saw was skewed by his perception, but he believes two are giving him everything they have. The third he's not so sure about. He's looking to dig up more dirt on that guy."

"Did you get names?"

"I didn't have time."

"It's okay." He kissed my forehead. "What else?"

"They know something's going on. There have been complaints regarding the skeletons. They've yet to actually find one. That frustrates him.

"He's not certain he could capture it. He's prepared to kill it himself—and he's heard of multiple ways to kill them, including fire—but he desperately wants to see one with his own eyes."

"Anything else?"

"Just flashes of him arguing with his boss, who isn't a true believer. How his boss got put in charge of a paranormal unit is a mystery to Detective Jackson. He has no respect for his boss and often feels as if he's beating his head against the wall interacting with him. He seems like a guy trying to get answers."

"Is he a threat to us?"

"Unless he's the best faker ever, he doesn't suspect us of being paranormal. Thieves and grifters? Absolutely. He even made a mental note to run Mystic Caravan through the system to see if we have any sexual deviants on the payroll."

Kade scowled.

"It's to be expected. That's why we're so stringent when hiring. We don't want any red flags when the police inevitably look at us."

"Right." Kade pursed his lips. "What do you want to do about him?"

"For now, there's nothing we can do. We need to wait to see what he does." I knew we'd see Jackson again. "He'll be back."

"What will he think when he sees the rest of our group?"

"Hopefully, it will reinforce his assumption that we're all grifters. I prefer he focus on the superficial."

He was quiet for several seconds, contemplative. Then he did exactly what I expected. "Have we been adult enough for one evening? Can we get to the romance now?"

I barked out a laugh. "Romance sounds good."

There was a wolfish glint to his eyes when he shifted again. "Finally, something I actually want to do."

"You'd better put that steak to good use. I'm expecting big things this evening."

"I aim to please."

5
FIVE

When I woke the next morning, things didn't feel as they had the night before. Sure, skeletons running around wasn't good, but they went down fairly easily. Unlike with zombies, I very much doubted bites could cause people to turn into skeletons, so we had that going for us.

Kade and I showered together—he was still feeling frisky—and then joined the others at the picnic area. Nobody was cooking breakfast.

"Cole said you wanted to talk," Raven Marko said. "He said we couldn't leave until you filled us in on a problem."

I cast Cole a sidelong look. "You could've told them."

He shrugged. "You're in charge." He looked happy. Monday in the circus world was a good day.

"Something happened last night," I started, launching straight into the tale. It took longer than I thought because I had to explain about the paranormal unit.

Nelson "Nellie" Adler swore under his breath. The warm weather in San Francisco meant he was dressed in a spaghetti strap dress, his wiry chest hair peeking out at every angle. "That's the last thing we need."

I held out my hands and shrugged. "It's not good. Everybody needs to be careful."

Nixie, who was seated next to Dolph, their thighs pressed together, stirred. "Will they be watching us?" she asked.

I shook my head. "That seems unlikely, but we have to be careful."

"We could extend the dreamcatcher," Raven suggested. "We could erect an outer ring that alerts if anyone tries to get close enough to spy."

"If they really want to watch us and avoid detection, they'll plant themselves in a windmill and put a telescope on us. They'll record everything we're doing. They don't have to be on top of us to spy."

"Then what's your suggestion?" Raven challenged.

"We have to be careful. That means you walk to the beach and strip there when you're going skinny-dipping," I ordered Naida. "That means no shrinking humans to dolls here period," I added for Nixie's benefit. "That means no beheading monsters," I said to Nellie.

"Ugh." Nellie threw up his hands. "And here I thought San Francisco was supposed to be fun."

I had to hold back a laugh. If I gave in to my urges, that would only encourage him. "We're just random people running a circus," I insisted. "He's already prejudiced against us. He thinks we're grifters."

"He's hardly the first," Raven said. "I can live with being looked at as a grifter. The other stuff..." She shook her head. "Tell us more about the skeletons."

"There's not much to tell. The closest approximation I can come up with is zombies."

"Do they spread anything with bites?" Raven was all business. "You said they looked as if they wanted to bite the woman."

"I don't see how that would work. The bacteria in the mouth spreads the infection for zombies. The skeletons had no flesh."

"That doesn't mean it can't be magically spread," Naida argued. "It could be a spell of some sort."

"Everybody needs to keep their eyes and ears open," Cole said. "No overt magic. Don't do anything weird." He cast Nellie a derisive look. "Do whatever you want as long as it indicates we're human."

"That's no fun," Nellie lamented.

"We do not want to get on this paranormal team's radar," Cole insisted. "That could be bad for all of us. Poet only got a brief glimpse inside this guy's head, but what she saw should be enough to freak all of us out."

"He wants to get his hands on one of those skeletons," I supplied. "He wants to experiment on it."

"Which means he wouldn't have any qualms about experimenting on us," Raven said. "We have to be prepared to modify his memory." Now she was talking to me. "If he does stumble upon the truth, we have to be ready to move fast."

I nodded in agreement. "That means potions," I said to Nixie. "We need to have them at the ready in case he has people with him. I can do it with magic, but we all know it's easier—and longer lasting—with potions."

"I have two," Nixie replied. "You're right about us needing more in case he has his men with him. I'm out of supplies, so I need to find a magic store."

Kade had his phone out. "There's something called the Twisted Thistle Apothecary near Masonic Avenue and The Love of Ganesha a few blocks away."

"You don't have to worry about me finding supplies here," Nixie said on a laugh. "There are a lot of options. I'll be fine."

"*We'll* be fine," Dolph corrected. "I'll go with you."

Nixie smiled at him, her expression soft and flirty. Dolph smiled back.

Because we were jerks, everybody let loose an annoying "aw" at the same time.

"Shut up," Dolph snapped, glaring at all of us in turn.

Everybody laughed.

"You're not funny," he snapped.

"It's okay, Pooky Bear," Nixie assured him, rubbing his arm. "They'll get over the teasing eventually."

"I won't," Nellie countered. "You stole my wingman."

Nixie sent him a dark look. "You'd better get over it."

"I'm good." Nellie shook his head. "You won't ruin my fun, girlie."

ONCE THE WARNINGS HAD BEEN spread, I headed to breakfast with Kade, Cole, and Luke.

Art's Cafe had a folksy feel, including a long counter where regulars sat and regaled each other with stories while sipping coffee and shoveling eggs and hash browns into their mouths.

The table we sat at had fun postcards under the vinyl top. They looked to have been collected from various locations, including Holland, Buckingham Palace, and Aruba.

"Good morning," a harried server said as she arrived at our table. She had a pen tucked behind her ear and wisps of gray hair escaping from a haphazard bun. "I'm Bea. I'll be your server. Can I start you with something to drink?"

"Coffees all around," Kade replied. "I'll have a grapefruit juice and water too."

"Waters all around," Cole added. "I'll have an orange juice, please."

"Cranberry juice for me," Luke added.

Since I didn't see tomato juice on the menu, I asked for orange juice.

Conversation was limited during Bea's absence. When she

returned, she was all business. "Do you know what you want?" she asked.

Because they fancied themselves gentlemen, my breakfast companions deferred to me.

"I'll have two eggs over medium, hash browns, whole wheat toast, and bacon, please." I sent her my winningest smile, but she was unmoved.

"I'll have the Hot Link Scramble with hash browns and whole wheat toast," Cole said.

Bea was a little softer with him, but not by much. "And you?" she prodded Luke. "Before you even open your mouth, know that we don't like a lot of modifications. Stick to the menu."

Luke was affronted. "What makes you think that I'm going to ask for modifications?"

"You have a certain look about you."

"I think I should be offended." Luke grumbled, then tapped the menu. "I'll have the Turkey with Avocado omelet with hash browns and an English muffin."

Bea turned her attention to Kade. "And you, handsome?" Now she smiled.

"Unreal," Luke complained. "If she winks at him, I really will never get over it."

Kade smiled at Bea as if she was the only woman in the world. He liked messing with Luke as much as the rest of us. "I'll have the Chef's Special omelet with hash browns and wheat toast. Thank you very much."

Bea took our menus and nodded. "Sure thing, handsome." Then she winked.

Luke glared in her wake. "What the hell is happening? The entire world has joined together to mess with me."

"We have," Cole said. "That's how much we love you."

To pass the time while waiting for our food, our conversation naturally turned to the skeletons. "I wish we knew more about the ones that have been seen throughout the area," I said.

"Are you talking about the skeletons?" a woman one table over asked, unabashedly eavesdropping on us.

"Yes," I replied. "We saw two last night. The cops weren't able to tell us very much."

"That's because the cops are hiding it." The woman shifted to face us. The man sitting across from her looked friendly enough, but it was impossible to hide his eye roll. He believed his breakfast partner was a bit of a kook. Given what we were dealing with, a kook was just what we needed.

"Why are they hiding it?" Cole asked. He recognized exactly what the woman was, and just like me, wanted to take advantage of the situation.

"They don't want anyone to know the truth." Her eyes sparkled. "If people knew, they'd panic. It would be a scene straight out of *The Walking Dead*."

"Molly," her boyfriend—he was obviously her boyfriend because only someone getting regular sex could look that exasperated and affectionate at the same time—growled. "Don't tell them your whackadoodle theory."

"It's fine," I assured him, offering up a different sort of smile. "We want to hear the whackadoodle theory." I decided to fully embrace the zaniness. "We love a good story, and after what we saw last night..." I cast a heavy look in Kade's direction so Molly would think I was just like her. "Let's just say I have a lot of questions. The cops weren't helpful at all."

"They never are," Molly agreed. "This is my boyfriend, Justin. He thinks I'm nuts. I've been tracking the skeleton thing for weeks now."

"Weeks?" I had to keep my expression neutral. "This has been going on for weeks?"

"It started at Mission Dolores Cemetery," she said.

Kade had his phone out and was typing. He knew as well as I did that the history of the cemetery was important. "It's considered the oldest cemetery in San Francisco," he said. "This is interesting. It says here that it's one of only a number of cemeteries remaining in San Francisco. It was once part of a much larger cemetery." His brow creased. "What happened to the other cemeteries?"

Justin had the answer.

"All of San Francisco's cemeteries were moved to Colma," he explained. "The city banned burials in 1900 because there wasn't enough room. I believe there were some health concerns because the city was so dense. The land is too valuable to waste on a cemetery."

"Wait." Cole extended his hand. "I never knew that. What happened to the bodies that were already buried?"

"Depends on who you talk to." Justin's shoulders hopped. "Some people swear all the graves were moved."

"There's no way." Cole shook his head. "That's a very labor-intensive effort."

"Most people agree." Justin's grin resembled a grimace. "A lot of the graves were just ... left there."

"And buildings were erected on top of them?" I demanded, horrified at the thought.

Justin nodded.

I glanced over at Kade for confirmation. It wasn't that I didn't believe Justin. It was just too horrible to think about.

"This article states that by 1900, all the cemeteries were filled and not being taken care of," he said. "I guess more than 150,000 bodies were moved, and it's estimated that between 50,000 and 60,000 bodies were left behind."

That was dumbfounding. "What about the headstones?"

"Old headstones were destroyed and recycled. Families were contacted and asked if they wanted to pay a fee to move their loved one's grave." He wrinkled his nose. "Oh, this is gross. If the families couldn't be found or said they couldn't afford it, the bodies were moved to a mass grave."

"Well, that's respectful," I muttered sarcastically.

He shrugged. "Supposedly a bunch of the remaining bodies are under the University of San Francisco and residential neighborhoods."

I was appalled. "So weird." I shook my head. "Why was this Mission Dolores Cemetery spared?"

"It doesn't say."

I focused on Molly. "Do you know?"

"No. Sorry." She was solemn. "I just know that's where the skeletons were first seen. They crawled out of their own graves."

I waited for her to continue. When she didn't, I had to prod her. "Then what?"

"They've been seen all over town," Molly replied. "The sightings are growing in number. People say it's a reckoning."

"For moving the graves?"

"That and all the sin in San Francisco. I can't answer that question because I don't know." I thought she was done, but then she lowered her voice to a conspiratorial whisper. "But you know what I heard yesterday?" She didn't wait for me to respond. "I'm not sure if it's true, but it kind of makes sense."

"What?"

"People are saying the skeletons were the victims of the city's Committee of Vigilance."

That meant absolutely nothing to me. "I'm not sure what that is," I hedged.

"They cropped up in more than one city because of the population explosion in certain areas," Justin volunteered. "I was a history major." His grin was quick. "I know a little about this stuff."

"What did the Committee of Vigilance do?" Cole asked, looking as if he already dreaded the answer.

"Well, according to the reports of the time, the population grew from 900 to 20,000 so rapidly that law enforcement couldn't keep up," Justin explained. "That led to groups of vigilantes forming to handle crime. They hung people and forced elected officials to resign. Each committee lasted a few months before relinquishing power."

"When was this?" I asked.

Justin screwed up his face as he thought. "I believe it was 1851 and 1856. I know they were five years apart."

"And their victims ended up in this cemetery?"

He bobbed his head. "They called themselves purifiers. There were claims of racism. I remember the case of a victim the group admitted they didn't have proof of guilt but hanged him anyway.

"The first committee executed four people and openly claimed they were working in defiance of the government," he continued. "The second committee executed several people too. They also instilled their own government after the fact. It was called the People's Party. Supposedly the vigilantes were against political abuse of power, but they simply established their own political abuses."

"That's how it usually works," Cole added. "Where else have the skeletons been seen?"

"All over," Molly replied. "They're more concentrated in Hispanic areas."

"Is there a reason for that?" I asked.

"I've heard people mention Dia de Los Muertos a few times. They say it's the Day of the Dead come to rule us all."

Conversation with the other table dwindled when our food arrived, and I waited until Molly and Justin had left to give my opinion on the subject. "There are plenty of Hispanic paranormal legends. Maybe we should do our grocery shopping at one of the Spanish markets."

Cole agreed. "No offense to Molly—I actually liked her—but she seems the type to fall for any story. As interesting as I find the vigilante stories, I can only find a record of eight people being killed. If skeletons are being sighted all over town, we're talking a lot more than eight."

"Those skeletons would be so old there would be nothing holding them together," Kade argued.

"Well, that's true of all skeletons," Cole said.

"Magic is holding them together," I said. "Magic is causing them to rise ... if they are rising."

"What's the other possibility?" Cole challenged. "If they're not digging themselves out of graves, where are they coming from?"

"Maybe they're not real skeletons and were never people. Maybe they're being conjured out of thin air and set on the town."

"To what end?"

"That's what we have to figure out." I finished my juice. "We don't need a lot of stuff this go-around, but we still have to stock up on the basics. One of the Spanish markets will easily fit our needs."

"Then let's head to the market," Cole said. "I'm as curious as you to find out what's going on here. I'm not particularly afraid of the skeletons—they were easy enough to dispatch—but whatever is controlling them is another story. There's something else out there."

6
SIX

We picked a market northeast of Golden Gate Park. I didn't want to waste a lot of time shopping—especially since we didn't need a lot of food this go-around—and this seemed like as good a place as any.

It wasn't a supermarket by any stretch, but it did have a nice produce section as well as a deli counter.

"What do we need?" Kade asked. "Do we want eggs and everything for breakfast?"

I shook my head. "Everybody likes to hit up the breakfast places here. Even on performance days, people still go out for breakfast. We need stuff for quick lunches."

"Lunch meat, cheese, bread, and condiments," he guessed.

I nodded. "And lettuce, tomato, onions, and sandwich pickles."

"We should grab some pasta salads and potato chips," Cole suggested.

"And maybe two boxes of cereal for breakfast in case somebody doesn't feel like going out," I added. "One high-sugar option for Nellie and Dolph. One healthier option for everybody else."

"Got it." Kade gave me a wink, which made Luke groan. "I wasn't even trying to irritate him, but I got lucky," he whispered to me before giving my butt a light swat and heading off toward the bread aisle.

I watched him go, caught between laughing and rolling my eyes.

"He and Luke are adopting a brotherly relationship," Cole noted.

"Is that how brothers really get along?" I was honestly curious.

"Yup. It's better than Luke's constant jealousy about the time you two spend together, isn't it?"

"I can't decide."

Cole laughed. "He's settling into adulthood. He'll never lose the part of him that is so thoroughly Luke, but he's not as bad as he used to be."

I narrowed my eyes. "You didn't even know him when he was really bad. He'd already started maturing by the time he met you."

"I've heard stories and seen the photos." Cole slung his arm around my shoulder. "What's bugging you?"

He always knew. Kade could pick up my moods, but Cole was a master. It was fascinating, especially because I hadn't particularly liked Cole when we first met. That was my magic reacting to his, but now I couldn't imagine my life without him. My friendship with him was different from the one I shared with Luke, but the bonds were just as strong.

"How do you know something is bugging me?" I asked.

He laughed as if I'd said the funniest thing in the world. "I know you, and you're troubled."

"These skeletons have been running around the area for weeks."

"Do you believe what Molly said at breakfast? That they originated in the cemetery she mentioned?"

"It's not that I think she's lying," I said.

"She's excitable," Cole supplied. "She's the type who believes any story she hears."

"That's not necessarily a bad thing."

"It's not good. She wouldn't ask the critical questions necessary to get to the truth."

I stopped pushing the cart and turned to face him. "If these skeletons have been around as long as she says, rumors and myths are already building. We might never know the truth of where they started."

The words were barely out of my mouth when a teenage girl popped around the end cap of the aisle and fixed me with a wide-eyed stare. "Are you talking about the skeletons?"

My mouth dropped open. I hadn't realized anybody was listening to us.

"Who are you?" I demanded before thinking better of my aggressive approach.

"Elena," she replied. "Who are you?"

"Poet." Now that I'd caught my breath, I realized that a teenage eavesdropper was better than the alternative.

Elena couldn't have been older than seventeen. She had rounded cheeks, big brown eyes, and long brown hair to her waist. She wore the typical teenage attire of the day, a belly-baring shirt and short shorts with fringe. The shorts were so short the pockets peeked out from beneath the fringe. Her pink toenails were prominent around the thong in her flip flops and she had a henna tattoo on her calf.

"Poet isn't a real name," Elena said. "Unless..." Her eyes widened. "Were your parents hippies?"

"I'm not sure what you mean by that," I admitted when I was certain I wouldn't burst out laughing and alienate the girl.

"My grandparents were hippies. They tell stories. Apparently, they went to a place called Woodstock in the olden days."

"I believe Woodstock was 1969," Cole countered. "I don't know that I'd consider that the 'olden days.'"

Elena grew incredulous. "That was fifty-six years ago. How is that not the olden days?"

Cole opened his mouth, then shut it. "You know what," he said finally. "You make an interesting point. That sort of *was* the olden days."

"Totally," Elena agreed. She moved closer to me, her eyes taking in my silver necklace. It boasted a veve as a pendant, the mark of Maman Brigitte, my great-great-however many greats-grandmother. It was a series of lines and crosses. Brigitte's symbol also included a heart. "That's cool. Are you into voodoo?"

I was knocked off kilter again. "You're familiar with voodoo?"

"We're Catholic," was Elena's simple reply.

"I'm not sure I understand."

"Voodoo has some roots that cross into Catholicism. I like to research religions when my mother starts arguing that I need to spend more time in church. Like, I'll look up as many atrocities that were done in the name of religion as possible just to make her mad."

I didn't know what to make of that. Elena was an odd but interesting girl. "New Orleans is one of my favorite cities. I have a great love for the voodoo culture." I was the first of the new loa order, so that was kind of true. There was no way I could tell her that Baron Samedi and Maman Brigitte—along with a whole slew of other loas—were real.

"Do the skeletons have something to do with voodoo?" Elena asked. "I heard you talking about them. That's all anyone talks about in this neighborhood."

I wanted Elena to think she was talking to a friend, not a strange woman in the market. "Do you live in this neighborhood?"

"Yup. This is my abuelo's market. I help him when I'm not in school."

"It's a very nice market."

Elena shrugged. "It's their way of keeping me from hanging out with the boys. My mamá says that I'm an accident waiting to happen. My older sister had a baby before she got out of high school. My parents don't want the same thing to happen to me, so I get to work here and stay out of trouble." Her expression told me her opinion on that subject.

"You'll be glad for it when you get a little older," I promised. "Have you seen the skeletons?"

Elena nodded. "They come at night."

"Only at night?" Cole asked.

Elena gave him a sidelong look, as if sizing him up, then she sighed. "You're gay." It wasn't a question, and her disappointment was palpable.

"I am," Cole confirmed. "Do you have a problem with that?"

Elena shook her head. "People should love who they love. I'm just bummed because you're hot."

Cole chuckled. "Sorry to disappoint. I'm way too old for you anyway."

"I like older men."

"Have you actually seen the skeletons?" I pressed before their conversation could continue. "We saw some last night."

Elena turned serious in an instant. "Where?"

"By the Mucky Duck."

"I heard about that. They say the cops were there fast, but it was still too late."

"We saw the police. They seemed interested in catching one of the skeletons."

Elena's snort was full of disdain. "They'll never catch one. Those things are designed for maximum destruction. They blow themselves up if they think someone might grab them."

"They blow themselves up?" I thought about the fine dust particles that remained after hitting the skeleton with my magic. Perhaps that didn't happen because I was such a badass after all.

"Yeah. They try to bite and kill people, but when they're outnumbered, they blow themselves up."

"How long have they been in this neighborhood?" Cole asked.

"Weeks." Elena held her hands palms out. "More than a month."

"Do you remember the first story you heard?" Cole knew exactly how to use his law enforcement background. He was a master at eliciting information.

Elena lifted one shoulder. "We were at one of the reunions. They're kind of what old people like you would call block parties."

I exchanged an amused look with Cole. We weren't *that* old. "What did they say?"

"They said skeletons were seen outside the cemetery. My family helps keep up the cemetery. They say it's our responsibility because we have family there."

I nodded to get her to continue.

"They have a lot of ideas," she said. "My mami and papá believe it's La Llorona."

I stilled. "La Llorona?"

"Do you know who she is?"

I licked my lips and glanced at Cole. "Vaguely," I replied. "I know the legend."

"What's the story?" Cole asked.

"It's the legend of the weeping woman," I explained. "She's a vengeful ghost in Mexican folklore who is said to roam near bodies of water mourning her children, who she drowned in revenge against her husband for cheating."

Elena nodded. "If you hear the cry of La Llorona you'll be hit with a string of bad luck and die."

Cole pursed his lips. "What does that have to do with the skeletons?" he asked.

Elena shook her head. "There are no skeletons in the original legend. That's why it doesn't make sense."

"Are they talking about anything else?" I asked. I had trouble believing La Llorona had anything to do with this. If she was real. In our line of work, we couldn't rule something like that out.

"The other one I've heard tossed about is El Charro Negro."

"I'm not familiar with that legend," I said.

"I am." Cole flashed a smile for Elena's benefit. "El Charro Negro roughly translates to the black cowboy. He's a legendary figure in Mexican folklore who I believe appears as a cowboy wearing all black."

Elena nodded encouragingly. "He's the ghostly horseman of death. He symbolizes the dark side of the human soul. He's supposed to be very handsome." Elena winked at Cole, making me glad Luke was otherwise engaged. "He dresses very well, like a fancy cowboy."

"A dandy," Cole volunteered. "He's often described as elegant."

Nothing about the skeletons could be considered elegant. That didn't mean all legends were right. I'd learned that firsthand when being introduced to Baron and Brigitte. Some things could be true and others exaggerated.

"The story I always heard growing up was that he comes at night," Elena started.

"Like the skeletons," I said.

She nodded. "He tempts people. He makes them offers but he's really bargaining for their souls."

I frowned. That sounded exactly like a certain loa I knew. Papa Legba offered people riches beyond their wildest dreams and took their souls in trade. By the time they realized, it was too late. "Okay," I nodded. "What does that have to do with the skeletons?"

"Nothing that I'm aware of." Elena was rueful. "When my abuelo told me bedtime stories, he often mentioned El Charro Negro. He said that he appeared on the street after dark with a bag of coins. He shook it, and the people who were attracted to the sound were those who could easily lose their souls. He said it was a lesson about something sounding too good to be true."

"But there were never any skeletons in the legend?" I pressed.

"No."

"Then why are people associating the skeletons with him?"

"They're afraid," Elena replied simply. "When it was just a rumor about skeletons escaping from the cemetery, everyone laughed. But the stories have been ramping up for weeks. People have seen them. They take over the streets. You can see them from the windows. They don't try to enter our houses, but they go after anyone out after dark."

"Have they killed anyone?"

Now Elena looked afraid. "They eat people."

"They completely consume them?"

"They chew on them until they're dead. Then they leave them in a pool of blood and move on."

"What do you think they want?" Cole asked.

"I don't know. Everyone is afraid. We don't have bonfires and street parties any longer. We don't have Sunday potlucks. Everyone is locked down at dusk. My abuelo isn't even keeping his market open until seven like he used to. He doesn't want to risk it."

"What about the police?" I pressed.

"They come sometimes, but it's not just our neighborhood."

The next question I had was tricky, but I had to ask. "Elena, you live in a Hispanic neighborhood, correct?"

She nodded.

"All the other attacks you've heard of, have they been in Hispanic neighborhoods too?"

"It started that way," she replied, "but now they're everywhere. And there are more and more coming. I think they're going to kill us all."

We talked to Elena for a few more minutes, then checked out with our haul. I waited until we were in Kade's truck on our way back to the park to speak.

"Do you think she was right about it starting in Hispanic neighborhoods?" I asked Cole. "That could be a clue."

Cole tapped his fingers on the armrest as he stared out the window. "It's possible. It's also possible that she's only hearing the stories from her neighborhood. It sounds as if her family keeps a tight leash on her."

"And she's bitter about it," I said. "If they're not careful, they're going to chase her away. The kid needs to breathe."

"She's too scared to leave now."

"If this was an isolated incident, maybe the skeletons were being used to scare one sector of the city into behaving."

"That's not what we're dealing with," Cole said.

"This is bigger. I'm interested in the fact that the skeletons self-destruct if they start losing. Someone doesn't want their skeletons studied."

"Because that might lead to a way to destroy them all."

I rubbed my forehead. "Maybe we can come up with a spell to stop the skeletons from self-destructing."

"You want to get your hands on one."

"Do you have a better idea?"

"No, but if we keep them from self-destructing how will the neighborhoods band together to protect themselves?"

"We have to make sure it works on one skeleton."

"How are we going to find one?" Kade asked. "We lucked into seeing them last night."

"We have to figure it out fast. We have less than a week, and then we're out of here. We can't leave these people to the skeletons."

"I'm not as worried about the skeletons as I am about whatever controls them," Cole admitted.

7
SEVEN

As we unloaded the groceries, everybody was working. They wanted to get through all of their daily tasks before heading out to enjoy the wonders of San Francisco. Kade and Luke walked to the Big Top, and Cole headed for the midway. That left me at loose ends, and there was only one thing I could think to do.

Raven's House of Mirrors needed little setup. We magically protected the mirrors for the move so there was nothing to do but give the space a dusting when we reached a new location. Raven was doing exactly that, a roll of paper towel at her feet as she sprayed the mirrors.

"I don't like that face," she said when she saw me, clucking her tongue and shaking her head. "What's up with you?"

"I want to use your computer," I replied. "I need to research San Francisco's haunted history."

Her brow creased. "What's wrong with your computer?"

"It gave up the ghost last week. I ordered a replacement that will be ready at the Apple Store tomorrow. I have my phone, but right now and I need a bigger screen."

"Knock yourself out." Raven abandoned her work and followed me to her office. "What are you looking for exactly?"

"I'm not sure." As I got comfortable at her desk, I told her about our breakfast conversation, and then about what Elena told us at the market.

"I don't see how this could have anything to do with La Llorona or El Charro Negro," she argued, as she lowered herself into one of the auxiliary chairs. "Those legends don't line up with skeletons running all around town."

"It got me thinking, though. Maybe there's something else in San Francisco's history that will explain it."

"Never say never, I guess."

I started typing, casting a broad net. The first thing I came up with was the ghostly policeman of Golden Gate Park. I read aloud.

"He roams the park at night looking for drivers to pull over," I started. "He's looking for people who don't have their headlights on. He issues citations but when the drivers try to pay their fines they find the officer who issued them died more than a decade ago."

Raven's eyebrows hiked. "Now that's dedication. What a miserable afterlife."

I smirked. "This is interesting. Apparently, people now wait to get out of the park before pulling over, and that results in the ghost officer disappearing."

"How did he die?"

"Um, he was killed in an accident patrolling the park. He crashed into a car that didn't have its headlights on and was supposedly killed instantly."

"Why do you say 'supposedly?'"

"Because I can't find a name for the officer. If this really happened, there would be a memorial somewhere here in the park."

I closed that window and looked for another. "Ah, here's one that will surprise no one. There's a White Lady of Stow Lake legend."

"There's always a white lady."

"Stow Lake is in Golden Gate Park."

"It seems this park is teeming with ghosts. What's it say about our white lady?"

"In the early 1900s a mother lost her baby in the lake," I started. "She was taking a walk with her three children. The baby was in a stroller. She got tired, sat on a bench, and was joined by another woman. She talked to the woman, and when she looked back the stroller was gone because it had rolled into the lake."

I frowned. "That story makes no sense."

"Yeah, you're missing something," Raven agreed.

"The mother who accidentally saw her baby drowned—wouldn't you hear the wheels rolling?—was distraught and killed herself."

"Let me guess," Raven said dryly, "she drowned herself in the same lake."

I bobbed my head. "She left her other two children behind. The baby's body was retrieved from the lake but the mom's body was not."

"That's a standard story. What's the deal with the woman who sat with the mother?"

"They say she was an imp."

"Always an imp." Raven rolled her eyes. "What else?"

"Ever since, people say that the ghost approaches guests at the park and begs for help finding her baby. She's often by the Pioneer Mother statue. The story is that the statue, depicting a woman with two children, is the home for this woman's spirit.

"Oh, and this is interesting," I continued. "At night, people claim the statue looks as if it has three children. Two older ones and one that's barely a toddler."

"Is there any truth to that story?"

"Let's see. There's a newspaper article from 2020. They investigated because a lot of people claimed to see her."

"How many of them were drinking or smoking pot?"

I smirked and read on. "Okay, this article goes into a little more depth. It says this occurred before the 1906 earthquake. The woman spotted a friend and they sat down to chat."

"So no imp?"

I shook my head. "The story is largely the same, although this doesn't mention the other children. The mother apparently lost her mind and ran into the lake. That's the last anyone saw of her."

"No one thought to pull her out of the lake?"

"Yeah, there are some holes," I agreed. "This article says she wears a white gown and approaches people on foggy nights. Others have heard her moan. With some digging, the writer says the first mention of the ghost is in a 1908 story that mentions a guy named Arthur Pigeon. He had a car full of partying women speeding through the park.

"Mounted police stopped them and when they talked to the occupants of the vehicle, they were all as white as ghosts," I continued. "The driver said they'd seen a 'thing' dressed in a white robe trying to stop the vehicle. It was described as a tall, thin figure that seemed to shine, with long fair hair and no shoes. The officer was dubious and asked if they'd been drinking. Then he asked to see where the ghost was. The women in the car refused, and Arthur had to show the officer back himself. There was no ghost."

"Shocking," Raven laughed.

"Ghosts are real," I argued.

"Women in white rarely are. They're legends created to make young women take care of their children. No fun for you," she wagged her finger. "Once you pop out a kid, your only job is to take care of it. Never mind that none of these legends exist to frighten fathers."

She had a point. Plus, she'd been around for a very long time. "Have you ever come across a true lady in white legend?"

"No."

I kept reading. "This is kind of funny. The police captain of the park station issued an order that any ghost matching the description be arrested on sight."

"They obviously thought it was a hoax."

I tapped my bottom lip and scrolled lower. "According to this article, San Francisco's history before the 1906 earthquake was lost because fire destroyed the city's police and coroner's reports."

"There might have been an actual police report about a woman and baby drowning," Raven said. "The odds are long, but still..."

"It does say the park was a common spot for suicides in the late 1800s. They even ran an article in 1900 called 'The Park Suicides' because it was a regular thing."

"Interesting. Does it say why?"

"They said the shrubbery 'appealed strongly to the troubled philosopher who seeks to rid himself of what he deems a burden,'" I read out loud. "They published a list of suicides in the park for a decade and found that one in every twelve suicides in the city took place in the park."

Raven leaned forward. "That's a significant number. How did they die? Does it say?"

"One by drowning. There were some poisonings, which is weird for a park. Why not do that at home? There were self-inflicted gunshot wounds. Oh, this says the one drowning was later ruled a homicide. Two twelve-year-old earthquake refugees living in the park reported seeing a baby's body floating in Lloyd Lake, which isn't far from Stow Lake. They dragged the lake, but no body was found."

I hummed to myself as I continued to plow through the article. "At least four of the suicides were women, and one was never identified."

"That wasn't uncommon back then," Raven said. "There were no exhaustive searches to be made at the press of a button."

I nodded in agreement. "There's another article from 2019. Seems the author followed some ghost hunters searching for the white woman."

Raven's snort was full of disdain. "Ghost hunters are nutty."

"Oh, look at this." I turned the laptop so she could see the screen.

I'd blown up a photo of a statue that looked like something out of a horror movie.

"Is that the Pioneer Woman statue?"

"Yup."

"Freaky."

I closed out of the windows. As interesting as I found the legend of the woman in white, I had trouble reconciling that story with the skeletons.

"Anything else?" she asked.

"Another incident in the park." I shook my head. That seemed a lot for one location. Sure, the park was huge—bigger than any park I'd ever visited—but the odds seemed long.

"Not another woman in white?"

"It's called the Portals of the Past at Lloyd Lake."

Raven sat straighter. "Sounds interesting."

I laughed. "So, going back to the 1906 earthquake—that seems to be a reoccurring theme in these stories, doesn't it?—there was a mansion at a different location. The fire that followed the earthquake destroyed about 25,000 buildings." I lifted my chin. "That seems like a lot."

"San Francisco had a dense population even then. They didn't have fire hydrants, so once the fires were out of control they essentially had to burn themselves out."

"Did you ever visit San Francisco back then?" I knew Raven had done a lot of traveling.

"I was here before the earthquake. I liked the city a great deal. I had every intention of coming back, maybe even living here for a bit, but that earthquake and fire were terrifying. I didn't want to deal with the worry that it might happen again. I also didn't want to deal with the cleanup."

"There's a memorial of a mansion that burned on Lloyd Lake," I supplied. "It was supposed to be a reminder of everything that was lost. The mansion belonged to a railroad tycoon named Alban Towne."

"Interesting name," Raven mused.

"Alban? Yeah." I kept reading. "A photographer spent time after the fires getting pictures. Apparently, he took what's considered an iconic image of the smoldering ruins of the city framed between the columns."

"There's beauty in everything," Raven said.

"The portals were moved from the mansion, which was several miles away, and placed by the lake in 1909 as a remembrance. People have reported seeing glowing balls of light floating around the lake and near the woods."

"That's more believable than a woman in white." Raven leaned forward to look at the photo I'd pulled up. "Glowing orbs could be anything, including witches."

"And witches can conjure skeletons," I mused.

She nodded.

"Sir Arthur Conan Doyle was interested in spiritualism. He visited the portals in 1923 to see for himself and even mentioned them in *Vertigo*.

"There are legends about the columns," I continued. "Some say they're a gateway to a different world. That's why they survived when nothing around them did."

"Plane doors?" Raven suggested, arching an eyebrow.

I leaned back and considered it. "Maybe something came through the door and is controlling the skeletons."

"Do you think these skeletons are actually being unearthed, or are they being created?"

"Josh, who is something of a history buff, said San Francisco moved almost all of its cemeteries out of the city to save space. If people couldn't afford to move a displaced loved one…?"

She made a face. "They paved over them."

"Half the city sits on graves."

"That must make basement excavation a nightmare."

I didn't mean to snicker, but I couldn't help myself. "It's possible there's a plane door, or we could be looking for something as simple as a witch who decided to use skeletons."

"You said that Elena mentioned that the skeletons destroy themselves when it becomes obvious they're about to lose," Raven said. "Have you ever heard of magic that does that?"

"That's what I was going to ask you."

"I haven't, but it might exist." She glanced out the window, then back at me. "Tell me about the cemetery that was supposedly the first place the skeletons were seen."

"Mission Dolores Cemetery." I typed in the name as I talked. "It's the oldest burial ground in the city. On 16th Street, was part of a larger cemetery. In 1889 they started reducing the size of the cemetery. There were 5,000 people buried there but they're remembered with a single marker now.

"Let's see," I continued. "A couple governors are there. Ooh, victims of the city's Committees of Vigilance. Josh mentioned that. They sounded fun. A famous boxer and ballot box stuffer named James Yankee Sullivan is there."

"How do you become a boxer and a ballot stuffer?" Raven asked.

"You have to be good at multitasking."

"Let me ask you this." Raven leaned forward, "do you think the cemetery is key?"

"It's possible."

"We need a paranormal from the community," Raven said.

"A Spanish bruja?"

"Do you have a better idea?"

I didn't. "Nixie said she had a list of magic shops. We should see if we can find one with Hispanic roots. That might be our best bet."

Raven stood.

"Don't you want to finish shining your mirrors?" I teased.

"Hell, no. I love Hispanic magic stores. They come up with some great curses. And they're really good with the conspiracy theories. Even if we hear ten stories we want to discard, there might be a good one to chase."

I stood to join her. "I'll text Kade and tell him we're heading out."

"You don't want to bring Romeo with you? Since when?"

"Since I've found that the women who work in these stores are more open to talking to other women."

She had her phone out. "I'll tell Percival to get lunch on his own. We can get something on the road. Then everybody can go their own way for dinner."

"Maybe someone will come across another group of skeletons," I mused.

"That might actually be the best thing for all of us."

8
EIGHT

After looking over Nixie's list, we chose a shop about five miles away. I drove Kade's truck, which wasn't easy to park given the small lot behind the store. Finally, I managed, but Raven laughed the entire way through my ordeal.

"It's not funny," I complained. "His truck is too big."

"What's he going to do when we move to Moonstone Bay and he has to get rid of it?"

"Actually, we can have one vehicle. I was thinking that Kade's truck might be best. It's not that old. Luke's truck has a lot more miles on it."

"Luke won't take that well," she warned. "Please let me be there when you tell him. I enjoy a good Luke meltdown."

"He'll be fine. I have every intention of getting him the best cart. We've already done some talking. Because we're getting a ship to transport our supplies, it makes sense to get the carts on the mainland and transport them over. I'm going to talk to Galen and see what he says about registering them and figure that out, but I was thinking we could sell all the other vehicles and the trailers."

"Geez." Raven's face went momentarily blank. "I didn't consider all of that, but it makes sense. The trailers won't be necessary. We'll take the tents and booths."

"And the House of Mirrors," I assured her. "We should be able to clear a decent chunk of change from selling the vehicles and trailers."

"And when—and where for that matter—are we going to do that?"

"Florida. Michigan is our last stop before our winter break."

"You plan to pick up the girls there?"

"They're champing at the bit. We're only two months from picking them up. They'll come to Florida with us. They can help with all the selling and packing. Some of us have winter places in Florida to sell."

"How are we going to do that in just a month?" Raven almost looked as if she was bordering on panic.

"We don't have to be there," I replied. "We can get a property manager to handle all of that."

"Wow." Raven let out a breath. "You're a lot more prepared than I am. I hadn't even gotten that far."

"I like to be prepared." I sent her a grin, then sighed. "It's going to be a lot of work, but we'll have a place to call our own. I talked to Hadley the other day, and she has a parcel of land in mind we can take to build houses.

"We'll have to live in the hotel for a few months, but we can use magic to help with the construction," I continued. "Apparently, there's a little village in a place she called the Barrens. A Mohan set up shop there for a long time. They've cleared the area of traps and nasty surprises."

"They had a witch doctor?"

"They didn't even know about it. The Barrens are a couple miles outside town. She's going to send me photos. If we like it, they're going to set about building a road in."

"How can she do that?"

"She's the mayor."

Raven's eyes went wide. "How is she the mayor?"

I laughed again. "They removed the DDA from power. She's the interim mayor. They're already moving on a bunch of stuff, and she's come up with some paperwork for us to have an attorney review. We'd have to pay taxes on the land, but it would be ours."

"What's the land like?"

"There's room for gardens. There's a big communal kitchen, which I kind of like the idea of. There are two bunkhouses that we can use for other things. There's one big house that the Mohan used, but with a communal kitchen I think we can surround it with smaller houses."

"Nobody would need a big kitchen then," she mused.

"It's just a thought. Nobody would have to stay there if they didn't want to. If anybody wants to secure their own apartment in town they can."

Raven shook her head. "It's all really coming together."

"Did you think it wouldn't?" I was honestly curious.

"No, I knew it would. I just thought it would be harder. It's as if things are working out magically."

I rolled my neck. "I'm excited to be able to call a place home. It's been a long time for me. Even longer for you."

She shrugged. "For a long time, I didn't think I wanted a home. Being on the move felt safer."

"That was because you didn't have trusted people around you. Now you do."

She nodded.

I walked into the magic store first. There were two workers, both beautiful Hispanic women.

"Hello," Raven said, her shoulders squaring as she looked around. She seemed shocked by the magic bouncing around us. "Brujas," she said as she took in the women. They looked equally as shocked to see us.

"Lamia," the one behind the counter replied as she looked Raven up and down. Then she turned to me. "I have no idea what you are, but you're fantastic."

My cheeks colored under the praise. "Thank you." What was I supposed to say?

"We're here about the skeletons," Raven announced, not waiting for me to decide how I wanted to broach such a sensitive topic. "My friend here saw two last night. We're confused as to what's going on. Some of what we've uncovered led us to you."

The woman who had greeted us furrowed her brow. "You think we have something to do with the skeletons?"

"No." I shook my head. "We heard that the skeletons were first seen outside a cemetery. A girl at a market this morning made it sound as if the skeletons are regularly seen after dark in her neighborhood."

"You mean a neighborhood like we live in."

I nodded. "We were looking for someone with actual magic. That's why we're here."

"I see." The woman licked her lips, glanced at her coworker, then nodded. "I will shut down for a bit so we can talk." She moved to the door.

"You don't have to do that," I protested, not wanting her to lose any business.

"It's fine." She waved off my concern. "It's better that we're not interrupted. Especially if you can help."

"That is the goal," I agreed.

Once she'd placed a sign on the door that said the shop would reopen in an hour, she led us to a small sitting area at the far side of the store.

"I am Esperanza," she announced. "This is my store." She gestured toward the other woman. "This is my cousin Maria. We are both brujas."

"I'm Poet," I replied. "I'm ... well, there really isn't a word for what I am. I'm kind of a hodgepodge. My roots are firmly planted in New Orleans." That was my way of explaining my type of magic without going into detail.

Esperanza nodded in understanding. "You have some bruja in you too then."

"Yes and no. My history is ... well, it's long."

"And you?" Esperanza turned to Raven. "It's been a long time since I've seen a lamia. Your people prefer the desert of late if I'm not mistaken."

"I don't live with my people," Raven replied before providing her name. "My family is one I chose, not the one I was born to."

"Ah." Esperanza poured iced tea for everybody. "And you two are together?" she asked after handing us glasses.

"Oh, no." I shook my head. "I mean, we're together here, but not as a couple."

"Are there more in your family?"

"Yes. We're with Mystic Caravan Circus."

Maria squeaked out a noise for the first time, emitting a tittering and making the sign of the cross. "I told you they would come," she hissed to Esperanza. "You're legends." Her eyes sparkled as they focused on us.

"I don't know about that," I hedged, uncomfortable.

"But you are." Maria bobbed her head. "We have followed your exploits. We know about the god in San Diego you killed."

"Actually, we gave him part of a soul, and last time I checked, he was spending his time falling in love."

Esperanza looked taken aback. "The rumors of Bael's death are not true?"

"Not even a little," I confirmed. "There was an unfortunate battle that has ended. We hope it stays that way."

"But you've been in a lot of places and battled much evil," Maria insisted.

"That's true," I confirmed. "We would like to battle this evil as soon as we figure out what it is."

"No one knows," Esperanza replied. "We have been searching for answers ourselves, but we haven't come up with anything yet. It's good you're looking too."

"We saw the skeletons after dinner last night. All the bars were open. There were people out."

"I'm willing to bet the people you saw were tourists, or locals who don't believe the stories," Esperanza said. "People in our neighborhoods believe. They've seen them. They're just now starting to branch outward."

"Do they have ties to your community?"

"Yes." There was no hesitation. "That doesn't mean the skeletons only want to hurt my people. In fact, most of the attacks I've seen have been on your people."

It took me a moment to translate that. "You mean outsiders."

"Yes. Now, it's possible the reason tourists have been targeted is because they aren't expecting trouble. They have not heard the stories."

"So they could be attacks of opportunity," Raven surmised. "The tourists are on the streets. The locals have enough fear and knowledge to be inside after dark."

"It could be that," Esperanza agreed. "It could also be that the tourists are the intended targets. Getting the army up and running didn't happen overnight. The numbers started small but have been growing."

"What was the first story you heard?" I asked.

"It was about a month ago. A woman was walking between houses after leaving a friend's place after a wine night. She was a little tipsy, thought she saw something white coming toward her on the sidewalk but then lost sight of it. She kept going and then the skeleton came out of the bushes to attack.

"She was frightened of course but managed to keep her wits and run to her home," she continued. "Once inside, she called the police. They came but found nothing."

"What did you think?" I asked.

"That she was drunker than she let on. I feel bad for that now, though. We've all heard stories. Many of us have seen the abominations."

"Are they real?" Raven asked.

Esperanza's eyebrows moved toward one another. "As opposed to what?"

"A golem, say. Perhaps someone created the skeletons and made them look that way for a specific reason."

Esperanza nodded in understanding. "Anything is possible, I guess. But that is not my feeling."

"Have you seen them?" I asked, hoping beyond hope.

"Twice," Esperanza replied. "The first time I was leaving this store. I held a séance for a small group. I do that sometimes for special parties. There were two on the sidewalk. They seemed to be just standing there. I was convinced they were decorations or something. Then they turned and started heading toward me.

"I had a choice," she continued. "I could've locked myself in my store for the night and waited them out or run to my car. I went for my car."

She licked her lips before taking a deep breath. "They tried to get in my way as I was leaving. More came out of the darkness. I decided to run them down."

"Let me guess: They exploded when you hit them."

She laughed. "Exactly."

"I thought my magic had done something strange to them last night," I said. "It turns out they apparently destroy themselves if they feel they're going to lose."

"I have come to the same conclusion," she confirmed. "I don't know why someone would do that. It must be a spell of some sort. Sometimes you can feel the magic zipping around at night. That's how I knew not to go outside the second time."

"What happened that time?" Raven asked.

"I went to the window two nights ago. I was on the second floor. When I looked out, there were skeletons everywhere, at least fifty. They were marching down the street, as if in a parade. They walked in front of my house, then turned a corner.

"By that time, we all knew to stay in after dark," she explained.

"Everyone locks their doors, but the skeletons do not try to get into our houses."

"I wonder why," Raven mused. "If they really wanted to exert maximum havoc, why not go into the houses?"

"Maybe they can't," I replied. "Maybe there's something about the spell that restricts them."

I had endless questions. "What else can you tell us?" I asked Esperanza. "Is there a god here? Is there some other creature that has threatened the area?"

"It's been relatively quiet for years, other than the normal paranormal issues in a city this big," she replied. "The vampires do their vampire things. The shifters howl at the moon and drink until they can't walk. We perform our normal rituals. There has been nothing out of the ordinary."

"I heard a story this morning," I said. "A man at the next table when we were eating breakfast told us that when all the cemeteries were moved out of San Francisco, a lot of bodies were left behind."

Interest gleamed in Esperanza's eyes. "Are you suggesting the skeletons are coming from beneath the city?"

"Is it possible?"

She tugged on her bottom lip. "I'll be honest and say that I never considered what you're suggesting. It does make a weird sort of sense, though."

"I was told that the first skeletons were seen near Mission Dolores Cemetery."

"I have heard the stories," she confirmed.

"From what I read, Mission Dolores used to be much bigger. The surrounding area was reclaimed for other things, and a lot of the bodies were left behind."

She sat straighter in her chair. "That would explain why that location was taken so early. It's not that the bodies were inside the cemetery. They could've been taken from the nearby grounds."

"But why? That's the part I can't wrap my head around. The skeletons might be a danger if there were a lot of them and you were alone, but we can take out huge swaths of them easily. They're not exactly the most solid soldiers."

"Maybe they're meant to be a distraction," Raven volunteered. "Maybe something bigger is going on and whoever is controlling this wants everyone to focus on the skeletons. This situation can spiral out of control before we even realize what's happening."

9
NINE

We had information, but not enough to lead us to a suspect. These skeletons hadn't decided to rise on their own. Someone had cast a spell, used a talisman, or called upon a god, or maybe even a demon.

That last one gave me pause. Seeing Bael at work in San Diego had made me realize there were beings out there who had far more power than I did.

"What's the plan?" Luke demanded as he approached the picnic table where I sat scrolling my phone for haunted San Francisco information.

"I don't have a plan yet," I replied. "I'm still researching."

"How can you not have a plan?" Luke was incredulous. "All you have to decide is if you want seafood or Italian."

It took me a moment to realize what he meant. I lowered my phone. "You're talking about dinner."

"Um … yes!" Luke threw up his hands. "What did you think I was talking about?"

"The skeletons."

"Why would I care about them?"

"They're killing people."

"I don't see how. The ones we took out last night weren't much of a threat."

I arched my eyebrow. "We?"

"I supervised," he replied.

"I guess it doesn't matter who did what," I muttered.

"That's what I said. I supervised."

"The skeletons on their own aren't my biggest fear," I said. "That honor goes to whoever is controlling them."

On a theatrically drawn-out sigh, Luke plopped down on the bench next to me. "What makes you think someone is controlling them?"

"They wouldn't be here otherwise."

"Okay, but why skeletons?"

"I don't know. It must be significant."

"Or they're convenient because of the whole moving-the-cemeteries thing."

"I'm starting to get frustrated," I admitted.

"You know the fix for that."

The gleam in his eyes told me he was about to say something annoying. I played the game anyway. "What?"

"Dinner."

A quick glance at my phone showed it was getting late.

"It's your night to choose the restaurant," he said. "I'm starving."

"I know exactly where we're going. I picked it out a few hours ago."

He remained suspicious. "It had better not be Korean barbecue."

"What's the matter with Korean barbecue? You like it."

"We're in San Francisco. We have a lot more options."

"Well, if Kade picks Korean barbecue when it's his turn, you're going to suck it up." I was firm on that. "I chose Italian."

Luke didn't look impressed.

"After, I thought we could go to the south viewing area and look at the bridge," I added.

That perked him up a bit. "What's the name of this Italian place? I want to make sure it's up to my standards."

"It's called the Magic Flute Gardening Ristorante."

"Really?" A smile crawled over Luke's handsome features. "I do like a magic flute."

I rolled my eyes. "Don't make this weird."

"What?" He was the picture of innocence. "I like magic flutes."

I flicked his ear, ignoring his yelp. "You're gross sometimes. I hope you know that."

Luke didn't look bothered. "I'm fine with that." He slapped my leg. "Now, get up. I want to eat. You can obsess about the skeletons over dinner."

"Fine. You are eating Korean barbecue if that's what Kade chooses."

"Of course." His tone was oily. "Whatever gave you the idea I was going to be difficult? I'm a diamond in the rough, Poet."

He was many things. Heck, sometimes he was a diamond in the rough, although that saying had always irritated me. It didn't matter tonight. "I'm ready. Now that you've brought it up, I'm hungry."

"Then let's get out of here. I want to see these magic flutes."

I glared at him. "You're going to turn this into a thing, aren't you?"

"Don't I always?"

THE MAGIC FLUTE HAD A CHARMING, low-key ambiance. Like all San Francisco restaurants, the exterior was fancy, with stylized windows and an ornate sign. Inside, the walls were yellow and orange, and there was an adorable walled patio.

"Do you have a table for four outside?" I asked the hostess.

"Absolutely." She smiled at me, but her gaze drifted to my reverse harem. They were three handsome men, and they drew attention wherever we went. I could practically hear the woman humming in her head as she thought "lucky girl." "Right this way."

"I'm going big," Cole announced once we were settled. "This menu looks amazing."

"We should get appetizers," I said to Kade. "It's going to be a long night if we go to the bridge."

"It's just a bridge." Luke made a show of being imperious, but I knew he was just as excited as the others to see the bridge.

Our server was all smiles as she approached our table. "Does everybody know what they want?"

"We'll start with the fried olives, calamari, and cheesy bread for appetizers," Kade said. "I'll have an amber ale. For my entree, I'll have the pesto chicken penne and the Caesar salad."

"Absolutely." The server sent him a flirty smile that didn't dip when she noticed his wedding ring. "And you?" She turned to Cole.

"A glass of the pinot noir, and the Italian sausage penne."

"I love Italian sausage the same way I do magic flutes," Luke offered, even though nobody cared.

The server was the only one who smiled. "What would you like?" she asked Luke.

"I will have the pom-mosa, and the salmon piccata."

"That's a very good choice." The server winked at him, which had Luke preening. Then she turned to me. "And you, ma'am?"

One of my pet peeves was being called ma'am. I absolutely hated it because it made me feel old. I also hated being called miss, but that was because it was almost exclusively used by older men, and it felt as if they were trying to put me in my place. I would've preferred a solid "Hey, you" to either ma'am or miss. I didn't voice my annoyance. There was no point. She was being respectful, even if the term poked every nerve ending in my body.

"I'll go with the cosmo, and the prawn scampi, please." I handed her my menu. "Thank you."

"No problem." The server smiled at each of my dinner companions in turn and then left us to our conversation.

"She called you ma'am," Luke said with a laugh. "You hate that."

"I *do* hate that."

"You realize that people don't call you that because they want to insult you?" Kade challenged. "They are trying to be respectful."

"It makes me feel old," I lamented.

"You're still young and hot."

"Of course I am." I patted his knee under the table. "Will you still feel that way when I deliver that kid you want so much?"

Kade looked bewildered. "Why wouldn't I?"

"I've heard there are stretch marks involved in the process."

"Oh, knock it off." Kade gave me a serious look. "You're in a mood, but not about being called ma'am. There's something else."

I could've denied it. Most people would've pretended they were fine. I wasn't most people. "I am struggling with who's behind all of this," I admitted. "Why summon a bunch of skeletons to attack the city?"

"It has to be a distraction of some sort," Cole said.

"It's the only thing that makes sense," I agreed. "And that's what worries me. This is a big operation. It's been going on for weeks. The people in the magic community have been trying to find answers, but they're not coming up with much of anything."

"What are our options?" Cole asked. "Who has the power to do something like this?"

"It could be a witch. That's always the obvious answer. San Francisco has a thriving Wiccan community."

"Yeah, but a lot of those people are really nature lovers who like the idea of conversing with the Goddess but don't actually believe there is the sort of magic we possess," Luke argued. "They might believe in love and revering nature, but if they ever saw a shifter they'd pass out."

"There are real witches here."

"A lot of paranormals too," Cole added. "The siren population here is almost overwhelming. There are huge nests of vampires. The shifter population is strong."

"Because those populations are thriving, other paranormals would make their way here to join in the fun," I said.

"The cost of living is really high, though," Kade argued. "Wouldn't that deter some groups?"

"Yes, but the snob factor appeals to certain people. Vampires especially love how expensive it is to live here."

"You don't believe vampires are behind this?" Kade looked dubious. He wasn't an expert on paranormals, but he understood vampires for the most part.

"Alone?" I shook my head. "I can see a born vampire getting involved with a witch and pulling something like this off, though."

"Without knowing the end goal, it's hard to come up with a culprit," Cole said. "For all we know, it could be a paranormal we've never heard of before."

"We just fought Bael and one of the strongest gorgons ever," Luke said. "What are the odds we'd get another 'out there' opponent so soon? Shouldn't we be expecting a run-of-the-mill witch for a change?"

"That would be a nice change of pace," I agreed, "but I don't think it's realistic. San Francisco has a lot of mystical stories. There are three connected to our park alone."

"Like what?" Cole leaned forward, intrigued. "What are we talking about?"

"Well, there's a story about a lady in white," I started.

Cole made a face. "There's a story about a lady in white in every city."

"The stories involving this lady are pretty strong."

"It could just be a ghost," Luke said.

The server picked that moment to deliver our drinks and appetizers, so we had to table the discussion for several minutes.

"San Francisco has a very rich haunted history," I said after our server left. "One story about the park involves a police officer who died after being struck by a driver who didn't have their lights on. Now he gives tickets to anyone speeding and not using their lights."

"That's kind of funny," Luke said on a half laugh. "Who would want to spend their afterlife handing out tickets?"

"It's not the strangest thing I've ever heard," Cole said. "Sometimes, when dealing with ghosts, they're trapped in the last moments of their life. They don't even realize they're dead in some instances."

"It's still kind of weird," I argued. "I mean, supposedly people try to get out of the park without stopping for the police because he magically goes away."

"That seems like a recipe for trouble, but I get it," Cole said. "What's the third one?"

"That one I find more interesting, and I wouldn't mind heading over to check it out tomorrow. There are columns from a huge mansion that burned following the 1906 earthquake."

"Are the columns haunted or something?" Kade asked, his forehead creased.

"Yes. They're called Portals to the Past. They were moved to the lake here, and people claim to see orbs of light."

Cole sat straighter. "They see orbs, not people?"

I nodded.

Kade glanced between us. "Why is that important?"

"Sometimes orbs of light are associated with plane doors. The moving of the columns could have been for a specific purpose."

"So we're thinking the columns are a plane door?" Kade cocked his head. "Why would we care about that given the fact that the skeletons are running rampant through the city?"

"It might be nothing," I replied. "It's interesting."

"It could also mean that whatever is controlling the skeletons is from another plane," Cole offered.

"Then what's our next step?" Kade asked.

"Dinner and going to look at the bridge," I answered. "I'm hoping a good night's sleep will have me firing on all cylinders tomorrow."

"The problem isn't that." Cole argued. "The problem is that this city has too many paranormals. Narrowing it down is going to be a problem."

"We don't have a choice."

. . .

DINNER WAS AMAZING. I FELT FULL—but not too full—and happy when we parked and walked to the south side overlook for the bridge.

Tourists were all over the place to get a look. We picked a spot with a lovely view of the lighted bridge.

"Nice," Kade said as he wrapped his arms around me from behind and kissed my neck. "This is the sort of outing I enjoy."

"It's pretty," I agreed, smirking when Cole and Luke started arguing about who had the better spot for a selfie. "Nights like this are my favorite."

The words were barely out of my mouth before the lights on the bridge flickered. Then they went out, plunging the bridge into darkness.

"What the hell is that?" Luke demanded, forgetting about his selfie in an instant. I could barely make out his features as he looked around. "How will the cars see to get across?"

"Their headlights," Cole argued, pointing. "They should be able to see. They just need to slow their pace."

A feeling of dread marched through me. I pulled away from Kade and leaned forward. Drums were beating in my head, except they weren't drums. It was a heartbeat.

Was it my heartbeat?

Was it the city's heartbeat?

I couldn't tell. All I knew was that the lights were going to turn back on and that I was going to see something awful. I was right, and the lights flared back to life a few seconds later.

"See, it's fine," Cole said.

It wasn't fine. I knew that even before I saw the skeletons flooding the bridge.

"Holy crap!" Cole was already scrambling. There were hundreds of them, and they were flitting between the cars.

I grabbed Cole and Luke and ordered Kade to grab me. I had to transport us to the bridge.

"Get ready," I ordered, not caring that people were watching. "We're going."

With that, we blinked out of existence and reappeared in the middle of the skeleton melee.

10
TEN

All three members of my reverse harem—a term I'd lovingly embraced when a young witch called them that in another city—were alphas, but they knew I could handle myself in a fight. They didn't rush to crowd around me as a shield.

We spread out and we went to work.

Luke shifted enough to give himself the claws he needed to attack the skeletons. Only those looking closely would be able to see, and even if they tried to tell the cops what they'd witnessed, it would be written off as hysterical ramblings.

He went after the closest skeletons, and much like the others, they exploded into dust as he ripped through them.

Cole had magic at his disposal but given the terrified people watching from nearby vehicles—traffic had ground to a halt—he couldn't put on a big display. He filled his palms with small bursts of magic and slammed them into the skeletons' chests. They exploded.

I dropped to my knees, allowing the bridge to illuminate with a soothing blue magic along the deck. My magic froze the skeletons in place, which allowed Kade, Cole, and Luke to start ripping through them.

Once they were frozen, I withdrew the dagger I often kept in my purse and started jamming it into skulls, keeping a brisk pace as I walked through the pack.

"Go!" Cole ordered to the idling cars. The occupants were frozen in place, their knuckles white from gripping the steering wheel. He managed to get the first line of cars off the bridge. The others were boxed in by skeletons.

"It would help if they'd start driving over them," Luke noted.

"They're afraid," I replied. I didn't blame them.

"Move," I ordered a woman in the car nearest me. I slammed my fist on the hood of her car. "Go!"

Her eyes were wide, but she was frozen in fear.

"I've got it." Luke ripped open her door, leaned down and pressed the gas pedal with his hand. The car lurched forward, taking down three skeletons in the process. As they exploded, realization finally registered on the woman's face.

"Keep going," Luke ordered as he pulled back. "Don't stop. Go home."

"I don't live here," the woman managed in a timid voice.

"Then go to wherever you're staying. Find someplace safe. You have to get off the bridge."

The woman followed Luke's instructions and raced forward. That gave me an idea.

"Clear a path for me," I demanded.

Kade and Luke stepped forward and took out three skeletons before I could blink. That gave me the room I needed. I slapped the car to my left, using my magic to propel it forward. If the occupant was surprised, he didn't show it. He gained control of the car and drove off the bridge.

I repeated my action time and time again. The space behind us was clear. We steadily cleared as we went.

"How long is this bridge?" Kade asked when we paused a moment to catch our breath. We'd been at it for thirty minutes.

"Almost two miles," Cole replied. He'd come to the same conclusion as Kade. "We cannot walk the whole way. We've only made it a quarter of a mile.

"We have to go bigger," Luke said, his eyes landing on me. "There has to be a way to clear these skeletons out en masse."

My brain was already working. I could think of only one possibility. Slowly, I swung my eyes to Cole. He nodded, and our magic comingled. I amplify his powers.

"Shield us," I ordered Kade and Luke.

They moved in front of us as I dropped to my knees, took a deep breath, and expelled my magic. I had a lot of power at my disposal, but the bridge was long. I gulped in a breath when I thought I'd reached the bottom of my well and found a bit of extra magic to cover the remainder of the bridge.

Cole grabbed my shoulder when I nodded at him that it was time. He steeled himself with a deep breath and sent his fire racing down the magical lines I'd put in place.

Fire exploded the length of the bridge and screams ricocheted around us. I kept my eyes pointed at the deck—I didn't want to make eye contact with any of these people—and waited it out.

The fire dissipated just as soon as it built, like a mini explosion. When I looked down the bridge, I saw dust flying in every direction.

"Well, *that* was interesting," Kade said as he helped me to my feet. "I think we got all of them."

That was good, because I was lightheaded. "Yay." My voice was weak, and it had Kade sending a sharp look in my direction. "One for the winning team."

"What's wrong?" He grabbed my waist with both hands and kept me upright.

"I'm fine," I lied. I was pretty far from fine. There was black around the edges of my consciousness, and I was deathly afraid I was going to pass out.

"She expended too much energy," Cole said, drawing Kade's piercing glare. "We both did. The bridge is just too big."

"We need to get her out of here."

I slapped Kade's hand lightly. "We're not done."

"We're done." He almost sounded panicked, and while I never wanted him to be afraid, he didn't have a say in the matter.

"We're not done." I pushed away from him, trying not to let my annoyance take over. It wasn't his fault. Of course he was afraid. If he'd expended so much magic he could barely stand, I'd be frightened too.

"Poet." That's all he said. My name. There was anguish associated with those two syllables.

"I'm fine." I forced a smile. To prove I was okay, even though I wasn't, I started walking. Traffic was moving again, so I moved as far to the right as I could. I didn't want to risk traumatized motorists taking advantage of the situation and running me over.

I didn't look over my shoulder to ensure that Kade, Cole, and Luke were following. That was a given.

"I think all the skeletons are gone," Kade said. His voice was gentle now. "You can rest, baby."

My natural instinct was to argue with him—I wasn't some weakling who needed to be propped up—but I didn't actually disagree with him. As far as I could tell, all of the skeletons were gone. That was a relief, because there was no way I could muster enough magic to fight them a second time.

I was just about to tell him that when the hair on the back of my neck stood on end. Something—something very big—was here. It wasn't the skeletons. Despite how many of them there were, they didn't ping my inner loa senses like this creature. This was something powerful.

"What is it?" Kade asked.

I scanned between the cars. Then I turned to stare directly in front of me.

She stood about two hundred feet away, her white dress whipping in the tremendous wind. Her body looked human, although it was ethereally pale and there wasn't an ounce of fat on her, and the lace dress she wore was dated. Her face resembled a skull, like a Catrina, the ones I'd seen sold at festivals in border states.

"What the hell is she?" Cole demanded.

"I don't know." My energy level hadn't improved, but I no longer felt as if I was going to black out. I started moving forward.

The woman—was she a woman or was she something else entirely?—didn't flee as I approached. She smiled, and the expression only added to her creepiness.

I closed in until I was about fifty feet away. She monitored my progress, her eyes remaining on me.

"What are you?" I asked when I was close enough for her to hear me over the traffic. I had to yell, but it wasn't as if the motorists had their windows down and were trying to listen. All they cared about was getting home. For all they knew, the skeletons were on their way back to finish what they'd started.

"What are you?" the woman asked, mocking my tone.

"I asked first."

She laughed, enjoying what had happened even though her entire army had been wiped out. "I am something you'll have to figure out on your own. That was quite the showing just now." She vaguely gestured toward the far end of the bridge. "There are more I can call on."

"Why?" I demanded. "What's your goal? Maybe we can come to some form of agreement."

She laughed as if I'd said the funniest thing in the world. "You can't give me what I want."

"Try me. I'm more powerful than you realize."

"Not more powerful than me." She was matter of fact. "This is my town. You don't belong here."

"Like we haven't heard that before," Luke muttered.

"You might have heard it, but you'd better listen this time." Something dark flashed in the creature's eyes. "Stay out of my business."

"And if we don't?" I challenged.

"I'll kill you."

I mustered a laugh, but it wasn't very intimidating. "Perhaps we'll kill you."

"Is that what you think is going to happen?"

"It has to." I wanted to fight her, throw as much magic at her as possible, but there was none to spare. I'd burned through my reserves eliminating the skeletons.

Worse, she seemed to know that.

"You need a lesson in respect," she said. "All of you." She finally acknowledged Kade, Cole, and Luke. Her gaze was dismissive when it landed on Luke. It was blasé when she glanced at Kade. Cole she gave a considering head tilt. Then she focused on me again. "It will be my pleasure to provide it."

She moved surprisingly fast, her hand catching fire. I wanted to shield us. No, I *needed* to shield us. There was no magic to bring forth, however.

Her magic lifted us off our feet. Up and over. We careened toward the water below. We hit so hard that the oxygen was forced out of my lungs as I plunged under the dark water. I lost track of which way was up.

It was like being trapped in darkness. I wanted to breathe, but I couldn't. I tried to swim, but my muscles felt as if they'd been carved from stone. My consciousness waned.

The last thing I registered before the darkness claimed me was a figure moving in at my side and an arm slipping around my waist.

Kade. It was Kade. I knew it without seeing him.

Then I was gone.

"WAKE UP!"

Kade's voice was screechy when I returned to the land of the living. How much time had passed? I registered three things immediately.

The first was that we were on solid land. I was wet, but not surrounded by water.

The second was that everything hurt, and I mean *everything*. Every muscle in my body suggested I'd just run a marathon. My joints felt as if they were inflamed, and even my bones ached.

The last thing was that I was freezing. I was in some sort of shock.

Slowly, I opened my eyes. The first face that swam into view was Kade's. He looked terrified, as if he was about to lose everything he loved. I wanted to make him feel better, but when I tried to speak, no words would come.

The second face I saw was that of Naida. Inherently, I knew she wasn't supposed to be here. She hadn't been with us when we went into the water. She was wet just like us—and naked.

"There she is." Naida's smile was reassuring, and she nodded to let me know everything was okay. "You're fine," she said. "They're going to take you back to the circus. Nixie will have a potion ready for you."

I wanted to tell her it wasn't necessary, but I was floating, and the words wouldn't come. All I could manage was a quick look around to make sure the others were there. Cole and Luke were on the ground a few feet away. Both were conscious, but Cole looked as if he'd been through a war.

"Sleep," Naida ordered. "You'll be better before you know it."

I allowed my eyes to close. I was vaguely aware of being lifted from the ground—that must have been Kade again—and then I floated in a sea of uncertainty until a multitude of voices became apparent.

"Just pour it down her throat," Raven ordered. She sounded as if her anxiety was spiking. "Don't mess around. There's no reason to be gentle."

The next thing I knew, someone was pinching my nose and my jaw was pried open. The potion didn't taste good—they never did—and I had to swallow reflexively or risk choking.

One swallow led to two, then three. The fourth was only half a swallow, and I forced my eyes open.

"Hello." Raven beamed at me, but her eyes were feral as she hunkered down. "Don't ever do that again."

Confused, I frowned at her words. "I..." My voice was a rusty hinge, and I had to swallow.

"Get her some water," Raven ordered.

Before I could register much else, a bottle of water was pressed to my lips. I didn't have a choice and was forced to drink it. All of it. I was gasping when I swallowed the last of the water.

"Well, that was unnecessary," I said when I could finally speak. My voice wasn't back to normal, but it wasn't as ragged as it had been.

"Do you know what happened?" Raven asked.

I took a moment to fully grasp my surroundings. I was braced against Kade, his body lending me warmth. Everything still hurt, but not at the level I had felt when waking the first time.

"There was a woman in white," I said. "She had a skull for a face."

"So I heard. Do you remember the rest?"

"I think so."

Raven didn't congratulate me on a job well done. We had saved thousands of people on the bridge, but she clucked her tongue. "You're a freaking idiot sometimes. Never expend that much magic again."

"It was my only choice. There was nothing else I could do."

"There's always another way. You'd better figure that out for next time."

Next time? We'd barely survived this time, and the woman in white didn't look as if she was even tired.

11
ELEVEN

Once I was feeling steadier—although nowhere near strong—Kade moved me to one of the canvas chairs. He was in mother hen mode, giving no space. He pulled his chair so close that it touched mine. Then he took my hand—I thought to hold it—but instead he pressed his fingers to my pulse and started counting.

Part of me wanted to be angry. I was fine, just a little shaky still, but he needed it. This was how he handled things on missions.

With my free hand, I pinched the bridge of my nose and stared at the sky. "Did anybody see where she went?" I asked, knowing full well the answer.

"It happened too fast," Luke replied. For once, he wasn't making jokes. "We were over the railing and into the water so fast."

"Once we were in the water, you and I were dead weight," Cole added. His eyes were sunken, and he looked exhausted. "The only reason we're still alive is because Luke and Kade saved us."

"We weren't drained," Kade replied. "Had you been at full strength you would've been able to swim for yourselves."

I pursed my lips, debating, then smiled. "Thank you for saving me."

The laugh he let loose was hollow. "I couldn't find you at first. It was too dark. Then I remembered I had magic."

"Kade's magic led us to the two of you," Luke added. "You glowed under the water, which allowed us to find you. Otherwise..."

"It was her show of force," I said. "She wanted us to know that she could kill us."

"Then why not just do it?" Dolph challenged.

"Maybe she needs us for something." She'd unleashed her skeletons on the area weeks before our arrival. Sure, it was possible she wanted to time the expansion to our arrival, but how would she know? Why would she care about a circus visiting San Francisco?

"I don't think it's us," Cole said. "In fact, I'd be surprised if she wanted anything from us. She almost seemed amused that we'd eradicated her army. We were like gnats to her, nothing more."

"If she's using the bodies beneath the city, she has plenty to choose from," I said. "She'll be able to raise a whole new army. She wasn't tired despite the army she unleashed on the bridge. We were exhausted getting rid of them. She was fine."

"That's because we have human in our blood," Cole said. "I'm an elemental, but there is still human in my blood. Same with you."

"I bet Baron wouldn't have been tired," Nellie said. "We should call him to help."

I pinned him with a dark glare. "Absolutely not. Don't even say his name."

Nellie rolled his eyes. "He's not evil. He's just not weighed down by human emotions."

Did he think that made things better? "He's a pain in the ass," I shot back.

"He's helpful." Nellie wasn't going to let it go. "This thing, whatever she is, could kill us. You said so yourself. She might not risk it if she knows there's a loa in town."

I shook my head. "We can't count on the loas to swoop in and save us. There will come a time when they won't be there to save the day. We need to be able to handle this stuff ourselves."

"You and Cole almost died," Nellie challenged. "You're our strongest fighters—"

"Hey," Luke protested.

"Do you have any idea how much trouble we would be in if we had to go up against this thing and we didn't have you and Cole?" Nellie persisted. "We would die."

"I happen to think I could take her on," Naida argued. She'd been so quiet that I hadn't even registered her presence.

"Why were you there?" I asked her. "How did you find us?"

"I was swimming," she replied. "The sirens were singing about what was happening on the bridge. They said there was trouble. I swam in that direction to see what it was and saw the four of you going over the side."

"You knew it was us?"

Naida's smile was rueful. "Kade and Luke had you at the surface by the time I reached you."

"She helped us get you to shore," Kade said.

The period was hazy, but I remembered. "You were naked," I said to Naida.

Naida smirked. "I'm always naked if I can arrange it."

"What happened once we got to shore?" I asked. "It's not altogether clear."

"I checked you over, realized you were magically depleted, and ordered them to get you back to the circus," Naida replied.

"Had they carried us the whole way back?"

"Let's just say we got our workouts in," Kade replied. "It feels like a bit of a miracle, but everybody was so worked up on the bridge that nobody saw us. When we got back to the observation point, it was empty, so we loaded you in and drove back."

"It was good timing too," Luke added. "The police were shutting down the bridge as we left. They didn't even look in our direction."

"I guess it's good we were outside the area," I said. "If we'd still been there, Detective Jackson would've had some questions for us."

"That's a given," Kade agreed. "It worked out ... except for the fact that there are probably cameras all over that area."

"Well, crap," I murmured.

"We'll handle it if he comes sniffing around," Cole said. "We'll say we were trying to help people and had no idea how big the problem was. If he saw us getting blown off the bridge by that creature's magic, we'll feign ignorance."

"Do you think he'll come looking?" Nixie asked. She was in front of Dolph, the big man's hands stroking her arms.

"I don't know," I replied, shrugging. "Even if he doesn't, he could spy on us."

"Poet is right," Raven interjected. "We can't get worked up about it. Not yet." She was grim as she snagged gazes with me. "Go to bed. You need to recoup your strength."

I WANTED TO STAY UP AND TALK TO Kade. I didn't even bother washing my face or putting on pajamas. He helped me strip out of my wet clothes and put them in a laundry basket. Then I crawled straight into bed. I was out before he rolled under the covers with me.

I slept so hard I didn't dream. Or, if I did, the dreams weren't important enough to remember. I was certain that I would see the woman in white's face in my sleep, but I slept soundly until I woke with a start the next morning.

Kade, who looked to have been trying to sneak out of bed without waking me, cursed under his breath when he realized I was up. "Sorry. I couldn't hold it any longer. I was just going to run to the bathroom."

Did he think he owed me an explanation for a basic bodily function? "Go," I ordered.

He raced to the bathroom. When he returned, he smiled before sliding in next to me. "Go back to sleep," he instructed, his hand moving up and down my back.

"What time is it?"

"A little before nine. You can sleep some more."

I tried to remember what time I'd gone to bed. "What time did we get back here last night?"

"You were out more than eleven hours."

I arched a challenging eyebrow. "I'm done sleeping." I never slept that long. Even when we were on our honeymoon and we knew before going to bed that we were going to sleep in, I didn't spend that much time down.

He sighed, the sound dramatic enough that he reminded me of Luke. "Fine." He brushed my hair out of my face. A quick look in the mirror told me I had a ferocious case of bedhead. "How are you feeling?"

I'd cataloged my entire body to ascertain just that when he'd been in the bathroom. "I'm good."

He didn't look convinced.

"I'm good," I repeated, irritation getting the better of me. "Don't worry about me. I'm great."

He cocked his head.

"Are you great or good?"

"Once I'm showered and fed, I'll be great."

That elicited a smirk, but it was full of relief rather than smugness. "I'm glad. I'm starving too."

"Then let's shower. I want to get some food—real food, not cereal—so we can make plans for the day."

"Okay." He was far too agreeable. That's how I knew the situation on the bridge had frightened the bejeezus out of him. "Whatever you want."

"Are you going to dote on me all day?"

"What do you think?"

"I think it's going to be a very long Tuesday."

. . .

I DIDN'T SPEND MUCH TIME WORRYING about drying my hair or bothering with makeup. I dressed in capris and an over-sized pink T-shirt, my hair pulled back in a clip shaped like a taco.

Everybody was near the picnic tables, drinking coffee and chatting. They looked up at Kade and me as we joined them.

"I'm fine," I announced before any of them could utter a word.

"You definitely look better," Raven offered. "How did you sleep?"

"I slept like the dead. No pun intended."

"You should continue to get your strength back throughout the day."

"I'm good." If they were all going to hover, things were going to get ugly. "Believe me."

Raven gave me another once-over, then nodded. "Before everybody splits up for breakfast, we should talk about what needs to be done today."

I poured myself a cup of coffee. "What do you think we need to do?"

"Research."

"We need information," Naida added. "We can't do anything until we know what we're dealing with."

"Any idea where to get that information?" I asked.

"I'm going to talk to the sirens," Naida replied. "They usually know what's going on, even if they don't want to get involved. Dolph is going to visit the vampires. He won't take Nixie because you know how vampires feel about pixies."

They wanted to suck them dry because they find pixie blood delicious.

"Nellie is going with him," she continued. "I'm taking Percival to the paranormal library."

"And I'm going to hit the paranormal bakeries," Nixie volunteered. "I'll get some sweets, and hopefully the bakers—who are often pixies—will have some information."

I nodded. "What do you want us to do?"

"Nothing," Raven replied. There was no give to her tone, and her expression practically dared me to push her on the subject. "Get your breakfast, then hang around here. We need you and Cole at full strength."

I grumbled under my breath. There was nothing worse than being infantilized, but she was right. I wasn't at one hundred percent yet.

"How about we go for breakfast and get some stuff done here," I suggested. "Then, once the food has done its job and I really am back to a hundred percent, I'll take a lap around the park. There are a few things I want to see, and the vendors at the craft fair will be setting up. They might have some information."

For a moment I thought Raven might argue, but she nodded.

"Awesome. I'm glad we're on the same page."

12
TWELVE

We were looking for diner food, not as easy to find in San Francisco as one might assume. The city boasted some of the best food in the world, but most of the restaurants had a specific theme. Everyday eggs and hash browns were rarely part of that theme.

When Kade found Rain Tree Cafe and I looked at the photos, it was exactly what we were looking for. We needed locals to talk—the tourists would gravitate toward the kitschier locations.

Kade held my hand for the walk but verbally sparred with Luke. It was part of their everyday routine, and it was almost comforting. That allowed Cole to check in with me.

"Did you sleep well?" I asked him.

"I didn't even make it out of my clothes," he said with a half laugh. "I fell face first on the bed. Luke had to undress me."

I arched an eyebrow.

"Don't be weird," he chastised. "Luke is actually good at doting. I woke up smelling like lavender oil. He didn't want me to stink in my sleep."

Dissolving into giggles, I earned a bright smile from Cole. "I don't think I moved all night either," I admitted. "I expected to dream but I didn't."

"I don't think I dreamed either. If I did, they weren't worth remembering. Maybe that's what happens when you're wiped to the point of exhaustion. What's the plan this morning?" Cole looked at the cafe as it came into view. "You were pretty specific with your breakfast request."

"We need locals," I replied. "We need people who have heard the stories flying around. The tourists can't help us."

He was quiet a beat as we waited for traffic to clear to cross. "Poet, have you considered what's going to happen if Detective Jackson comes calling to ask us about last night at the bridge?"

Even now I didn't have answers. "I guess we'll have to deal with it on the fly."

"He might know what we are," Cole said. "He's not a normal cop. He sees the skeletons for what they are."

"Maybe so," I agreed. "That doesn't mean he *knows* knows. He might think I'm a simple witch and you're a simple warlock. The odds of him actually knowing what we are—what Kade and the others are—seem pretty slim."

He nodded. "When you think about it, two pixies, a magical strongman, a dwarf from another plane, a lamia, the new breed of loa, a mage, an elemental, a couple of shifters, and a clown who likes to get freaky wearing chaps, kind of blows the mind."

Another giggle escaped. "If he comes, he comes. We'll deal with it."

"You're not as afraid now that we're going to stop traveling," Cole, surprised, realized. "You're at peace with it all."

"I'm not at peace," I countered, except that wasn't right. "Okay, I am," I corrected. "I'm not as worried about having to return to these cities. If we tick off the cops, they'll have to get over it. It's their only choice."

"I like that." Cole bobbed his head. "The thing is, Jackson is different. You know it as well as I do. He's aware of our world. He might not know everything, but he knows more than any other detective we've encountered. He could spell trouble."

"What do you suggest I do about it?"

"I don't know. I'm not suggesting this falls on you. We need to brace ourselves for the inevitability that he'll be back."

"I can't focus on Jackson right now. That woman in white is our primary concern."

"Yeah, about her." Cole shifted gears. "There's a woman in white story wherever you go. It could be a small town with a couple thousand people or a city of millions. What we saw last night wasn't a woman in white. What if she used the legend?"

"To what end?" I asked. "What would be the benefit?"

"I don't know. We don't know her goal. She didn't seem keen on killing us. She just wanted us out of her way."

We took a break from the conversation to get seated in the cafe. Our waitress Evelyn, a huge messy bun on top of her head, immediately appeared.

"Do you know what you want?" she asked, seemingly uninterested in whether we were ready to order or not.

"Yes. I'll have the California omelet with a side of bacon. Coffee and orange juice."

"Got it."

"Banana pancakes with two eggs over medium and a side of bacon," Kade said. "And coffee."

"Make it the same," Cole said. "But blueberry pancakes. And orange juice, please." He smiled at Evelyn. She didn't smile back.

"And you, sweetheart?" she asked Luke.

Luke grinned. "Did you hear that? Sweetheart." He preened.

Evelyn stared at him. "I don't have all day."

Luke's smile disappeared. "I'll have the Hawaiian crepes, an espresso, and a glass of water, if you don't mind."

"Oh, I mind all of it," Evelyn drawled before taking the menus from us. "I just mind some of it more than the rest."

I was caught between amusement and annoyance as I watched her go. "She seems ... nice."

"Don't mind her," a voice to our left said. I glanced over at an elderly man grinning at us from one of the stools at the old-timey counter.

I smiled back without hesitation. "She seems a little crabby," I replied. "I guess it's fair. Everyone is crabby at work, right?"

"They are," the man agreed. He smiled at Evelyn as she moved behind the counter. "Isn't that right, love of my life?'

Evelyn gave the man a dark look. He was at least twenty-five years older and had the sort of flirty energy considered crass these days. He kept ogling Evelyn's rear end wherever she walked past. "Abe, how many times do I have to tell you?" she challenged. To my surprise, she smiled before saying, "Not if you were the last man on Earth." Then she patted his cheek and set about getting the drinks.

"Did you see that?" Abe asked as he swiveled on his stool, his eyes sparkling. "She loves me."

"Is that what that was?" Kade asked with a laugh, his arm sliding over the edge of the booth to tuck me in at his side.

Abe waved off Kade's lazy smile. "You're still young and everything you and that girl do seems fresh and new."

Kade glanced down at me. "Is that true? Are things still fresh and new?"

"For now," I replied. "If you get stale, I'll know to trade you in."

Abe hooted and Kade rolled his eyes. Now seemed like the time to push my agenda. "You're obviously a local," I started, leaning into Kade's side to absorb his warmth. "We're looking for something interesting to do." I paused a beat. "Are there haunted tours?"

"Haunted?" Abe's forehead creased. "As in ghosts?"

"We like that sort of thing." I kept my smile light. "We've been hearing stories since we got into town, and we want to explore San Francisco's haunted history."

Evelyn bobbed her head as she stopped near Abe. "This whole

town is exploding with ghosts. Did you hear what happened on the bridge last night?"

I swallowed hard. "We heard something," I hedged. "I'm sure you know more."

"There were ghosts on the bridge." For the first time since we'd entered, Evelyn was animated. "Hundreds of them. They were attacking the people in their cars."

"They weren't ghosts," Abe argued. "I saw some of the news footage. They were something else."

"They looked like ghosts," Evelyn argued.

"Then you need glasses." Abe was no longer wasting time flirting with her. "Those things weren't normal, but they weren't ghosts." His eyes were solemn when they connected with mine. "They were something else."

"What?" I asked. Deferring to him might get him talking.

"A reckoning maybe."

"What do you mean?"

He sighed, long and drawn out. "This is how I see it," he said. "God created this world a specific way. He doesn't expect us to be perfect, but he doesn't expect us to be heathens. What's happening here is because of the heathens."

I had a lot of questions. Unsure if I should continue, I risked a glance at Cole. He also looked uncertain.

"Don't listen to Abe," Evelyn barked. "He gets worked up over the strangest things. He believes girls shouldn't wear dresses without tights."

"It's not my fault there are so many perverts out there," Abe complained.

"Why don't the perverts adjust their behavior?" Evelyn shot back. "Why is it on the girls to accommodate?"

"It's called modesty."

It was obvious Abe's sensibilities were a bit misogynistic. That didn't mean he couldn't be helpful. "People are saying there was a woman on the bridge," I volunteered before Abe and Evelyn resumed their discussion. "Amongst the ghosts who weren't really ghosts. Did you see her on the news?"

Abe sat straighter, his interest increasing. "I didn't hear about a woman."

I didn't want them to assume we'd been on the bridge. "I heard people talking," I lied. "They said there was a woman in a white dress."

"The woman in white hangs out at Golden Gate Park," Evelyn said.

I was encouraged by the fact that she knew the story. "Maybe it was her." I feigned innocence. "Does she have a skull for a face?"

"Does who have a skull for a face?"

"The ghost at the park. The people we overheard said the thing on the bridge had a skull for a face."

Evelyn and Abe fell into silence.

"We're intrigued," Cole offered. "We've always been interested in that sort of thing. I'm sure San Francisco has a rich history of paranormal activity."

"Oh, that's for sure." Evelyn responded. "You can't go a single block without hearing a ghost story here."

"What's your favorite?" Cole asked, his charm on full display.

"My favorite ghost story?" She seemed thrown by the question. "I don't know," she said after several seconds. "I was always partial to the one about the lady in white at the park. Her baby rolled into the lake and drowned. She threw herself in and drowned too."

"I think I've heard that one," I mused, "but I don't think it happened here."

"That story is shared in every freaking town," Abe scoffed. "That's not the best ghost story. The best ghost stories are from Alcatraz."

Until he mentioned it, I'd almost completely forgotten about Alcatraz. I'd briefly brought it up when describing the area to Kade, but then it had completely slipped my mind.

"Alcatraz was a prison," Kade said before I could find the words. "Why would it be part of the ghost history?"

Abe pinned Kade with a look. "Are you kidding me, boy?" He shook his head, almost looking as if he was pitying Kade. "There's no more haunted place in all of San Francisco than Alcatraz."

"Because bad things happened to the inmates there?" Cole assumed.

"Bad things happened to everyone," Abe said. "Inmates, guards, visitors. No one came out of Alcatraz with a happy ending."

I flicked my eyes to Evelyn to gauge her response. "It's true," she said when she realized I was looking at her. "People say there were already malevolent spirits on Alcatraz when they started housing prisoners there. That's why some of the prisoners got worse during their incarceration."

"I'm not sure I understand," I said.

"Some people say that if you're innocent and go to prison that you can keep your soul intact," she explained. "But the innocent prisoners there became as evil as the guilty ones."

"Because of the spirits?"

Evelyn lifted a shoulder. "All I know is that I think those tours of Alcatraz are a bad idea. If there's evil out there, what's to stop it from hitching a ride on one of the tourists and coming back here to do more evil?

"The natives cursed that land when it was taken from them. It should've never been used as a prison because it's already a sad place," she added. "When you add that much sadness to a curse, only bad can come of it."

I didn't hate the idea of checking out Alcatraz Island. I took advantage of Evelyn and Abe becoming focused on one another enough to embark on a new argument and glanced between my booth mates. "You guys want to go on a ghost tour?"

"No," Kade answered.

"Oh, come on," I prodded. "You'd love a historical place like Alcatraz."

"That's true," Kade confirmed, "but I don't want to run into a bunch of skeletons there."

"We have no proof the skeletons came from the island," Cole reminded him.

"We don't, but if you guys want to see it, there's a chance that evil skull lady will be there. I don't want Poet getting wiped out again."

"The goal isn't to get wiped out," I said. "It's to get ahead of this."

"Besides," Cole added, "even if it's a dead end, we'll learn a little something."

Kade let loose a long-suffering sigh. "Fine," he conceded, "but if something bad happens, I'm totally going to say 'I told you so.'"

I kissed the corner of his mouth, grinning. "Fair enough."

13
THIRTEEN

We had three options for night tours of Alcatraz. We chose the 7:05 p.m. tour because none were convenient for dinner. We figured we'd have a lunch of sandwiches at the circus and then dinner a little earlier than usual. Luke was bothered because it meant that drinks were out of the question. I ignored his complaints and headed to my tent to finish setting up.

I expected to be alone, but Cole joined me. He had his phone out and read from various websites as I worked.

"This says that D Block is the most haunted area on the island," he supplied. "That's where the prisoners were kept in solitary confinement."

I was happy to listen to him.

"Cell 14-D is considered the most haunted cell," he continued. "Visitors say that there's a chill and they hear chains and knocking. A man died in the cell in the 1940s. The story claims he was screaming about a creature with glowing eyes the night before."

"Can you confirm that someone actually died in the cell?" I asked.

Cole typed a bit, then nodded. "The guy's name was Rufe McCain."

I made a face. "Weird name."

He cocked his head. "Oh, wait. That's short for Rufus. McCain attempted to escape from Alcatraz in 1939 with four other prisoners. They were in an isolation unit and sawed through bars on the window. They made it to the water's edge, but that's where they were found by guards. Three of the men—including McCain—surrendered. The other two were shot, and one died from his injuries.

"Due to the escape attempt, McCain was sentenced to almost two years of solitary confinement," he continued. "That's how he ended up in D Block. The prisoners in D Block were locked in their cells twenty-three hours a day."

"Which means he was probably crazy at some point," I guessed. "That much isolation can seriously harm mental health."

Cole nodded. "They were returned to the prison population after serving their time. He got a work detail." He used his thumb to scroll. "On December 3, he was stabbed by one of the guys who tried to escape with him. Henri Young. Young stabbed him with a sharpened wooden spoon and McCain died five hours later. Young refused to say why he wanted him dead."

"How did McCain scream about a demon with glowing eyes?"

"None of this is in the same article." Cole went back to reading. "Oh, this is interesting and was not in the Wikipedia entry. The night they tried to escape, they constructed a makeshift raft. They were paddling away and McCain waited until that moment to admit he couldn't swim. He begged them to go back and reinforce the raft ... and they did."

"And that's when they were captured," I assumed.

"Yeah, and it might explain why Young wanted him dead," Cole said. "Once in solitary confinement, Young was angry. He threatened guards. McCain, however, gained the trust of the guards and managed to get on a work detail. When he delivered food to Young one night, Young tried to stab him.

"Once they were released in general population together, reports say, McCain wanted to kill Young," he continued. "He shared that with other inmates. Young reported that McCain made a cutting motion across his throat when they made eye contact that same day. Young claimed he feared for his life when he stabbed McCain in the stomach."

"What happened to Henri Young?"

"His lawyers claimed he didn't know what he was doing and tried to put Alcatraz on trial. The jury found that conditions on the island were to blame, and that infuriated the warden. Young was found guilty of killing McCain, but only three years were added to his sentence."

"That still doesn't explain the demon thing," I pointed out.

Cole navigated to another article. "It says here that the Miwok people have always considered the island haunted by evil spirits. They were brought to the island—in shackles—in 1859. There's not much here on them."

"Maybe none survived to tell the tale," I suggested. "Go back to 14-D," I insisted. "I want to hear about the glowing eyes."

"I'm trying to find it. It says it was a different inmate, but I can't find a name. He was screaming about glowing eyes and was strangled the next day."

"Interesting."

Cole kept reading, and I kept putting books on my shelves. They were mostly for looks. The good books were kept in the House of Mirrors, where guests couldn't stumble across them.

"This is interesting," Cole said after several seconds of silence. "Still no name on the inmate, but supposedly the ghost who haunts the cell is the one who screamed about the demon eyes. This says he died of natural causes, but the previous article said he was strangled."

"Legends take on a life of their own sometimes," I mused. "Any other ghosts?"

"Quite a few. There's the Lady in Green, who is often seen in the washroom of the warden's apartment. No name here either, but she was in her forties when she killed herself. She was visiting her husband and is often seen through the window of the bathroom."

"That doesn't fit our lady in white narrative."

"There's also the Ghost of the Birdman, Robert Stroud. He was put in solitary confinement for more than seventeen years for murdering a guard."

"Why was he called the Birdman?"

"He raised birds in his cell. I need more information on this guy. Let's see what I can dig up."

I left him to his reading and carried my crystal ball to the small table in the middle of the tent.

"Look at this guy." Cole lifted his phone to show me a balding man with a narrow face and a nose that reminded me of a bird's beak. "Creepy, huh?"

I laughed. "Sure."

"Stroud became a pimp at age eighteen. That was up in Alaska. In 1909 he shot a bartender and was sentenced to twelve years on McNeil Island in Puget Sound. He was considered dangerous because he often fought with inmates and guards.

"In 1916 he killed a guard and was sentenced to death by hanging," he continued. "That sentence was commuted, and he was given life imprisonment in solitary confinement."

"Death would be better," I said.

"To me too," he said. "While in Leavenworth, he cared for three injured sparrows in the yard. Within a few years, that grew to more than three-hundred canaries. He wrote a book called *Diseases of Canaries* that was actually smuggled out of Leavenworth and published."

"How?"

He shook his head. "It doesn't say. He became respected in

ornithology circles and ran a business from inside prison. That made prison officials angry, and they transferred him to Alcatraz in 1942 after they found out he'd been making alcohol in his cell."

"Apparently his solitary confinement was not as bad I thought," I mused.

"He was supposed to serve seventeen years at Alcatraz. He was diagnosed as a psychopath with an IQ of 112."

"How is his IQ important?"

"I'm not sure." Cole was completely focused on his reading. "He couldn't have his birds at Alcatraz, so he wrote a history of the penal system. Then, during what's been termed The Battle of Alcatraz in 1946, he tried to protect other inmates."

"That doesn't sound like a psychopath."

"Stroud climbed over the third-tier railing and lowered himself to the second tier, where he started closing the solid steel doors to isolation cells to protect those inside," Cole continued. "Stroud told the warden no one was armed, that all the cells were closed, and to stop firing into D Block."

"So weird," I said. "It's sounds like two different men. The murderer and the man who risked his life to protect fellow prisoners."

"The setup bugs me for another reason," Cole said. "There are notes here suggesting that Stroud was being watched extra closely for, and I quote, his 'overt homosexual tendencies.'"

"There was a movie made about him. Burt Lancaster portrayed him, and got to meet Stroud. Stroud claimed the reason he was never released was because he was an admitted homosexual."

I reached out and touched Cole's arm. Stories like this bothered me. They had to be even worse for him. "I can't believe I'm feeling sorry for a murderer," I said.

Cole continued. "Stroud was kept in Alcatraz until 1959. When his health started failing, he was transferred to a medical facility for federal prisoners in Springfield, Missouri."

I took it all in, considering. "Why would his ghost haunt Alcatraz?"

"That's a very good question. I mean, he didn't have it easy there, but he didn't suffer a terrible fate either."

"There must be more," Cole said. "I'll keep reading." He hesitated. "Unless I'm bothering you."

"I find your presence calming," I admitted. "Kade is calming too, as long as he's not around Luke. Luke is almost never calming."

"He can't help himself. He's high-energy."

"I almost always find you calming."

He winked and went back to his research. "At one time they took a psychic to Alcatraz. She was with a CBS news team. This was in 1984."

"Now we're getting somewhere." I smirked.

"Her name was Sylvia Brown, and she was sent to C Block to find a troublemaking ghost."

"Did she actually identify anyone?"

"She said the ghost was Butcher Malkowitz. He haunted the prison laundry. He was described as tall, with squinty eyes, and was reportedly a hitman for the mafia. He made so much noise in the laundry the Park Service felt the need to get rid of him."

"Did Sylvia Brown manage that?"

"No. He didn't want to leave."

"And Stroud's ghost? Where is he most often seen?"

"The former hospital, which is where I guess he spent most of his time."

"Hmm." It was a lot to take in. "Anything else?"

"Cell Block C," he said. "That's where the psychic found Butcher. Apparently, the ghost swings the heavy steel doors shut and it freaks people out. The only story that pops up is that people hear banjo music in the showers."

"Banjo music?"

"Al Capone apparently liked to play his banjo in there."

"No way. I refuse to believe the ghost of Al Capone spends his time playing the banjo in a shower."

Cole laughed. "I think the other ghosts sound more promising."

"But are we looking for ghosts? Those skeletons didn't appear to have souls. They were just vessels used to frighten everyone on the bridge."

"It's not the ghost stories that interest me the most. It's the native stories about the island."

"Ah, the evil spirits." I bobbed my head. "It does have a sort of *Poltergeist* feel to it, doesn't it?"

Cole's forehead creased.

"You've never seen *Poltergeist*?"

"When I was a kid maybe. I don't remember."

"Well, luckily for you, I love ghost stories. The whole premise of *Poltergeist* is that strange things begin happening in a family's house. Chairs move. One of the kids is almost eaten by a tree. Another kid goes missing through a portal."

"What a cheery movie," he drawled.

"At the end, they find out that their neighborhood was built on top of a former cemetery. They only moved the headstones, not the bodies."

Cole raised his chin. "Was the movie set in San Francisco?"

I had to think. "No. They never named the city. I think it was supposed to be California."

"Do you think the skeletons are poltergeists?"

"Not even a little." I vehemently shook my head, earning a smile from him. "The thing about the spirits on the island does make me think, though. We both know that if you treat people terribly it can leave a mark on the land."

"Then this dates back to when natives were housed on the island?"

"There are all kinds of injustices in the world. If that many innocents have their blood spilled on a piece of land, how doesn't it go bad?"

"Doesn't that turn it into a *Pet Sematary* situation?"

That made me laugh harder. "That was ancient Native American land," I conceded.

"And it did involve things that were buried coming back again."

"Like the skeletons." I grew quiet as I ran the idea through my head. It should've been laughable, and yet I couldn't rule it out. "Let's say that the land was marked by atrocities. It was a prison even before it was a penitentiary."

"And then things got worse," Cole said. He started typing again. He was frowning within seconds. "Native children were taken to the island and forced to work. They were abused. They weren't allowed to speak their native languages.

"Hopi men were held at Alcatraz for a year when they refused to hand over their children," he continued. "Even though you could see it from shore, it wasn't explored until 1775. The U.S. Army immediately took over the island once the United States acquired California. Barracks were built in 1850. It was used to house prisoners during the Civil War. The Army eventually left Alcatraz in 1934. Violent crime was exploding at that time, and the feds needed a prison for the worst of the worst."

"Maybe all the terrible things that happened coalesced to form a new kind of evil," I offered.

"I'm not opposed to that theory."

"But?" I prodded.

"Why now? Alcatraz saw the last prisoner leave in 1963. In 1969, Native Americans of many tribes took over but couldn't afford the upkeep. In 1971, U.S. Marshals moved everyone off the island, and it's been a tourist trap ever since."

I blew out a sigh. "How did a creature spring from that set of circumstances when only tourists have visited for fifty years? It's not as if something recently occurred. Let's say this entity was trapped on the island; how would it have been released in the last few months?"

"Maybe something happened with a tourist."

"Seems unlikely. Why didn't it happen before? It's not as if they're breaking fresh ground over there."

I rubbed my cheek. "I guess we'll find out tonight. Is it just the four of us?"

"I got a couple extra tickets, just in case. I thought Nellie or Raven might want to go."

"I'll ask. Something tells me that Nellie will be up for the trip."

My mind whirred with possibilities. "It might have nothing to do with Alcatraz. This could all be a waste of time."

"It's not a waste if we can rule out Alcatraz."

"You don't think our skull lady is tied to the island," I said.

"Alcatraz was a place of hardship and horror, but mostly for men."

"That thing we saw last night might not be male or female. It could've just picked a look." I dropped my head into my hands and closed my eyes. "This is so frustrating. We have nothing to go on."

"We need to start eliminating stories."

14
FOURTEEN

We had sandwiches at the picnic tables and then decided to branch out across the park. I was looking for proof that ghosts really were hanging around the park, and any stories about skeletons I could find.

First up was Portals of the Past. The columns were on Lloyd Lake, just off John F. Kennedy Drive. To my surprise, several people were fishing in the lake. A father fishing with a young boy waved at us as we approached.

"Nice day for it," he said.

I didn't have to touch him to get inside his head. Eric Pierson was an open book.

He was a loving father and husband. The best thing that had ever happened to him was meeting his wife Claudia in college. He'd fallen in love with her at first sight, but it had taken him six months to get up the courage to ask her out. Despite a severe case of endometriosis, his wife had delivered their son Oliver without complications. She wanted to have another baby, but he was uncertain because the doctors had warned it might be dangerous. He was happy with his family, and as much as he wanted another child, he didn't want to risk his wife in the process. He was hoping she would agree to adoption.

"It's a beautiful day," I agreed.

"What are you fishing for?" I asked Oliver.

The boy, all blond hair and gangly legs, smiled at me. There was a shyness to him, but he radiated goodness.

"Fish," Oliver replied, gesturing toward his pole. "I'm going to catch the big one."

"Oh, yeah?" I smiled.

Kade gave me a cursory look. It wasn't normal for me to engage with people this way. I was friendly enough, but I had to do so many readings a week that on off days I normally kept my distance from strangers.

"Show me what you're catching," Kade instructed, hunkering down next to Oliver.

"We're here with the circus," I announced. "We're setting up for the big festival and decided to come over because we read about this." I gestured toward the columns.

"Yeah, it's a big deal," Eric said. "People claim they're a gateway to another world."

There was no low hum under the ground to suggest a nearby plane door. Any stories that had popped up about the columns were either woefully outdated or the stuff of imagination.

I looked around and was relieved to find the other people who were fishing had left.

"Listen." I grabbed Eric's wrist and froze him in place. Then I placed my other hand on his forehead.

"What are you doing?" Luke hissed.

I cared about Eric's family. After hearing about so many bad things, I wanted to make sure something good happened. "You have to be strong when your wife says she wants another baby," I told Eric.

"She's going to work hard to get you to see things her way, but you need to be strong," I insisted. "She won't survive another pregnancy. You will adopt other children. Don't let her get pregnant again. Do you understand?"

Eric's eyes were vacant, but he nodded. "I've been trying to tell her."

"Try harder. This is important. You'll lose your family otherwise." I anchored the information in his subconscious with an extra bit of magic, then stepped back. "Do you know if they'll be setting up food trucks early for the festival?" I asked.

It took a moment for Eric's eyes to clear. There was no suspicion in his voice when he responded. "I don't think so. I don't really know."

"Okay." I kept my smile in place, then looked at Oliver, who was telling Kade a story. "I hope you catch the big one," I said to him as I motioned for Kade to join me.

"I'm going to." Oliver had no idea anything had happened. He was just happy to fish with his father.

I waved at Eric as we returned to the walkway. "Have a nice day," I called out.

"You too." Eric wasn't looking at us as we left. He'd already forgotten us.

"Why did you do that?" Luke asked when we were out of earshot.

"Because life is dark sometimes, but their life doesn't have to be. There was no reason not to try to give them a happy ending. They're good people."

Luke made an exaggerated face. "That wasn't much of an explanation."

"Leave her alone," Cole warned, his gaze piercing when it landed on his boyfriend. "You weren't there to hear all the horrible stories we hiked through this afternoon."

He knew me so well. "It was dark and depressing," I agreed.

"Is that why you did it?" Kade asked, capturing my hand.

"I did it because it was the right thing to do."

That was all I needed to say.

We left Lloyd Lake and headed toward the festival grounds.

People were already setting up. Workers were putting flags in the ground for tables in what would be the craft area. Stages were being erected for musical performances. All around, the park buzzed with activity.

And then I saw him. Detective Jackson stood next to an unmarked dark SUV, his arms folded across his chest as he watched the activity play out. He seemed more interested in us than anything else.

"Uh-oh," Cole said when he saw Jackson.

"Think he's here for us?" Kade asked.

"There's only one way to find out." I started in his direction.

Behind me, somebody—probably Luke—hissed. They all scrambled to keep up.

"Detective Jackson," I called out, schooling my face so I looked concerned rather than aggressive. "Have you found out anything about the skeletons?" I said it loudly enough that he jerked his eyes left and right to ascertain who might have heard me. When he turned back, there was a grim set to his mouth.

"Careful, Poet," Cole whispered. "He's already agitated."

Perhaps it was time to see how far I could push him. "I'm only asking because I haven't been able to sleep the last two nights," I added. "I was hoping you could tell me you have it figured out." I stopped directly in front of him.

Jackson, however well trained, worked his jaw.

"Ms. Parker, correct?" He smiled, but it was flat. "Or, is it Mrs. Denton? I never asked if you took your husband's name."

It was a weird way to slap me back. "I kept my own name," I replied. "Poet Parker has better alliteration."

"Your husband doesn't mind?" He didn't ask the question of Kade. His eyes were trained solely on me.

"Not even a little," I replied. "In fact, he's considering taking my name."

Kade made a choking sound.

"We're still debating it," I said.

"Sounds fine either way." Jackson shifted from one foot to the other. "You were asking something." He acted as if he couldn't remember the question

Fine. If he wanted to play games, I was good at them. "Skeletons," I said and in a voice that was about twice as loud as it needed to be. "I wanted to know if you'd found any answers about the skeletons."

His smile faded. "We're not sure what we're dealing with."

I tried to get inside his head again. Again, I saw bits and pieces. There was enough to tell a story, but it didn't feel complete.

"You must have some idea." I went as far as wringing my hangs together. "Something is obviously going on here."

"Obviously," Jackson agreed. "Have you seen anything since the other night? You're staying in the park. We've heard reports of skeleton sightings."

For the first time since meeting him, I was certain he was lying. "Oh, really? Where?"

"In the park."

"The park is huge. It would help to know exactly where they were seen so I can warn my people."

"If your people haven't seen them, I doubt they will," Jackson replied. He was on more solid footing now, and I couldn't help wondering if I'd made a misstep. "Speaking of your people, that's quite an eclectic group you've got."

He was going on the offensive.

"Thank you." My smile kept getting wider. "I'm pretty fond of them."

"One of them apparently likes to strip naked on the beach and go skinny-dipping."

My smile disappeared. "Is that against the law?"

This time when he smiled, he almost looked amused. "I pulled some files on you guys," he said. "Interesting reputation."

"How so?"

"Well, there was an incident in a cemetery in New Orleans," he started. "People say costumes were involved."

I could lie with the best of them in situations like this, so I decided to put my ability on full display. "People were dressed as loas for a parade. That was so fun."

"What happened in the cemetery?"

"What always happens in a New Orleans cemetery. People got drunk and made asses of themselves."

"You included?"

"Are you asking if I was drunk? I was tipsy. It was New Orleans, after all."

Jackson's eyes narrowed. "And in Little Rock. Something to do with a big fire."

"We didn't have anything to do with that."

"You were there."

"It's Little Rock. Almost nothing happens there, but when it does, they're prone to blaming outsiders."

Jackson's eyes narrowed further. "And Michigan?"

We'd had more than one big incident in Michigan. The state was a hotbed of paranormal activity. "I'm not sure what you're referring to."

"Detroit," he replied. "That's your hometown, right?"

He surprised me enough that I almost tripped over my own nerves. "I see you've been busy."

"I find your group very interesting."

"Why is that?"

I would've welcomed him giving voice to his suspicions.

"I can't fathom being on the road for so long," he replied. "You're like actual nomads. Other than your homes in Florida. But you don't spend much time there."

He really had been digging.

"Now you're moving where again?" he asked. "I can't remember if you told me."

"Should I take this to mean you have no explanation for what happened with the skeletons?" I asked, rather than answer the question.

"We're working on it," he replied. "What about you?"

"What about me?"

"Are you working on it?"

"How would I work on it?"

"I don't know, but you seem very interested."

"Who wouldn't be interested in finding out why skeletons are running around?" I challenged. Was this a good time to tell him what I'd found out? It was a risk, but I tried it anyway. "I mean, hearing that no matter what you do, they explode the way they do, how can you not find that fascinating?"

He pushed himself away from his SUV. I didn't back away, leaving only three feet separating us. "What do you mean they explode?"

"That's what everyone says. They explode if it becomes apparent they're going to lose." I was convinced I had the upper hand at this point. Then he dropped an anvil on me.

"Did they explode on the bridge last night?"

I reminded myself to breathe with a silent scream in my head, and somehow, I kept my face impassive.

"I'm not sure I understand," I replied.

Jackson cocked an eyebrow. "No?"

"I just said so."

"Well, that's a bummer. There was an incident on the bridge last night, and I thought maybe you knew something about it."

"I can't understand why you'd think that." *Just come out and accuse me of being a witch,* I silently seethed.

"I guess you missed quite a show." Jackson flashed another flat smile, then pulled out the fob to his vehicle. "It was nice seeing you."

I thought about refusing to move but Cole and Kade had firm grips on my arms.

"You've done enough for one afternoon," Kade said in a low voice.

"He knows," I replied as we walked back to the park. "He knows we're paranormal."

"He's trying to get us to screw up and admit it," Cole said.

"I'm not going to break." I was firm on that. "He can sit there and wait for me to break until he dies for all I care."

"That's a healthy attitude," Cole drawled.

"What else do you expect me to do?" I demanded.

"Nothing. You can't do anything right now. I don't think he can do anything either. It's a standoff."

15
FIFTEEN

We talked to people setting up throughout the park. About half of them had heard of the skeleton infestation. And half of those were convinced it was some sort of prank.

"It's not that unheard of," Kade argued as we waited for our table at Crab House at Pier 39. "You can't even get people to agree on the most basic of things now. I swear, if there was a global zombie invasion, people would run at them screaming 'government hoax' instead of protecting themselves."

"People get busy," Kade said. "We didn't see Dolph and Nixie were involved until long after it happened because we were busy with our own stuff."

I gave him a dark glare. "That was a mean thing to say."

Kade burst out laughing. "I'm just saying that it's not all that out there that they might not realize what's going on in their city."

"On top of that, just because your neighbor says that your other neighbor ran from a skeleton last night doesn't mean you'll believe it," Cole added. "If you don't believe in this stuff, if that's your natural state, until you see it with your own eyes..." He trailed off and held up his hands.

"Even if you see it, you'll try to rationalize it," Kade said. "That happened to me when I joined you guys. I saw you and Luke doing weird stuff—stuff that should've had me asking harder questions—but I kept rationalizing it away."

"That's because you were warm for her form," Luke said. "If you'd seen Raven and I doing weird stuff, you would've confronted us. Because it was Poet, you didn't make a big deal out of it."

Kade opened his mouth—likely to argue—and then snapped it shut.

"Did I just win an argument?" Luke looked thrilled with himself.

Cole and I laughed. Kade turned sour. Thankfully, that was when the hostess returned to take us to our table.

"This way," she said, her eyes dancing between the men with me. I was curious which struck her fancy. When she settled on Luke, I was secretly relieved. "Your server will be with you shortly," she said. "I hope you have a lovely meal." She winked at Luke.

"See!" Luke practically crowed. "I am the champion!" He raised his fist into the air.

Cole grabbed his arm and tugged it down. "People will think you escaped from an asylum."

Luke rolled his eyes. "You're not supposed to call it an asylum any longer."

"I heard you refer to a mental health hospital as a nut barn two weeks ago," Cole shot back.

"That was different."

"How?"

"It was me." Luke's smile was mischievous. It was the sort of smile that regularly got him out of trouble.

Once we were settled at the table, we focused on our menus.

"Let's get the garlic bread, the garlic truffle fries, and the crab cakes as appetizers," I suggested.

Kade's eyebrows hopped. "Hungry?"

I shrugged. "I might need to expend some energy on the tour."

Realization washed over him. "Expecting to find trouble tonight?"

"Probably not," I replied, "but better safe than sorry."

"I'm getting a cocktail," Luke warned. "I don't want to hear any grief about it either."

"Nobody will give you any grief," I promised him. "I'm having one too. One," I stressed. "Nobody can get tipsy."

"Oh, we're getting tipsy after. We're going to hit a bar."

That didn't seem likely because we were going to spend hours on the tour—it included a ferry ride—but I smiled all the same. "Whatever makes you happy."

The server had a big section, so she didn't spend much time chatting us up. We decided to place our whole order at once, so I put in for the appetizers and added the rest.

"I'll also have the Killer Combo, a Lemon Drop, and a glass of water."

The server smiled. "And you?" she asked Kade.

"I'll have a Mexican lager and the Super Combo."

"Sounds good," Cole said, handing over his menu.

Luke was another story, of course. "I'll have the Cucumber Basil Martini—but not too much basil, just enough basil—and Shrimp Tomato Basil Garlic pasta."

"Not too much basil again?" the server guessed.

"Oh, no." Luke shook his head. "It's fine to have the normal amount of basil in the pasta. The delivery method is different."

She didn't call him on being a pain. "Great. I'll be back with your drinks and appetizers shortly."

Luke watched her go, his expression dark. "I like the hostess better."

I rolled my eyes. "The server has a big section. Give her a break."

"Let's not bicker about this," Kade said. "Let's talk about something else."

"Sure. What do you want to talk about?"

"Well, for starters, what should we expect on this tour?"

I'd already looked it up, but I pulled up the page again anyway. "We take a ferry to the island."

Kade made a face but remained quiet.

"The ferry leaves from Pier 33, not far from where we are now. Raven and Nellie will meet us there."

"No Percival?" Cole asked.

I shrugged. "Raven didn't say. How many extra tickets do you have?"

"I got five extra because I wasn't sure."

"We can give the extras away when we're boarding. I'm not going to get worked up about the money."

"It's not worth it," Cole agreed.

"The ferry ride takes about fifteen minutes," I continued, grinning at the relieved look on Kade's face. "If we'd gone during the day, we could've stayed as long as we wanted, but I think the atmosphere will be better after dark."

"Unless the island is suddenly overrun with skeletons," Luke argued.

I kept reading. "There's a cell house audio tour. We'll have a ranger with us and an audio presentation."

"I prefer to wander around on our own," Luke complained.

"Not at night. I'm pretty sure the insurance for something like that would be astronomical."

"There are some special programs and exhibits, including a cell door demonstration." My brow creased. "What's to demonstrate about cell doors?"

"Probably how they closed during a lockdown," Cole replied. "It's more interesting than you might think."

"They're going to show us spots that were used for escape attempts. They call them hidden spots, which I guess were inaccessible to prisoners. We'll see a night view of the bay. That's about it."

Cole leaned back in his chair. "What are you expecting to get out of this tour?" he asked as the server returned with our drinks.

For the first time since she'd come to our table, her face became animated. "Ooh. Are you guys going on the Alcatraz tour?"

I nodded and sipped my cocktail. "Are you familiar with it?"

"I've been a few times. I'm really into the haunted aspects of the island."

I decided to take advantage of the opening. Her name tag read "Serena," so I decided to become friendly with her. "Serena?"

She nodded to confirm her name.

"We're a little nervous," I lied. "What can we expect to see? Have you seen a ghost?"

"Oh, you can't see ghosts." Serena solemnly shook her head. "You hear them." She lowered her voice. "The whole thing is creepy. I've been out there during the day, too. We used to take field trips to the island when I was in school."

"How many times have you been?" I asked.

"I've lost count." Serena offered up a dismissive wave. "I only go now during special ghost tours. You can go with actual ghost hunters."

I wanted to kick myself. That would've been better than the official tour. A quick look at Cole told me he felt the same. "Well, maybe during our next visit."

"You'll enjoy the tour," Serena assured me. She should've been working public relations for the island. "I get creeped out thinking about the things that happened on the island, but it's important to remember those things."

"You mean the way the prisoners were treated?" Cole asked.

"Yeah." Serena turned momentarily sad. "I get being tough on crime. I really do, and I'm not opposed to it. But back then they didn't have things like DNA tests or blood splatter experts."

I nodded for her to continue.

"I think innocent people ended up in Alcatraz, and they were treated horribly."

"I read that locations like Alcatraz were chosen because they were assumed to be escape proof," Cole interjected. "Once they had a prisoner escape, they knew they couldn't keep the prison going because the mystique of Alcatraz was officially gone."

"I've never heard it phrased that way, but it makes sense." Serena looked momentarily wistful, then shook her head and emerged from her reverie. "You guys are going to have the best time. I still remember my first trip to Alcatraz at night. There's just a different feel to the island. I don't know how to explain it."

"Sounds amazing," I enthused. "We're really looking forward to it."

Serena took off to wait on her tables, leaving us to discuss other things.

"I want to share what I've managed to drum up on Detective Jackson," Cole announced.

"How did you come by this information?"

"I still have contacts in law enforcement," Cole replied.

Why hadn't I thought of that sooner? "What should we know?"

"Jackson grew up in San Francisco. He went to the police academy here in town. His instructors marked him as gifted right from the beginning, and he rose through the ranks quickly. He's extremely well respected."

"How did he get on the monster squad?" Luke asked.

"He requested to create the squad himself."

I shifted on my chair. "Why would he want to do that unless he already knew something about the paranormal world?"

"A fair question," Cole replied. "I was on a monster squad as well. Carl—my contact—said there's nothing in Jackson's records that will answer our question."

"Bummer," Kade lamented.

"But there is gossip." Cole directed his smile at me.

"It must be good for you to be smiling like that," I said.

His grin widened. "No one knows if he's paranormal," he explained. "Some believe he is, but you're supposed to declare something like that if you get that far up the chain of command."

"How many people actually follow those rules?" I challenged.

"You'd be surprised."

"Did you declare that you were an elemental?"

"To my immediate supervisor? Yes. To others in the department? Not necessarily. But I did follow protocol."

"You're such a rule follower," Luke teased, poking his side.

Cole grinned at him. "This isn't the time for flirting."

"Yeah, yeah, yeah. Go on with your story."

"As it stands, Jackson is not listed as a paranormal, but rumors persist about his abilities."

"Spell it out for me," I prodded.

He pulled out his phone. "I took some quick notes. So, the basics first. Jackson is twenty-nine."

That threw me. "I would've pegged him as mid-thirties."

"Maybe he lied on his application," Kade suggested.

"I'm not sure it matters," Cole said.

"It matters if he's paranormal," I pressed. "That could change everything."

Cole bobbed his head. "I don't have that information. I have a few stories about his exploits."

"Lay them on me."

"His first big accolade came when he wiped out a nest of vampires on Treasure Island. Apparently, they'd taken it over, to the point tourists were afraid to go there. He handled that."

"He took out an entire nest by himself?" Luke asked dubiously. "How many vampires are we talking about?"

"It says fifteen."

"No way." Luke vehemently shook his head.

"Unless he's paranormal," I supplied.

Cole shrugged. "His other big claim to fame is stopping a zombie invasion before it got a foothold. Three years ago, there was a voodoo queen annoyed with her philandering boyfriend."

"Ah, isn't it always the philandering boyfriends?" Luke teased.

"She decided to take out the entire town, so she went big," Cole continued. "The initial outbreak was fifty zombies."

"Where did she get the bodies if there are no cemeteries for fresh burials?" Kade asked.

"Funeral homes."

"Jackson apparently figured out right away where the bodies were coming from and shut down every funeral home in town," Cole said. "That frustrated people, of course, but then he put together a hunting team. They lost five people after the initial fifty."

"What happened to the voodoo queen?"

"He cornered her, offered her a chance to go to jail. She refused, and he shot her in the head."

"He meant business," Kade said.

"That's what everyone says about him," Cole confirmed. "He doesn't mess around. He's brutal right from the start."

"That's how things don't get out of control," I said. "He just goes for it, and then makes whatever claim he wants after the fact."

"Exactly," Cole agreed. "He says things like 'three hundred people would've died if I didn't do this,' and there's no way to argue with him."

"If he does something that results in innocent people dying, he'll get pushback," Kade said. "Until then, he remains the hero of San Francisco."

"Have your contacts heard anything about the skeletons?" I asked. "There must be some chatter."

"They're treating it like a zombie infestation," Cole replied.

"But it's not."

"I don't know what to tell you." Cole held out his hands. "Right now, Jackson has all the leeway to operate as he wants. He can set the city on fire, and no one will push back."

I pressed my lips together, considering. "What about us? Has he put anything in his reports about us?"

"Carl can't give us that sort of information. Jackson basically does what he wants, when he wants, and doesn't have to provide any information to higher-ups. As long as he gets results, they're happy with his methods."

"It's possible the higher-ups don't want to know," Kade said. "If they're predisposed not to believe, it's easier to operate in the dark and put everything on Jackson. He can be their hero and their scapegoat."

"That makes him dangerous," I said. "He'll keep getting whatever he wants until things go sideways. By then, it will be too late."

16
SIXTEEN

Raven, Percival, Naida, and Nellie met us at the dock for the tour. We had one ticket to give away. The woman told us she couldn't afford the tour and just wanted to see the ferry leave. Amelia Pritchett was so excited for the trip that she decided to attach herself to us.

"Nice," Nellie said dourly. He'd dressed in pants, rare for him. When issuing the invitation for the tour I'd warned everybody to dress warm. Apparently the wind on Alcatraz Island was no joke. It was off-putting to see Nellie in pants and a hoodie.

"Don't," I warned him in a low voice.

Nellie made a face. "How are you going to do anything if she's constantly hanging around?" he challenged.

"What exactly do you expect me to do?" I was honestly curious to hear his answer.

He shrugged. "When do we ever go on an excursion like this and not have something happen?"

I hated that he had a point. "It will be fine." I smiled at Amelia, who was talking a mile a minute to Cole and Luke. She was in her forties and her reaction to being included made me a little sad. She seemed lonely. "Just leave her alone," I instructed.

Nellie harrumphed. "When this goes sideways—and it will—remember who warned you."

I glared at him as he moved to the railing to watch as Alcatraz loomed large in front of us.

Kade moved behind me and wrapped his arms around my waist as he planted a kiss on my neck. "It was a nice gesture," he offered.

"But?" I prodded. I could always tell when there was a but in my future.

"She might make things hard for us," he said.

I'd already come to that conclusion, but there was nothing I could—or would—do about it. Amelia was happy with her good fortune. "It's going to be fine."

"Of course it is." Kade kissed my neck again. "Maybe nothing will happen and we'll be able to pretend we're normal people for a change."

That sounded nice, and maybe a little boring. I patted his hands. "Don't bet on it."

OUR TOUR GUIDE'S NAME WAS JETT SUTTON. He smiled constantly, which matched his energy level. I found that more grating than Amelia's nonstop chatter.

We were at the back of the group when we disembarked from the ferry. Jett immediately started pointing things out.

"This is the bookstore and ranger first aid station," he said, pointing to a building on our left. "These were residential apartments back in the day."

He yammered on about the parade grounds and the water tower. He explained that there once was a duplex for the warden and the captain of the guard. There were family quarters at one time on the island and bachelor barracks.

"Alcatraz Island even had its own power house," he said, his eyes gleaming. "There are more tours to and from the island now than there was transportation to and from the island back then."

He led us to the biggest structure, the main cell building.

"So, a few facts about Alcatraz Island as we make our way to the building," Jett started. "The island was initially developed as a fort. It was declared a military reservation in 1850 by President Fillmore and transitioned into a prison in 1907. It didn't join the Bureau of Prisons until 1933.

"The prison officers planted a huge garden, which is still maintained today," he continued. "Some of the children who lived on the island have formed their own alumni association."

We were getting closer to the main cell house, and the atmosphere felt heavy. I kept one ear trained on Jett. His information was interesting enough.

"There was no death row on the island," he explained. "There were no facilities for execution. Prisoner violence was a huge problem, and a fair number of inmates committed suicide here."

"Well, that's a cheery topic," Luke muttered.

I sent him a quelling look and kept listening.

"Despite some of the stories, officially, no prisoner ever escaped from the island," Jett claimed.

I narrowed my eyes and waited, knowing there was more.

"Despite that official line, three prisoners—Clarence Anglin, John Anglin, and Frank Morris—are unaccounted for. They spent years planning their escape, including making fake heads out of papier-mâché and human hair. They drilled holes into the utility corridors behind their cells.

"They built rafts from raincoats and crafted paddles," he continued. "When it was time, they crawled through the holes and climbed pipes before escaping through a ventilation shaft. At the beach, they jumped into the water."

"What happened then?" Amelia, breathless, asked.

"Nobody knows." Jett held out his hands. "All three men had attempted escape before. The FBI interrogated family members. Boat operators were asked to be on the lookout for them. It's assumed they drowned. A few days after they disappeared, a sealed packet of letters was recovered. Later, some paddle-like pieces of wood and rubber were found.

"Another inmate named Allen West who was supposed to go with them but didn't make it out of his cell in time provided officials with information. The plan was to get to Angel Island and then cross Raccoon Strait. No one knows if they stuck to that plan or if the wind pushed them off course.

"Once on dry land, they planned to steal clothes and a car, but no thefts of that nature were ever reported," he explained. "No credible evidence was ever found that they survived."

"But no bodies were ever found so there's no proof that they died," Cole suggested.

Jett bobbed his head. "Exactly."

"But they did escape," I argued. "I mean, they might not have survived, but they did make it off the island."

"They did."

"So it's kind of a false claim."

Jett shrugged. "It is what it is."

He led us into the cell house, which was as eerie as they come. My inner warning system started to ping. I looked around, searching for a source, but saw nothing.

"What is it?" Kade hissed, picking up on the change in my energy.

"Trouble," I replied.

"Where?"

"I don't know."

Without being told what to do, our group spread out. We became the outer wall of protection around the other tourists. Cole and Luke were at the front, staring down the murky corridor of cells. Kade and

I were at the right, but there was nothing to see. At the back of the group, Raven shook her head when meeting my gaze. Did she feel that energy? Was she just going off my instincts? It was Nellie on the left who finally alerted us.

"Incoming," he bellowed.

The energy had built to a fever pitch, and I did the only thing I could. I used my magic to take over the group of tourists and force them into cells. They marched forward, two to a cell. Then I sprung the mechanism to lock them inside. Jett was with them and seemed to register a bit of surprise, but I clouded his mind.

We all jolted as the cell doors rolled shut with a deafening clang a split second before the skeletons oozed out of the darkness.

"Here we go," Raven said. She grabbed the nearest skeleton by the cervical vertebra that was once its throat, staring directly into its eyes before it went poof in her hand. Her nose wrinkled. "Well, that's no fun."

"I wish I had my ax," Nellie lamented right before punching a skeleton in what would've been its crotch. The skeleton went up in a ball of dust. "It's kind of like a video game," he noted as he kicked another skeleton, grinning like a wild man when it exploded. "How many points do I have?"

I was determined to get a good look at one of these things.

My loa powers kicked into high gear as I approached a solitary skeleton. I slammed a protective dome around it, hoping to cut off whatever communication might be taking place. I managed to make it inside the dome and touch the skeleton. It didn't poof. If the thing could have an expression, I would've guessed it was one of confusion.

Something akin to panic reverberated off the creature, and it lunged for me. I slapped its hand away, marveling at the fact that the skeleton remained intact despite no connective tissue holding it together. When it went for my eyes with its bony fingers, I stepped out of the dome and stared at it.

"It's held together by magic," Raven said. She'd joined me as the others easily dispatched the other skeletons. Nellie was right. It did sort of feel like a video game. "It's not very strong magic." She stepped inside the dome and tried to grab the skeleton by its head.

In an effort to help, I moved inside the dome with her and grabbed the skeleton's wrists. Finger bones went every way as the skeleton tried to tear itself apart. I'd managed to stop the explosion, but that didn't mean the skeleton was durable.

"Nothing," Raven said before grabbing my hand and dragging me out of the dome.

We watched with wide-eyed wonder as the skeleton slammed itself against the edge of the dome. Instead of going up in one big explosion, it began to shatter itself against the barrier. Bones fell one at a time until there was nothing left but a heap. The skull on top of the pile seemed to glare at us.

"What in the hell?" Raven spun away and moved to one of the few skeletons remaining. I followed her. "Create another dome," she ordered.

I did as instructed. The tourists were locked in their own heads imagining a tour around them.

Once the skeleton was locked in the dome, Raven stopped it from trying to ram itself against the invisible wall by sheer force of will. "Stop," she ordered, her lamia powers coiling in the small space. "I order you to stop!"

I raised an eyebrow. "Is this like 'stop in the name of the law?'" I teased.

"Don't confuse me with law enforcement." Raven sneered.

"Yes, we can't have that," a voice said from behind us.

Slowly—so slowly I felt as if I was trapped in a pit of molasses—I turned. There, in the dim light, stood Detective Jackson. He had four of the biggest, burliest men I'd ever seen with him. They had their arms out at their sides, as if preparing for battle, yet there was nothing to fight. We'd taken care of that.

"Hello," I said.

Behind me, the last remaining skeleton threw itself against the dome wall and crumbled to the ground.

"Oh, man," Raven complained, throwing her hands into the air as she swiveled. "You distracted us and ruined it."

"I see." Jackson crossed his arms over his chest.

I jutted out my chin, daring him to say something.

The silence stretched out between us.

"Aren't you going to come up with a lame story to tell me what you're doing here?" he asked, exasperated that I hadn't buckled and spoken first.

"We're on a tour," I replied.

Jackson's eyebrows migrated toward his hairline. "I've never seen an Alcatraz tour that went this route." His eyes scanned the cells, where everyone was frozen. "Isn't that the guide?" He pointed to Jett.

"Yes. He's been great. I'm going to give him a five-star review on Google. He's high energy and knows a lot of great facts."

Jackson shook his head. "Are you seriously going to stand here and pretend this is normal?"

I decided to turn things around on him. "Are you going to stand here and pretend it's normal for you to be here this late?"

"I'm a police detective."

"I tell fortunes at the circus."

He made an incredulous face. "What does that have to do with anything?"

"What does you being a detective have to do with anything?" I shot back. "Are you arresting someone here?"

"I haven't decided yet." Jackson looked pained as he shook his head. "I need an explanation for what happened here."

"We're taking a tour," I repeated.

"That doesn't explain the skeletons."

A smug smile bubbled up. "Skeletons?" I looked around. "I don't see any skeletons."

"There are skeleton parts in whatever those bubble things are." His face lit with triumph as he gestured toward the two domes.

"Hmm?" I dropped the dome magic, cringing and crowing at the same time as the bones exploded and turned to dust. "I'm not sure what you're referring to."

"You're unbelievable." Jackson stepped forward, and for a moment I wondered if he wanted to strike me. Kade, Cole, and Luke moved in and surrounded me.

"I don't recommend it," Nellie told Jackson. "You might have four hunks of beef hanging with you, but we have our own strength."

Jackson almost looked surprised to see Nellie. "Where did you come from?"

"If you ask my mother, I came from her loins ... and did a lot of damage because my head was so big."

Jackson's lips curved down. "I didn't see you here with the others."

"I'm small. I often escape detection."

"You're the guy who's usually in a dress." Smugness returned to Jackson's face.

"I do have a wonderfully expansive wardrobe," Nellie agreed. "As the bearded lady, I have to perform at least three times a week. I need options."

"You're the bearded lady?" Jackson's eyes went wide.

"Be careful," Raven sang out. "You don't want to say the wrong thing."

Jackson held up his hands. "We won't get anywhere if we keep going around like this. We need to have a conversation."

I was agreeable to that. "Okay. Let's talk."

"Not here." Jackson gestured to the people in the cells. "We can't talk in front of them. Let them out, and we'll go elsewhere."

"Or, you can go elsewhere now and we'll finish our tour." I wasn't ready to call it a day. Plus, I wanted to control this meet and greet. "Meet us at the circus and we'll have that talk you're so fired up about."

"You expect me to come to you." It wasn't a question.

"You'll want to meet everybody in our group. Spying on us isn't the same as actually meeting us."

He let loose a resigned sigh. "Fine. I'll meet you at the circus. You need a lesson on who you're dealing with."

A condescending chortle escaped Raven. "Funny, I was thinking the same thing," she said.

17
SEVENTEEN

Kade wanted to know exactly what was going to happen when we were face to face with the police detective. I had no idea what to expect. Jackson was a wild card. There was nothing to do but deal the cards and play the hand.

When we got back to the circus, we found him sitting at one of the picnic tables. He was alone, the men he'd had with him at Alcatraz nowhere to be found. He was either bold or had them positioned near the circus grounds, watching.

"How was the rest of your tour?" he asked as I accepted a beer from Dolph, who stood in the kitchen area with Nixie, a protective wall of muscle keeping her from danger. He glared at Jackson.

"It was interesting," I replied, happy that my voice was calm and there were no nerves on display as I regarded him. "I had no idea that Alcatraz had such an interesting history."

Jackson made a face. "Do you know how many movies have been made about Alcatraz?"

"Those aren't my types of movies."

"Ah, let me guess." A sneer took over Jackson's features. "You're a romcom girl."

"Hey," Luke barked. "Romcoms are a freaking treasure."

I smirked, then shook my head. "I lean toward horror."

"Then what you saw tonight was right up your alley."

"Not really," I replied. "I don't get off on people being in danger. Is that your thing?"

"I'm a police officer."

"That wasn't really an answer."

He scowled and shook his head. "I don't think I'm a fan of your attitude."

"You're not the first person to tell me that." I moved to the table—the others had purposely refrained from sitting with him—and sat. "This is how this is going to work," I started.

He jolted. "You don't decide how things work. I'm the authority here."

"Are you, though?" I cocked my head. "This is our territory."

"How do you know I won't use my magic to blow you away?"

The way he phrased it had me grinning. "You're funny."

"I'm serious."

"There's a reason we wanted to meet you here." I took another sip of my beer. "We have protections in place. You couldn't have gotten this far into our area if you had magic." That wasn't technically true. Intent mattered when it came to the dreamcatcher. He didn't need to know that.

He narrowed his eyes.

"This is how it's going to work," I said again. "I'm going to ask you a question. You're going to answer. Then you may ask me a question."

He growled, then held up his hands in surrender. "Fine. Ask your first question."

He probably expected me to ask about the skeletons. I had to ease him into this. "What do you know about the paranormal world?"

He looked taken aback. "That's what you want to know?"

"Yes."

"I know a great deal about the paranormal world. Probably more than you, in fact."

That made me grin.

"What?" he demanded when I didn't say anything. "You're an expert?"

"I'm waiting for you to actually answer the question."

"Geez." His bad temper was apparent as he shook his head. "I know about a lot of things."

"Give me an example."

"I know about vampires ... and shifters ... and sirens."

"Okay. Who here is a shifter?"

He fidgeted on his seat. "Him." He pointed at Kade. This was a test, and so far he was failing miserably.

I shook my head. "Try again."

"None of them are shifters. You're all just low-level witches running a grift."

I had to fight to contain my laughter. "Is that what you really think?"

"You guys are playing a game here."

"We're really not."

He stared hard into my eyes. "Prove it."

"Prove what?"

"That you're more than just witches looking for money."

"How would you like me to prove that?"

"Show me some magic." His smile was feral. He didn't think I would come through. Or, if I did, he had his men in position to take video that he would try to blackmail us with.

I held out my hand.

He stared at it as if I was offering him candy and enticing him into a white van. "What do you want?"

"I'm the fortune teller," I reminded him. "My magic comes from here." I tapped the side of my head with the hand I wasn't holding out to him.

He balked. "You're not going to try to hypnotize me? You're not going to make me bark like a dog at the sound of a specific word?"

"That wasn't my plan. If you would like me to do that, I can probably manage it."

He stared at me.

I stared right back.

Finally, he made a disgruntled sound and placed his hand in mine. "Do your worst."

I kept my face placid. "You really are twenty-nine," I said after a moment. "I would've pegged you for mid-thirties the night we met. You have a grizzled quality."

"I've seen a lot." He didn't look wowed with what I'd told him so far. "You could've found that information with a Google search."

"You have two sisters. One older, one younger. The older sister is married to a man you can't stand, Dave. You want to do great bodily harm to Dave because you believe he's abusing your sister."

Jackson's eyes bulged. "Who told you that?"

"You just did. It's all in your head. You might be worried about the skeletons right now, but your sister hasn't returned your call from earlier and your bad mood is really because you wanted to check on her after the scene at Alcatraz. We screwed up your night.

"Your sister is okay," I assured him. "She's gearing up to leave her husband."

"She would've told me if that was her plan."

"She's embarrassed. You told her the day before her wedding that her husband was bad news, but she brushed you off. Your feelings were hurt. She's afraid to tell you the truth because she doesn't think she deserves your help."

His eyes narrowed. "Where is she now?"

"Making plans. She won't leave him until next week. She has an apartment to move into with her kids. But she needs to leave before then."

"When?"

I smiled. "You're going to her as soon as you're done here, and you're going to move her out. Take the men you have watching us from the trees. Not because there will be a fight, but because you'll need witnesses. Otherwise, your brother-in-law—and what a tool he is—will file a report and claim you threatened him. You'll survive the inquiry, but those in your department who are jealous of your upward momentum will use it against you."

Jackson looked flabbergasted. "Are you telling me the truth?" he asked finally.

I released his hand. I'd seen everything I needed to see. I'd been looking for more than a way to get past his defenses. His sister served that purpose. The other things were enough to earn my trust.

"Listen, you're not a bad guy." I glanced at Kade to let him know I meant it. "You're a little brusque, but that's because you're younger than most of the people you order around.

"Your men are loyal to you," I continued. "They trust you. To them, you're a complete and total badass. That doesn't interest me, though."

"What does?" He crossed his arms over his chest.

"The fact that you watched us take out a cadre of skeletons but you're still worried about your sister's husband," I replied. "She's softer than your younger sister. You worry about her, too, but for different reasons.

"Your younger sister has a mouth on her and always stands up for herself," I continued. "You think that one day she's going to tell off the wrong person. Your older sister would never tell somebody off, and you're sick to your stomach thinking about her being abused by her husband."

"She would never admit it." Jackson looked out into the darkness. "I knew it. Deep down. She wouldn't tell me."

"You're going to swoop in and save her tonight," I promised. "Her husband will be difficult. You'll get a restraining order, and he won't be a problem for long."

Jackson jerked his eyes back to me.

"He likes to mouth off too. You won't have to do anything to him.

Even when he starts making threats about custody. He'll never see the inside of a courtroom."

Jackson's mouth fell open. "He's going to die?"

"He likes to drink and drive, right? Thankfully, when he takes out himself, he won't hurt anyone else."

Jackson moved his jaw back and forth. "Why should I believe you?" he asked finally.

"Because I also know that when you were fourteen years old you had a crush on a girl named Lizzie Carruthers." Now I smiled. "She was petite and sweet ... and you had hearts in your eyes whenever you looked at her."

He swallowed hard.

"You were too shy to ask Lizzie to go steady then, but you got the courage to ask her to prom when you were sixteen. You spent a year and a half with her. They were the best year and a half imaginable. Then she went to college on the East Coast and you broke up."

"The distance was too much," he admitted. "We were too young."

I leaned forward. "Lizzie is moving back to San Francisco. She'll say it was for work when she 'accidentally' runs into you the day after her return. She's coming back for you."

He looked dumbfounded. "I don't understand how you're doing this."

"It's what I do. Tonight, what you saw at Alcatraz, is what *we* do."

He glanced between us, wetting his lips. "I thought you were bad guys," he said. "I knew that first night there was something different about you. I thought I saw..." He trailed off and glanced at Cole.

"Fire?" Cole guessed. He held out his hands and conjured a small ball of blue flame. Then he extinguished it. "You did."

"We didn't need the fire," I explained to Jackson. "The skeletons are hexed so that when they're about to lose they explode."

"Which is why you were trying to isolate that skeleton," he guessed.

"I was hoping to find a thread of magic to follow."

"Why are you involving yourselves?" He was plaintive. "You're in no danger. You could protect yourselves and do nothing." He shifted again. "I saw you on the bridge. I saw the light show. You could've died, but you still fought."

"That is also what we do. We try to help wherever we are."

"I checked on you." He drummed his fingers on top of the picnic table. "There are stories about happenings in San Diego."

"Boys doing terrible things to women?" I asked. "Girls retaliating by wilding out in packs?"

He nodded.

"They were caught in a war between a gorgon and a demon."

"A gorgon?" He looked confused. "Like, Medusa?"

"Yes and no. It was one of her kind."

"And you killed it?"

"We fixed things so the gorgon split her soul with the demon. It was basically a love story run amok. It's fine now. We don't need to go into the details."

"What are you?" he demanded. "You're not a witch."

"It doesn't matter what I am, and I'm not here to share our secrets. We're here to help you with the skeletons. Unfortunately, other than one brief interaction on the bridge with what looked like a human skull beast, we have no idea who's doing this."

"You don't think it's a zombie invasion?" Jackson deflated a bit. "That's kind of what I was hoping."

"They're not biting people and turning them," I noted. "They're not multiplying through infection. In fact, I think whoever is doing this is tapping all the bodies that weren't moved when city officials booted all the cemeteries from town. There's a ready-made army of bones beneath this city, and our enemy is using what's convenient."

Jackson fell silent for a beat before turning a pair of dumbfounded eyes to me. "I never thought about that."

"Well, again, it's what we do." I rolled my neck. Weariness was starting to catch up to me. "I need specifics about the skeletons. A few of the people we've talked to have told us they've been around a few weeks."

"Yes, but never in these numbers." Jackson was all business now. "Until a few days ago, we might hear about one or two. They were easy to kill. We assumed they were looking for something specific because they would appear in an area, poke their noses around, and then take off."

"That's funny," Luke volunteered. "Because skeletons don't have noses."

I gave him a quelling look and turned back to Jackson. "When did they start showing up in droves?"

"I guess it was Friday, right before you guys showed up. That's why I assumed it was you."

"It's not us," I assured him. "Just to be clear, I need to understand. One or two were showing up and acting as if they were searching an area?"

"Yes."

"And their numbers exploded this weekend."

"It was as if they were suddenly supercharged."

Discomfort rolled through me, and I darted a look to Raven.

"The chalice," she said. "We know that a huge amount of magic was released when we destroyed it. It's possible some of that magic went to other places."

"What chalice?" Jackson demanded. The suspicion was back on his face.

"The Chalice of Fuerza," I replied. "It was hidden away in San Diego. Multiple factions were searching for it. We found it and destroyed it because it was dangerous. It's possible the magic that escaped as we were trying to destroy it went to other areas."

"Like here."

I nodded.

"What does that mean for the skeletons?"

"I don't know."

"It's possible that whoever is controlling the skeletons got impatient," Raven said. "She could be looking for something similar here, and perhaps hearing the chalice was destroyed lit a fire under her. I say 'her' only because of the creature Poet described on the bridge."

"If there is a chalice here, what do we do?" Jackson asked.

"We find it," I replied. "We don't know that there is a chalice, though. We have to do some research."

"Then let's do it." He got to his feet.

I laughed at his gung-ho nature. "Not tonight."

"Why not?"

"Two of us expended so much magic last night that we're still not back at a hundred percent," I replied. "Plus, I need to think. There are multiple possibilities."

"I want to get rid of this thing. It has to go."

"You're assuming there's a thing," I reminded him.

"I hate when there's not a thing," Nellie offered.

"Right?" Luke burst out laughing and gave him a high-five.

I glared at them before returning my attention to Jackson. "Leave a card with your number. Hopefully, we'll have a better understanding of what's going on tomorrow."

He didn't look happy, but it was obvious he wanted to get to his sister. "Here's my cell number." He handed me a card. "We need to get ahead of this."

"We're on it," I promised. "We'll figure it out."

18
EIGHTEEN

After Jackson left, I gave Naida the silent okay and she twirled to expend her magic. I watched it spread out from around us, bouncing off the dreamcatcher and alerting to two different spots.

That was where Jackson's people were watching us.

With a nod, I told Raven to mute the area. We needed to have a discussion.

"We're covered," she said after throwing out a scatter spell that would keep them from eavesdropping for the next twenty minutes. "Make it fast. They're going to be suspicious."

"Once he escorts his sister out of her unhappy home tonight," I said, "Jackson will want to work with us."

"Do you really think he's a good guy?" Cole asked.

"He's trying to do the right thing. His methods might not always work, but he is trying." I ran a hand through my hair. "He's not my concern right now, although I should've asked him how he came to be at Alcatraz tonight. I forgot all about it."

"You think he was following us," Kade realized.

"How else would he have ended up there at the right time?"

"It makes sense." Kade was grim. "I'm more interested in how the woman in white knew to send the skeletons tonight."

"She could be watching us too," I supplied. "We're on her radar because of the thing at the bridge."

"She had been releasing a few skeletons a night," Cole said. "Then she suddenly released a horde."

"Are you asking if the chalice played into this?"

"It was supposed to give magical beings more power. She's a magical being."

"But she started on this endeavor before that happened. If the chalice plays a role, it's because she got a surprise power boost. She couldn't have foreseen that was going to happen."

"Why would it come to her?" Raven asked. "That magic was supposed to dissipate. Instead, she got a jolt. What if other magical beings—the sort we don't want to get a power upgrade—come out of the woodwork with more magic at their disposal?"

"I thought we were done with the chalice. It can't be a coincidence that her power grew tenfold in the aftermath of the chalice's destruction."

"I don't much believe in coincidences," Raven said.

I rubbed my forehead. It had been a long day, and I was starting to get a headache.

"Maybe we're focusing on the wrong thing," Cole volunteered when it had been quiet too long.

I slid my eyes to him. "What should we focus on?"

"The skeleton lady," he replied. "What is she? I've never seen a creature like her. Have you?"

"Exactly like her? No." I shook my head.

"We need to start figuring it out. If we don't know what she is, we can't fight her. We have to come up with a plan."

"Let's call it a night." I stood. "Tomorrow, we'll start figuring it out."

. . .

MY DREAMS WERE DARK, SKELETONS PUSHING me into the hidden areas of Alcatraz. Even though they'd been a little fuzzy after the fact, none of the guests on the tour questioned what had happened near the cells. Jett said nothing, though I did notice him giving the cells odd looks as we left the area.

After our morning cuddle, Kade and I showered and headed out to meet Cole and Luke for breakfast. I got the surprise of the day—and not a good one—when I found a familiar face drinking coffee at one of the picnic tables with a handful of my friends.

"Oh, man," I whined when Baron Samedi, my loa great-grandfather, lifted his chin. "I should've seen this coming."

Kade let loose a low chuckle. "I'm surprised he didn't show up sooner."

Resigned, I marched to the table. "What are you doing here?" I demanded.

Baron, his face streaked with the white makeup he often wore when drinking in the French Quarter, swallowed his coffee and smiled. His white teeth were a stark contrast against his dark skin.

"Hello, granddaughter," he boomed, his smile so wide it almost ate his entire face. "You don't seem happy to see me."

I didn't respond to that. I would come off as rude, and despite how annoying I found him, Baron had helped us on more than one occasion. "What are you doing here?" I repeated.

"The magic world is roiled," he replied. "You can trace the lines of discontent from here to home. I figured I'd better check on you."

I pursed my lips, considering, then sighed. "You might be helpful." I sat across from him and accepted the mug of coffee Cole pressed into my hand. "You're kind of a skeleton."

That wasn't exactly correct. As a loa, Baron often wore skeletal makeup. When he was in New Orleans, that was fine. The loas were popular figures in the French Quarter, and with all the drinking going on, no one questioned them. In a magical fight, they adopted different faces that also resembled skeletons. Could the woman in white be a loa?

"Can you raise skeletons like zombies?" I asked as the idea began percolating.

Baron's eyebrows hiked. "To do what?"

"Search for something," I said. "And if you do raise them, do they try to bite people?"

"You're painting an interesting picture," he noted. "I'm intrigued. I need to hear the whole story before I can answer."

I filled him in over coffee. My stomach rumbled, but I pushed my hunger aside. When I finished, he was intrigued. "You talked to her on the bridge?"

I nodded, unsure why that was important. "She didn't say much of anything, other than her fight wasn't with us and we should get out of her way."

"You didn't heed that warning."

I glared at him. "They're hurting innocent people and terrorizing the city. We don't normally walk away from situations like that."

"Right. Right." He bobbed his head. "I forget sometimes that you're such a do-gooder."

"You're essentially a god," I reminded him. "Shouldn't you be a do-gooder?"

"No." There was no hesitation. "That's not how it works. The world can't thrive if one side takes over. If everyone is good, that goodness takes on an insidious quality. If everyone is bad, well, that one is obvious. There must be both light and darkness."

"Well, I happen to think the world would be better without so much darkness," I argued.

"That is your way. You'll learn, though." He stood. "It's time for breakfast."

I glared at him. "You were supposed to tell me if that white skeleton lady is a loa."

"You already know she isn't." His upper lip curled into a sneer.

"You would've recognized her magic now that you're part of the line."

I was fairly positive she wasn't a loa when I asked the question, but I wasn't ready to let him off the hook. "What is she?"

"I don't know, but I have some ideas."

"Perhaps you'd like to share them," Cole prodded.

"Over breakfast. I'm nursing a wicked hangover. Papa and I went out on Sunday."

"Sunday?" I scratched my cheek. "Why are you still hungover if your outing was Sunday?"

"We started Sunday. We just wrapped up last night."

I rolled my eyes until they landed on Kade, who was grinning. "Great. We'll see how you feel after breakfast."

LUKE PICKED A RESTAURANT CALLED Wooden Spoon for breakfast. It boasted the standard fare that we liked and the more upscale things he enjoyed, making it a good fit for all.

We'd made Baron wash his face so people didn't assume he was some kind of weird street preacher. With his top hat and raggedy clothes, he stood out. The city had its eccentrics, but he couldn't remotely pass as a local.

"Grits." Baron demanded. "It's not breakfast without grits."

"You're not in the South," I reminded him.

He made a face, and I wanted to ask why he was here if he missed home so much.

Once our coffee and juice had been delivered, conversation turned to the skeleton lady. "What is she?" I demanded.

Baron shrugged. "She's not a loa."

"How can you be certain when you haven't met her?"

"I know where all the loas are currently. None are on the West Coast."

"You said you had ideas," I pressed.

"My guess is that she's a ghoul."

I couldn't stop my eye roll. "She's not a ghoul." My response was automatic. I'd crossed paths with more than a few ghouls. She didn't fit the bill.

"And now it's my turn to ask how you can be certain?" Baron challenged.

"She wasn't picking her teeth with the bones of her dinner," I replied without hesitation.

"There's more than one type of ghoul."

"I'm well aware. She doesn't match any of the ghouls I've met."

"That doesn't mean she's not a ghoul."

I wanted to argue with him—my mood was poor, and he hadn't helped it any—but I changed course. "What type of ghoul do you think she is?"

"The type born out of great loss."

I frowned and glanced at Cole, who was listening raptly.

"You need to be more specific," I said.

"Some beings are born of necessity," he replied. "Some of strife. Wendigos, for example. More often than not, their birth comes out of cannibalism."

"Are you saying this thing is a wendigo?" Cole asked.

"No, although she's probably not that different from a wendigo. I bet if you get a full picture of her past that she suffered a great tragedy."

"Maybe that's why she's emulating the woman in white thing," Cole mused. "Women in white are usually mothers who have lost children."

"Where did her magic come from?" I asked. "If she was a human who lost something, or went through a terrible ordeal, where did the magic come from?" I was triumphant. I'd won.

"Where did your magic come from?" Baron asked.

"I was born with it."

"Maybe she was. The loss might have allowed the magic to grow into something terrible."

"But why is she just making her move now? Did this tragedy occur recently?"

"If so, maybe we can find a record in news reports from the last few months," Kade suggested.

Baron shook his head. "There's no way this is a fresh hurt. This sort of power takes a long time to build."

"Why now?" I pressed.

"You said she was looking for something," he responded.

"That was suggested to us," I countered. "They seem to be searching."

"They're not entering houses," Cole said. "If they really were searching for something, why are they casting such a wide net?"

"Perhaps this creature was locked away somewhere," Baron suggested. "Perhaps it was captured by magic and recently escaped."

"But it didn't have as much power until a few days ago," I argued. "We thought it had something to do with the destruction of the chalice."

He considered it, taking a long time to sip his coffee. "Depending on the type of magic she possesses, she may have received a power burst from the chalice."

"You didn't tell us that was a possibility." My tone was more accusatory than I expected, leaving me surprised at my vitriol. I adjusted quickly. "I'm just saying that if that magic is going to be fueling a bunch of paranormals, we could be in trouble."

Baron didn't look troubled. In fact, he shrugged it off. "What would you have done differently?"

"I don't know."

"You had to move fast," he reminded me. "If you hadn't destroyed the chalice, Agnes or Bael would've gotten their hands on it. Either one of them becoming ten times stronger would've meant a death sentence for a lot of people."

"People are dying here," I argued.

"Are they?" He tilted his head. "How many?"

"I don't know. A few at least."

"A lot of people could've died on that bridge," Cole argued, siding with me even though he didn't look convinced that I was on the right side of this conversation.

"'Could' being the operative word," Baron said. "You don't know that they would've died. Perhaps this creature chased whatever she was looking for to the bridge and you ruined it for her. Maybe she wasn't going to hurt anyone."

"What about at Alcatraz last night?" I asked. "Why did she chase us there? If what she was looking for was at Alcatraz all this time, why did she pick last night to send her minions in?"

"I don't have the answers you're looking for," Baron replied in his even tone. "I can only suggest she's looking for something specific, and now that you're on her radar, perhaps she thinks you can get it for her. I'm here to help."

"Because you felt the magic rippling out from San Francisco," Kade murmured. "Do you think we're in danger?"

"Something big is going to happen," Baron replied. "There's no getting around it now. Everyone in the magical world can feel something. San Francisco is about to become the epicenter of something big."

"Are the residents in danger?" I asked.

"They always are when something like this happens."

"Yes, but—"

"No buts." Baron was firm when shaking his head. "I have contacts here. Some very old contacts. I will touch base with them. They might have a better handle on what's about to happen."

"What about us?" Cole asked. "What are we supposed to do?"

"Things are already set in motion. Do what you normally do."

He remained matter of fact, and that irritated me to the nth degree.

"You give me heartburn," I complained. "Has anybody ever told you that?"

"Your great-grandmother." Baron grinned. "You remind me so much of her."

19
NINETEEN

Back at the circus grounds, I left Kade, Cole, and Luke to run through the final checklists to make sure we were ready to open the next day. I set off on foot, thinking I was alone. Baron had other ideas.

"This is a beautiful place," he noted at the Monarch Bear Grove, a heavily wooded area that had an old-world atmosphere. "It's hard to believe that in the middle of a city this big there are still pockets of this sort of beauty."

"You can't find this in New Orleans?" I asked as I hunkered down to look at the base of one of the trees. There were footprints, only they looked like bone imprints.

"New Orleans is a beautiful city," he argued. "The most beautiful city in the world."

When I glanced up at him, he seemed wistful. "You don't have to stay in New Orleans. You can go wherever you want."

"I would never leave New Orleans. That's my home." He sighed. "It's nice to visit other places, though." He turned his attention to me. "What are you looking at?"

"Does that look like a skeleton print?" I pointed.

He leaned down and stared at the indentation. "Yes," he said. "Is that important?"

"It's proof the skeletons have been running around the park even though we haven't seen them."

His expression was blank. "I'm not sure why that's important."

"We've been in the park three nights now. The dreamcatcher went up the first night."

Realization dawned on him. "If the skeletons have been in the park why hasn't the dreamcatcher alerted?"

"The dreamcatcher is designed to draw in evil entities. If they were close, they should've been drawn to us."

"Why weren't they?"

"I'm asking you."

He smirked at my sharp tone. "So much like my Brigitte. That's why you're my favorite. Why did your dreamcatcher fail?"

"It didn't fail."

"Have you tested it?"

"It doesn't fail. We would know. It's part of us. When we're inside of it, we can feel it humming."

He looked intrigued. "So you were using loa magic from the start. Very interesting."

How was that interesting? Wait, it was interesting. Ugh. I hated him sometimes. "I didn't get my loa power boost until we were in New Orleans. I absorbed Marinette's power."

"You may have had loa powers before. Your upgrade may have enhanced them."

I said on a sigh, "That doesn't matter right now."

"What matters most right now is who this creature is. Who is she at her core? Was she always magical? Did something happen to make her magical? Why does she take the form she does? Why did she decide on skeletons?"

"I think she chose the skeletons because she has easy access to them." I moved away from the first footprint and settled next to a second. "Apparently, between 1920 and 1940, the bulk of the cemeteries were moved out of San Francisco. They wanted to repurpose the land."

Baron's eyebrows hopped. "How did that work?"

"I did some reading. Burials were banned in San Francisco in 1901, but the removal of the bodies didn't take place for almost twenty years. It was a long process. Health hazards were the biggest concern. We know that's crap. They wanted the land for businesses and houses. It was much more valuable than a cemetery could ever be.

"After new burials were banned, the cemeteries weren't maintained," I continued. "A lot of the bodies were interred in mass graves. The city's aquatic park used the stones collected from the cemeteries for construction. Some of the unclaimed headstones were used as walkways."

"Doesn't seem very respectful."

I stared at him a beat, considering. One thing New Orleans did better than most cities was respect its dead. The loas were basically the highwaymen of the dead. To them, San Francisco's decision to eradicate the cemeteries would be disrespectful.

"Do you think doing something like that, moving people from their final resting places, can cause magic to coalesce in a certain way?"

"Are you asking if I believe moving the cemeteries created a supernatural being?"

I shrugged.

"I'm loath to say that anything is impossible—we live in a world where almost anything can happen—but to create a being like that you need a lot of anger and sadness."

"The skull woman was dressed in white. Everywhere we go there's a woman in white legend. They all play off a woman losing a child."

"You think this creature lost a child."

"Her choice of outfit is purposeful, but I can't say why I believe that."

"You have good instincts. If you believe that, even if it's just something inside you suggesting it, there's no reason to doubt yourself."

He was good when it came to bolstering my self-esteem. I appreciated it, even if I did find him annoying on most occasions. "She's not a true woman in white. She's not a ghost. Unless..."

Interest sparked in his eyes. "You believe she was a ghost and then became more."

"Is that possible?"

"Again, we live in a world where anything is possible. As for ghosts becoming corporeal, it has happened. Even if they don't become corporeal, they can still affect the world they left behind."

"And poltergeists are basically angry ghosts."

"That's a little simplistic, but sure." He tapped his bottom lip. "The way your mind works is amazing. I would've never considered anything you just suggested."

"But you don't know if you believe it."

"I have no reason to. I have no reason to disbelieve it. We don't have enough information."

"Right." I blew out a sigh. "Let's keep going."

"What are you looking for?"

"More proof that the skeletons have been here. That they're somehow immune to the dreamcatcher. If that's the case, we need to figure out a different way to draw them in."

"For such a smart girl, you're missing the obvious explanation."

I narrowed my eyes.

"You said it yourself. The dreamcatcher draws in individuals who mean to do harm. That goes for humans and monsters. Perhaps the skeletons mean no harm."

"People have died."

"Have they?"

When I thought about it, I realized that there was no confirmation of deaths. We'd heard stories about skeletons biting people. It had seemed that first night that the skeleton wanted to bite the woman we saved. "Oh, crap," I said.

"I'm no expert, but it seems the skeletons might not have any intent either way. If this creature is controlling them, her intent might overrule everything else."

"And she might not be ordering them to hurt people," I said. "She might have ordered them to look for something. Any injuries could be a byproduct of their appearances."

"Without intent, the skeletons can't be lured."

"Right." I bobbed my head.

"So what will you do?"

I had no idea. "I need to talk to Raven."

"You're open to suggestions from others. That's good."

I cast him a sidelong look. "Of course I am. Why wouldn't I be?"

"I always think I'm right."

"Where has that gotten you?"

"To a time my kind almost went extinct. That's why it's good you're not that way. You will carry us forward. I told everybody you were the right choice. Now they have no option but to revere me."

"You always bring the conversation back to yourself."

"Why change what's been working for me for thousands of years?"

I WANTED TO DITCH BARON but he insisted on accompanying me to the House of Mirrors. The second we walked inside, he became distracted with his own reflection and dawdled.

"If you're coming, then we're going this way," I said impatiently, pointing in the direction of Raven's office.

"This is a glorious room," Baron replied as he looked at himself from a hundred different angles.

He showed no sign of following me, so I left him to worship himself.

"What's up?" I asked Raven from the doorway of her office.

She was intent on her computer. That's when I remembered I'd yet to pick up my new computer. It had to be done today.

She lifted her chin and stared at me. "If you're about to ask if I'm in the mood to babysit, the answer is no. When it comes to Baron, the answer will always be no."

I smirked. Raven and Baron knew each other before I was upgraded, as Baron liked to refer to it. They had a tempestuous relationship that had only grown more fraught as he more frequently graced us with his presence.

"He's out staring at his reflection." I sat in the chair across from her desk. "He was feeling philosophical, and actually got me thinking."

"I don't believe that. He's too full of himself."

"He's back to normal. He actually said—with a straight face—that the House of Mirrors was glorious. Of course, he was staring at hundreds of his reflections at the time."

"He is nothing if not predictable," she said. "What did he have to say? It's so rare that it happens I might want to mark it in my calendar for posterity."

"I found skeleton footprints, proving they've been in the park."

Her eyebrows moved toward one another. "And you want to know why they haven't made their way to us."

I shouldn't have been surprised that she understood. "Have you been thinking about it too?"

She nodded. "It doesn't make sense."

"Baron pointed something out: intent matters with the dreamcatcher."

"Oh, geez." Raven nodded. "The skeletons have no intent. Wait, if zombies cross the dreamcatcher, it alerts. They technically don't have intent because they're brain dead."

"Baron brought up another good point." I shifted. "Do we have confirmation that anyone has been attacked by these things?"

"Didn't you say the first skeleton you saw was trying to bite a woman outside the bar?"

"Yes, but what if we assumed that?"

"The women at the magic store said people have died."

"They didn't have names."

"Maybe they haven't injured anyone."

"Or people may have injured themselves trying to get away," I replied. "Maybe they're self-destructing because they're not supposed to hurt anyone. What if their purpose is to find something?"

"Find what?"

I held out my hands. "I don't know, but San Francisco has a lot of legends. Maybe we should look at those legends for answers."

Raven started typing. "Let's see if I can find anything about legends in the area. The lady in white at the lake is right on top."

That was to be expected.

"The ghost cop and Alcatraz are here, no surprise. There's a story about a tribal princess sleeping in Mount Tamalpais. That probably doesn't work for us. Supposedly there are a bunch of secret tunnels under Chinatown. There's a legend about suicides in Sutro Forest. That's not too far away."

I lifted my finger. "What's the story?"

"It says that a bunch of people—mostly men—went into the forest to kill themselves. They all hanged themselves at separate times. The forest is haunted."

"You said it was mostly men."

She nodded.

"Any names?"

"No, but that doesn't necessarily mean anything." She tapped her fingers on her desk. "The names of suicide victims aren't often reported unless they're famous."

I nodded. "Anything else?"

"There's something called the Sutro Bath sacrifices. Anton LaVey, the founder of the Church of Satan, was nearby. He was supposed to have conducted animal sacrifices and seances in the tunnels beneath the church. They say that if you light a candle at the end of the tunnel an invisible force takes it and throws it in the ocean."

"That's likely hysteria whipped up by the presence of the church. Those stories don't work for me when it comes to the skeleton lady."

Raven cocked her head. "I'll do some research to see if we can tweak the dreamcatcher. I'm leery about it because if we draw in a bunch of other people who might be evil but without intent we're going to be swamped with bad guys."

"And because we don't know what the skeletons are up to, there's no way to pinpoint one activity to draw them in with the spell."

She held out her hands. "I don't know what you want me to do."

Briefly, I closed my eyes. "I feel as if we're missing something that's right under our noses."

"That's because you're hard on yourself. We could be a million miles away from the answer and you would still feel guilty. We have to let this play out."

20
TWENTY

It was our last night of freedom in San Francisco, with the circus starting the next day, so we went to my favorite restaurant. Fog Harbor Fish House was a must visit whenever we were here, and even Luke didn't complain when we headed to Fisherman's Wharf for dinner. I thought it would be just the four of us, but Baron wedged himself into the backseat of Kade's truck.

"I love a foggy harbor," was all he said when I sent him a questioning look.

I smiled and shook my head. As much as he irritated me, he amused me too. He had a zest for life that I wouldn't have associated with someone who had lived as long as he had. He treated each day as if it was a party.

We got a table on the water, and I was almost giddy as I grabbed the menu. "You're going to love this place," I told Kade.

Kade smiled indulgently and rubbed my back. "I'm looking forward to it."

I frowned when Baron, who had taken the spot at the head of the table, reached around from the other side and started rubbing.

"Me too," the loa said.

We'd gotten more than a few odd looks when we'd followed the hostess through the restaurant. Thankfully, Baron didn't paint his face with the typical skull makeup he donned when drinking in the Quarter.

"We'll start with cocktails," Baron said when the server appeared.

Connie, judging by her nametag, gave him a sidelong look. "Okay," she said, drawing out the single word.

"He was rehearsing for performances in the park," I lied. "He didn't have time to shower and change."

Connie looked relieved. "He's part of the festival."

I bobbed my head "He's kind of full of himself," I added. "He likes when people stare at him."

"I do," Baron agreed solemnly.

"Well, you're doing a good job." Connie was much more relaxed when she pulled out a handheld device to take our orders. "Drinks."

"I'll have the Patron El Alto Fashioned," Cole said.

"I'll have the Alcatraz Escape," Kade added.

Luke was all smiles. "I'll have the Purple Haze, and she'll have the Lipstick Lemon Drop." He jerked his thumb at me.

I frowned. "Why don't I get to choose my own drink?"

"You were going to pick the lemon one anyway," Luke replied.

"That's fine with me," I told Connie.

"And you?" she asked Baron.

"That all sounds good to me," he said.

Confusion knit her eyebrows. "But which one?"

"Why choose?" Baron waved his hand as if she'd said the most ridiculous thing in the world. "Bring them all."

Her eyes flicked to me. She couldn't possibly understand that it would take an actual keg to make him even a little tipsy.

"It's fine," I assured her. "He's not driving."

"That's a lot of alcohol. Have you had his liver tested recently?"

"We're just hoping that he's not sitting on the good furniture when it finally fails."

She smiled, then caught herself. "Okay. Do you want appetizers? I can put those in while you decide on your entrees."

If I was going to spend a lot of time with Baron, I was going to need a lot of food to stuff into my mouth to cut off the snarky comments. "Appetizers are a good idea."

"Definitely," Cole agreed. "We'll get the blue cheese garlic bread, the fried scallops, the red chili garlic shrimp, and the baked tomato bruschetta."

"I'll have that too," Baron said.

I shook my head when Connie sent us a questioning look. "He'll share with us."

She still looked confused as she headed to the kitchen.

"We'll have to leave her a huge tip," Kade said. "Like, massive."

"I have a feeling this meal is going to be the equivalent of the cost of a sofa at our new house."

"It's on me," Baron replied.

I gave him a sharp look. "Do you even have a credit card?"

"Of course." Baron dug in his pocket and came back with a platinum American Express, a black Luxury Card, and a Chase sapphire card, all made of titanium.

"What the hell?" I grabbed the black card. "How do you have these?"

"I've been around a very long time, Poet. I've amassed quite a bit of money."

I wasn't convinced. I handed the card back to him. "Dinner is definitely on you."

"I'm going big," Luke said with a grin.

I had every intention of going big too. "We should've added the mussel fries to the appetizers."

"And the oysters," Baron added. "I'll find our lovely server." Before I could stop him, he was off on a hunt.

I watched him go, dumbfounded. "It's like having a teenager to take care of," I complained.

"I was never that bad as a teenager," Kade countered.

"I was," Luke replied. He picked up the sapphire credit card from the table. "I never had access to one of these. That was probably for the best."

I studied the menu, allowing myself to relax even though it didn't feel as if we'd gotten much accomplished for the day. "I'm getting the garlic roasted crab and a salad." If Baron was paying, I didn't care about dropping sixty bucks on an entree. "Steak again?" I teased Kade.

"Surf and turf. The mashed potatoes are garlic so I guess we'll be stinking together."

"We can brush our teeth before heading out for drinks."

He looked taken aback. "I didn't realize we were doing that." Unease practically rolled off him in waves. "Is that wise?"

I shrugged. "I won't hide at the circus all night. I love this city. I want to have fun, and we really haven't had a chance for drinks yet."

"But what if the skeletons come calling?"

"Raven and I talked about that. We're starting to wonder if the skeletons are actually a threat."

Cole's eyes went wide as he dropped his menu.

I shrugged. "I know it sounds weird," I acknowledged. "But they aren't killing people."

"That first night we saw one attack a woman."

"Did we really?"

Cole's forehead creased. "I don't understand what you're getting at," he admitted.

"Baron made a good point this afternoon," I started.

"I always make good points," Baron said as he reclaimed his seat. "The other appetizers are coming." He rubbed his hands together. "What good point did I make this afternoon?"

"When I said the dreamcatcher wasn't failing," I said.

He cocked his head. "Ah, the part about the skeletons not being drawn in because they lack evil intent. A true testament to my brilliance."

I glared at him. "Can you not take things to a weird place?"

"According to your grandmother, that's impossible."

Momentarily, I wished for Brigitte. She always knew how to put Baron in his place. Unfortunately, they fought like the Kardashians and Taylor Swift.

"What was I saying again?" I asked when I realized conversation had ground to a standstill.

"You don't think the skeletons are evil," Cole replied.

"What if the skeletons aren't self-destructing because they're about to get caught, but because they're about to become dangerous?" I challenged.

Cole opened his mouth, then shut it. He didn't get a chance to continue because Connie returned with our drinks at that moment.

"It'll be a bit before your appetizers come out," she said. "Do you want to order your entrees?"

Kade and I placed our orders. Cole was almost mechanical ordering the seafood platter. Luke kept his smile firmly in place ordering the crab, but without the garlic. Baron being Baron, he ordered three entrees.

"I'll have the seafood penne, the garlic crab, and the seafood platter," he said. "Make sure there's garlic on everything."

Connie's eyes were the size of saucers. "Um..."

"It's fine," I assured her. I grabbed one of his credit cards, which were still scattered on the table. "Just think of him like he's your crazy uncle."

"My crazy uncle doesn't have a black card. He walks around with mothballs in his underwear," Connie replied. "I'll be back with your appetizers shortly."

"We're really going to have to tip her well," Luke said.

"It's fine," Baron said. "Waitresses love me. I get a lot of action from the waitresses in the Quarter. I bet I could do well here too."

That was not a subject I wanted to discuss. "We're talking about the skeletons now."

Baron grew serious. "I've been thinking about your predicament for the better part of the afternoon. When I wasn't distracted by the handsome devil in the House of Mirrors."

"Who was the handsome devil in the House of Mirrors?" Luke asked.

I shot him a dark look. "He was obsessed with his own reflection."

"Ah, right." Luke bobbed his head. "I've spent hours in there before. You need to be careful. If you spend too much time ogling yourself, it's like taking a gift away from the world. Plus, you'll get too used to perfection so everything else in life will feel like a disappointment."

"I can't believe this conversation is continuing," Kade muttered.

I patted his knee under the table. When Luke and Baron got together, they were even more grating than usual. It was as if they both picked the worst things about their personalities and fed on them as a unit.

"I'm not saying that the skeletons aren't a threat," I said, taking control of the conversation once again. "There are certain things that suggest our first assumption might not have been correct."

"Tell us more." Cole leaned back and rested his arm on the back of Luke's chair. From all outward appearances, he seemed calm. I knew better. He didn't like my theory. He needed me to convince him.

"For starters, the skeletons are not difficult to take out. There are enough skeletons beneath the city to do real damage, yet they haven't. They haven't even come close." I sipped my cocktail before continuing. "Raven and I did a deep dive this afternoon. We can't find a single skeleton victim."

Cole pulled out his phone and started typing. When the appetizers arrived, I dug in with everybody. We plowed our way through them as if we hadn't eaten in days. Cole spoke only after Connie cleared the appetizer plates and brought the entrees.

"You're right," he said finally. "I can't find a single confirmation of a death. There are a few injuries."

"Were they biting injuries?" Luke asked.

Cole shook his head. "The injuries were sustained when people tried to fight the skeletons. Or run from them. There are some sprained ankles, bumps and bruises from falls. Someone broke a wrist hitting one in the face."

"No one died?" Kade said. "Didn't you guys hear stories about people dying?" he asked me.

I nodded. "But you can't always take those stories as fact simply because some people *think* they heard something."

Kade's face was blank. "Then we should leave the skeletons be?"

I shook my head. "Absolutely not. They're still a problem. We don't know what they were going to do on the bridge the other night."

"They also attacked us at the prison," Cole pointed out.

Cole rubbed his forehead. "I can't look at those things and not see them as a threat. I get what you're saying, though. Things aren't exactly how we thought they were."

"Not even a little," I agreed.

"Then what do we do?" Luke asked. "How are we supposed to move forward if we don't actually have an enemy?"

"I think she's looking for something," I replied. "I think she got a power boost from the chalice. Other than that, I just don't know."

Baron looked up from his plate. He'd already mowed through the seafood platter and was elbow deep in his pasta. "Ah, yes, the power boost. Run me through that again."

"When this first started, only one or two skeletons were seen here and there. At the time we destroyed the chalice, her power seemed to grow exponentially. She can now unleash an army of hundreds of skeletons. I'm not the only one who got an upgrade."

Baron shoved more penne into his mouth and chewed. "Interesting," he burped. "I didn't think hard enough about the fact that the magic had to go somewhere."

"Not all of it dissipated," I said.

"A lot would've been absorbed," he agreed. "I wonder what this thing was before her upgrade."

"You said she was like a wendigo."

"I used a wendigo as an example of a being that created itself," he corrected. "You brought up the figment, another example. One of those transformations was a choice, the other wasn't."

"What do you mean?"

"Figments wish themselves into being," he replied. "They choose their form and embrace it. Wendigos often spring from great suffering. Starvation. Mourning periods that never end. If you were to sit them down and ask if they wanted to turn into a monster, they would say no. Their feelings of self-loathing and general hunger cause it to happen. It's not a choice."

Now I understood, and it was an interesting observation. "This creature might not have chosen this outcome."

"And it might be grappling with what it has done," Baron added.

"I still don't understand the plan," Luke said.

"You can't have a plan without the creature," Baron replied. "You need to find her and figure out what's what. Otherwise, you'll lose."

"Well, aren't you cheery?" Kade drawled.

"After a few more drinks, I will be." Baron winked at Kade. "The spirits aren't very strong here, but I'll make it work. Where are we going after this?"

That was a very good question. I needed a prominent location if I was going to draw the skull woman to me.

21
TWENTY-ONE

Stuffed to the point I wanted larger pants, we made our way back to the circus. Everybody changed—I wasn't the only one who had practically eaten her way out of her waistband—and then we headed out. We wanted a bar within walking distance so nobody had to be the designated driver.

We let Luke choose the bar—it was easier than having to deal with a meltdown—and it was the name that decided it. He'd told us days earlier that he didn't want to visit an Irish bar. Once he saw the name Durty Nelly's, however, that insistence went out the window.

"It's going to be great," he assured me as we walked with Baron between us. Behind us, I heard Cole and Kade chatting in low voices. They seemed happy not to have Baron taking over their conversation.

"I just want a few hours to relax," I replied. "We probably won't get that, though, so don't get too drunk."

Luke sent me a sidelong look. "Why not?"

"The skeletons come out tonight. You know it as well as I do."

"You don't know," Luke challenged. "Maybe the beatdown we put on them at Alcatraz will send them into hiding."

I shook my head. "This creature doesn't care about sacrificing the skeletons."

"You said she wasn't a bad guy."

I slowed my pace. "I said I didn't think anyone had died so maybe her motivations were different."

"Sounds like the same thing to me," Luke said blandly.

It was times like this I wanted to hurt him. Badly. "I can't make a decision on anything until I have completely thought things through."

Baron, who had drifted ahead, halted. When he turned to me, his grin was fond. "Your grandmother says things like that. It's one of the reasons I love her the way I do."

I shot him a dirty look. "Now is not the time for you to be a weirdo. If you're going to be part of this team—and you seem determined to—then you need to get it together and start thinking outside the box too."

If Baron was bothered by my admonishment, he didn't show it. "I do my best thinking when I'm drinking."

That was a bald-faced lie. It had to be. I nodded all the same. "Fine, get your drink on."

Durty Nelly's had a bright yellow exterior with blue trim and a red door. It was jarring, but in a good way. Inside there was a long bar, stickers and signs all over the walls, and tables scattered everywhere. There were televisions in every open area, and it looked as if people were gearing up for a trivia competition.

Luke bobbed his head. "I'm really good at trivia."

I rolled my eyes. "You're terrible at trivia."

"Um ... I'm the best trivia-er—that's a word, right?—who ever lived."

I couldn't stop from laughing. "Maybe we'll play a round. Not until we have some drinks in us."

Luke nodded. "I'll order. What do you want?"

Durty Nelly's didn't have an extensive cocktail menu. That was fine for me, though, because I wasn't in the mood for anything fancy. "Just get me a bottle of something light," I instructed.

Luke's eyes narrowed into suspicious slits. "Since when do you want beer?"

"I don't want to get drunk tonight."

"You think we're going to find her on the way home."

"We won't. She's going to find us."

Luke opened his mouth, then shut it. "Maybe I'll just stick to beer too," he said.

WE DRANK. WE WATCHED LUKE PRETEND he was straight to hit on a woman and prove he was the handsomest member of our group. Cole wasn't bothered by the effort. He laughed until he bent at the waist to catch his breath. We played trivia, and even did surprisingly well despite the serious teams in contention. When Luke, Kade, and Cole broke off to shoot pool, I breathed out a sigh of relief. With Baron up at the bar trying to hit on a woman, I took advantage of the solitude to just breathe.

In and out. In and out.

The atmosphere was getting more tense by the minute, though I couldn't identify why.

Then she was there. The skull woman walked through the door and headed straight for my table.

I waited for the bar patrons to panic. No one even looked in her direction other than a few cursory glances. That's when it hit me. She'd glamoured herself. I could see the real her. It was likely the others—with the possible exceptions of Baron, Cole, and Kade—saw a human woman sitting across from me.

"Well, this is a surprise," I said before I took a long pull on my beer. I was nervous, but deep down this was what I'd wanted. A chance to talk to her. If we could come to an agreement, we would be able to move on and ... what? What did I expect to happen here? I had no idea.

"You're not surprised," the woman—was she a woman?—insisted. "You knew I would come after your showing in the prison last night."

"I hoped you'd come."

She chuckled.

"Let's get the pleasantries out of the way. What should I call you?"

"Call me whatever you want."

"My name is Poet," I continued, as if I hadn't heard her. A name might be useful for trying to dig up information on her.

"What kind of a name is Poet?" The creature looked annoyed.

I waited, and after a few seconds of uncomfortable silence, she made an exasperated sound deep in her throat.

"You may call me Catalina."

"Catalina means pure." It was also a name popular in Hispanic circles.

"Your name isn't even a name," Catalina sneered. Unlike the skeletons she commanded, she had a nose. "We need to have a discussion."

I nodded to propel her forward. This was what I wanted.

"You need to back off," she continued. With that, she moved to stand, suggesting she was going to leave.

"That cannot be our entire conversation," I barked.

"I have nothing else to say to you," Catalina replied.

"We have a few things to talk about." I patted the table to get her to sit. "You know you want to."

Catalina rolled her eyes but did as I asked. When I looked over, I saw Kade, Cole, and Luke watching me from the other side of the room. I sent them an almost imperceptible shake of the head to keep them in place.

"You're wise to keep them away," Catalina said. "I don't have much patience, and from what I can tell, the blond one is too annoying to let live."

I narrowed my eyes. "Stay away from my family."

"Family?" she sputtered. "You're all with the circus. That doesn't make you family."

"That shows what you know. We *are* family, a good one." I struggled to get my temper under control. "You don't get to dictate terms during this discussion. You're not the only magical one here."

"I could crush you like a cockroach. I showed you my power on the bridge. The only reason you're still alive is because I didn't choose to kill you."

"That's fair." Lying to her wasn't going to get me anywhere, so I went with the truth. "You also didn't take us on when we were at our best. We expended a lot of magic fighting your army. That won't be the case tonight."

Her lips, blood red without any makeup, tipped up. "Is that so?"

I backtracked, but only slightly. "I don't want to kill you. That's not my goal."

"What is your goal?"

"To keep people safe."

"What makes you think my goal is any different?"

I shrugged. "The skeletons mostly."

"They're on a mission."

"What are they seeking?"

Genuine surprise registered on her features, but she shuttered it quickly.

"You sent them to specific neighborhoods before you got your power boost."

She shifted on her seat, registering even more surprise. "How...?" She trailed off.

"The Chalice of Fuerza," I volunteered. "We destroyed it in San Diego, but a lot of magic escaped in the process. The timing suggests you received some of that magic."

"What is the Chalice of Fuerza?"

"Aztec magic."

"The magic of my people."

"I guess that may be true." I gave her another long look. "Catalina is a Latin name."

"Technically it's Greek."

"Yes, but it's used in Latin circles mostly now."

"What makes you think that I'm from this era?" There was a coldness to her tone that had me taking a moment to consider things.

"I just have a feeling."

"Do you do that often? Have feelings I mean."

"I do."

"What do those feelings tell you now?"

"That you're more powerful than you expected to be. That you're looking for something. You're not killing people just to kill them, which means there's still hope for you." I leveled a deadly glare on her. "If you stop doing what you're doing. Even if your skeletons didn't try to kill anyone on the bridge, there could have been a catastrophe."

"The only catastrophe would've been of your making."

"Tell me what you want," I prodded. "I might be able to help you."

"You can't."

"You don't know that."

"But I do." She looked up when a Hispanic woman walked past, allowing her glamour to slip for the briefest of moments, as if she was conducting a test.

The woman was taken aback, genuine shock rocking her. "La Ciguapa," she hissed, turning back around and hurrying toward the door.

"La Ciguapa?"

Catalina laughed, but there was an edge to her features now. "Back to what we were talking about," she said. "Stay out of my business."

"Tell me what your business is, and maybe we can come to an agreement," I countered.

"No."

She wasn't giving me anything to work with. "I'm going to tell you what I think," I offered, changing tactics. "You're looking for something that has sentimental value." It was a leap, but I was committed to it. "You don't strike me as someone looking for world domination."

She made a face. "World domination? You're a dramatic little thing."

I silently thanked my stars that Luke wasn't here for this conversation. If she thought I was dramatic, he would knock her for a loop she might never recover from. "You're not actively trying to hurt anyone. Except for us. Even so, I'm not sure you wanted to hurt us last night as much as you wanted to send a message."

Her lips quirked, but she didn't say anything.

"You don't want us in your way," I continued. "You think we're a danger to your plans. Hurting people isn't your aim."

"If you believe that, why are you sticking your nose in my business?" She looked genuinely curious.

"Your intentions aren't enough. That thing you did on the bridge the other night, people could've panicked and died."

She was quiet, as if considering, then shook her head. "I made a promise to my son. I swore to him that I would get this done eighty years ago, and I will."

A son? "Where is your son?"

Sadness permeated her features. I knew right away she wasn't softening toward me. Something inside of her might have gone momentarily soft, but that emotion wouldn't extend outward. "Stay out of my business." She stood. "I know what you are. I will do what's necessary to keep you out of my way." She took a step away from the table, then glanced back at me over her shoulder. "Back off."

I had no choice but to make her understand. "I can't."

"Then you'll die." On a sigh, she turned away from me. She walked away before I could say anything else, disappearing through the door.

I considered chasing her, but engaging in a magical showdown on the street seemed like a bad idea.

I was alone only a few seconds before Cole, Kade, and Luke returned.

"Are you okay?" Kade brushed my hair away from my face. "Did she threaten you?"

"We were going to come over, but were afraid to ruin the moment," Cole added.

"It was good you stayed back," I assured him. "She wasn't going to hurt me. At least not tonight."

"What did she want?" Luke asked.

"To warn me to stay away."

"That's it?" Luke's eyebrows moved toward one another. "That's all she wanted?"

"That's what she said."

"But you don't believe her," Cole surmised.

"She said she made a promise to her son eighty years ago. She's not worried about collateral damage. She said she'll kill us.

"There's something about her." I licked my lips, then exhaled heavily. I remembered the woman who had thrown Catalina for a loop, and told them about the brief exchange. "La Ciguapa. We need to figure out who that is."

Cole nodded. "Maybe we should do that back at the circus grounds."

Luke whined. "I'm not done getting my drink on."

"Then you stay here with Baron." There was no give to Cole's tone. "I doubt very much he'll leave this early. You can be his wingman."

Luke considered it, then shook his head. "I don't want to be separated from you and Poet." He glanced at Kade. "I would be fine being separated from you."

Kade rolled his eyes until they landed on me. "We can have drinks at the circus grounds. I think, much like everybody else, this is something we need to hash out."

22
TWENTY-TWO

Luke continued sulking at the circus grounds. Nellie shoved a beer in his hand, and he got over it quickly.

"She looked normal," Luke said as he held court. "I had no idea she was the skull lady until Cole said something."

"It was a glamour," I countered as I sat at a picnic table with Cole. He was looking up La Ciguapa.

"So she can appear normal," Raven mused. "I wonder why she doesn't do that all the time."

"Maybe she doesn't feel it's necessary," Kade suggested as he stood behind me and rubbed my shoulders. "If she's not out in public all that often, what would be the point?"

"She didn't use it on the bridge," Raven pointed out.

"She might not have thought she was going to show herself," Cole said. "She only appeared after we intervened."

Raven tapped her bottom lip. "Good point."

"Anything on the La Ciguapa thing?" I asked Cole when silence had descended.

"There's some, but not as much as I'd like." He rolled his neck. "It says here that she's a mythological creature of Dominican Republic folklore."

"That makes sense if the stories we heard about the skeletons are true. They were targeting Hispanic and Latino neighborhoods to start."

"Looking for something," Raven supplied. "She's looking for something in those neighborhoods."

"I essentially told her the same thing," I said. "She didn't confirm it. She didn't really deny it either. She just went all 'don't get in my way or I'll kill you' and took off."

"This entry says there's more than one," Cole said. "They're referred to as a ciguapa or ciguapas."

I nodded for him to continue.

"They're described as females," he continued. "They have either brown or dark blue skin."

"Oh, they're like giant Smurfs," Luke enthused. "Why didn't we get one of the blue ones? That would be so cool."

I shot him a quelling look, then turned back to Cole. "Why are they blue?"

Cole shrugged. "Maybe they're *Avatar* fans."

"You mean *Dances With Wolves* fans?" Nellie shot back. "That's all that movie is, and with too many special effects thrown in to make it fancy."

"I'll take your word for it," Cole replied.

"Just keep going," I prodded.

"They have long glossy hair that covers their bodies," Cole said.

"Like fur?" Luke looked horrified.

"I think more like the kid from *The Ring*," Nellie said.

Cole nodded. "I would go with Nellie's interpretation," he agreed. "They're supposedly mountain dwellers."

"San Francisco is surrounded by mountains," Raven added. "Mount Davidson, Mount Sutro, and Twin Peaks."

"Not to be confused with the very excellent television show," Luke said.

I ignored him and listened intently as Cole kept reading.

"This says their feet face backward," he supplied, his forehead creasing. "That has to make walking pretty difficult. They're nocturnal, which fits what's going on here. "Due to their feet, you're not supposed to be able to tell which direction they're going. Some people believe they bring death, and others say you shouldn't ever look them in the eye or you'll be bewitched."

I leaned back into Kade's massage and grunted when he hit a particularly tender spot.

"They don't talk," Cole added. "They chirp or whine."

"They sound like demented birds." Nellie shook his head. "You know how I feel about birds."

"Yes, you think they're unnatural," I said.

"They're creepy." Nellie's lower lip came out to play. "They crap everywhere, but that's a different problem."

"Ah, here we go." Cole straightened. "Their appearance changes depending on who they interact with. Some find them beautiful, some grotesque."

"That could be the glamours," I mused.

"They're considered wild creatures and often compared to mermaids, suggesting they're beautiful but cruel."

Catalina was beautiful. At least the glamour she'd chosen had been. Even underneath, however terrible, the skull was also somehow beautiful.

"They're considered deceitful and apparently want to isolate wayward travelers," he continued. "Although, other legends say they're benevolent."

"The legends are all over the place," Kade said.

"There doesn't seem to be a clear narrative," Cole acknowledged.

"Or the ciguapas aren't one thing," Raven argued.

"The reason the legends are all over the place is because they're trying to make the ciguapas conform to one mold. As we know, conformity never works."

Nellie flexed his muscles in his spaghetti strap dress. "Right?"

I smirked. "What else?" I asked Cole.

"According to this, the only way to capture a ciguapa is to track them at night during a full moon with a black and white polydactyl dog."

My mouth fell open. "Well, that's specific."

Cole laughed. "I'm not sure we'll be able to find an extra-toed black and white dog on short notice."

"How do you even figure something like that out?" Kade asked. "To become legend, something has to happen more than once, right?"

I shrugged. "You have to take legends with a grain of salt. There's always a bit of truth in there.

"The one other entry I found refers to the ciguapa as a succubus," Cole said. "She's known to lure wandering lonely men to their deaths. She lures them with her chirps—"

"Because that always does it for me," Nellie said dryly.

"She invades kitchens and villages to steal food, hypnotizes men the second they lay eyes on her, and then devours them whole while trapping their souls for eternity," Cole said.

"Sounds like the typical 'women are evil' legend that can pop up anywhere," Raven argued. "I wouldn't put a lot of faith in it. There might be a few things in there that are true, but it's one of those stories that spreads when men get lured by a beautiful woman. It's easier to blame the other woman than the married man."

"Her being a succubus is interesting, but I don't think it's right," I said. "She's not focusing on men. She's looking for something."

"They may be a subset of demons and don't care about correcting misconceptions," Raven said. "That would be my guess. Being able to glamour herself comes straight out of the legend."

"But we're flying blind on the rest of it," I said.

"It's no different than fighting one demon and assuming a second demon will be the same. Sure, they're both demons, but they have different powers and abilities. Not to mention motivations. If she is a ciguapa—and the reaction you described makes me think it's possible—she could be capable of any number of things."

I rubbed my forehead. What she wasn't saying was that it was possible the woman who saw Catalina in the bar simply latched on to a story from her childhood.

"She doesn't seem to want to kill us," Dolph interjected. "Maybe we should leave her be."

"What if she hasn't killed yet because she's not desperate enough?" I challenged.

"By then we could be long gone," Cole added. He exhaled heavily as he lowered his phone. "It's a mess," he said.

"That doesn't make her our enemy," I offered. "Maybe we can get through to her."

Raven folded her arms across her chest. "You have to be prepared to kill her if this starts spiraling. I know she hasn't technically crossed that line, but she might still be a threat."

On a groan, I nodded. "I know. There's a big piece of the puzzle still out there."

"We still have a few days," Raven said.

"Tomorrow is Thursday," I reminded her. "We have several long days ahead of us, and because this is a festival, the circus is open until late afternoon Sunday. We leave Monday."

"That's four days," Raven pointed out. "We've only been at this four days and the first day doesn't really count because we didn't realize there was an issue until late that night. We can still figure this out."

I wanted her to be right. I *needed* her to be right.

"Let's get some sleep," Cole suggested, breaking the tension that had settled over our group. "Everybody is on their own for breakfast tomorrow. The circus opens at eleven o'clock, so we need everybody here at ten to handle last-minute setup.

"As for the ciguapa, if that's what we're dealing with, we'll start figuring things out tomorrow," he continued. "We need rest."

. . .

I SLEPT RELATIVELY WELL DESPITE THE EXCITEMENT of meeting Catalina. I expected dark dreams, but they didn't appear. When I woke, I felt rested if not relaxed.

Before I could focus on the circus, however, I needed breakfast.

Kade chose Mama's on Washington Square with me in mind. It was famous—long lines on weekends and good word of mouth—but all I cared about was the food.

"They're called M'omelettes but they're omelets," the server Theresa informed us.

"Awesome. Um, I will have the scrambled Florentine and whole-wheat toast. With tomato juice and coffee, please."

"You got it." Theresa winked at me, which threw the whole winking game into a topsy-turvy place.

Kade chuckled as he rubbed my back. "Maybe you'll win," he whispered.

I shrugged.

"What's your most famous M'omelette?" Luke asked Theresa, his most charming smile on display.

Theresa, not charmed, shrugged. "Probably the Northwest."

Luke read the description and instantly frowned. "Salmon does not belong in an omelet."

"People like it," Theresa protested.

"Sick people." Luke shook his head. "I'll have the Californian with whole grain toast, an orange juice, and a coffee."

"Okay." Theresa rolled her eyes, then winked at me a second time as if we were sharing a joke. "What about you?" she asked Kade.

"Banana pancakes, a side of bacon, and grapefruit juice, please."

"I can do that." Theresa's smile was easy with him. Then she focused on Cole. "And you, sweetheart?"

Cole seemed less like himself this morning. He wasn't talking much, and he had no smile at the ready. Still, he was polite to Teresa. "I'll have the huevos rancheros, please. With whole-grain toast and orange juice."

"Do you want coffee?' Theresa asked.

"Please."

I kept my smile in place as Theresa headed off to put our order in. Then I gave Cole my full attention. "Do you want to tell me what's going on?"

"I'm fine."

He didn't look fine. "Cole..."

Luke gave me a shake of his head from across the table. "Don't push him, Poet," he admonished. "He didn't sleep well last night. That always makes him cranky."

I couldn't hide my surprise. Here I was assuming that I would have the bad dreams, but it was Cole.

"I was just restless," Cole replied, refusing to meet my eyes. "Nothing to worry about."

"Cole—"

"Don't." Agitation flashed in his eyes. "I don't mean to be crabby. I just have a bad feeling about how all of this is going to play out."

"Bad feeling?" Kade asked. His hand was on my back, but his eyes were on our friend. "What do you think is going to happen?"

Cole sat there and blinked for what felt like a long time. Then he licked his lips and sighed. "I dreamed of a dark-haired woman who tried to seduce me."

Everybody stilled.

"I don't think that means what you think it does," I said.

He rolled his eyes. "I'm not worried that I'm suddenly straight." He looked as if he wanted to remain stern but then he laughed. "Good grief. You really think that's what I'm worried about?"

I shrugged, uncertain. "Maybe a little," I conceded. "I've had dreams where I've been married to penguins. Sometimes your subconscious does weird things."

"I once dreamed I was married to Raven," Kade added. "She was insatiable."

I tracked my gaze to him. I couldn't believe he'd actually admitted that.

"Oh, crap," Kade muttered when he snagged gazes with me.

"That was a really stupid thing to say," Luke agreed, smiling wide. "You should've said you dreamed that you were married to me."

"That would've been a nightmare," Kade shot back. He held out his hands as he regarded me. "I don't have a thing for Raven. It was just a dream."

"It's fine," I assured him, managing to keep my expression neutral through sheer force of will. "Dreams aren't important. I had a dream about Dolph the other night. He can do amazing things with a trapeze."

Kade's expression turned dour. "You're just saying that because you want to punish me. I don't have a thing for Raven."

"If that's your story," Luke trilled.

Kade jabbed a finger in his direction. "You're not helping."

"I didn't know I was supposed to be helping." Luke was all faux innocence and impish delight. "Sorry." He wasn't sorry.

"I don't want to talk about Kade's love for Raven," I said. "I want to talk about Cole's dream." I stared him in the eyes. "Your dream doesn't mean anything. I once dreamed I gave birth to a dog."

Luke's hand shot in the air. "I have a theory about that since I'm a shifter."

Nobody acknowledged him.

"I'm not upset about the sex angle," Cole assured me. "I used to have dreams about having sex with women when I was younger. They were vastly outnumbered by my other dreams, but it's not unheard of. That's not what's bothering me."

"What is it?"

"What I read last night. The dream felt ... pointed. The woman had long dark hair and kept making this chirping noise to draw me in."

Realization dawned. "You think it was Catalina. Like, a real dream."

"Was she trying to lure Cole in his dreams?" Luke made a face. "That's kind of a waste of time."

"It's not good news either. She's coming for us."

"Unless it really was just a dream," Cole countered.

"Even if it was, your subconscious is telling you we're out of time. I'm right there with you. We need answers."

Luke nodded sagely. "We need to get ahead of this."

"You need to protect Kade in his dreams," Cole said. "It didn't work on me, but it might work on him."

"No way." Kade adamantly shook his head. "Poet is the only one for me."

His innocent response was enough to make Cole snicker. "Never say never."

23
TWENTY-THREE

We were swamped from the moment the circus opened. I needed to strategize for our battle with Catalina, but there were too many people clamoring for readings. I had to focus on my customers. And what a weird array of customers it was.

"You want to do what?" I eyed Francesca Mortimer with what I hoped wasn't horror. I'd learned to school my face over the years, but I was shocked.

"It's not a big thing," she insisted. "I need to know how to break my parents up and get my father put in jail."

I licked my lips, debating, then sighed. I had to know more about this. "Did your father do something to you?" If that was the case, I would help her.

"Yes." Francesca was emphatic. "He said I have to get a job."

I waited for her to continue. When she didn't, I cocked my head. "And?" I prodded.

"I don't want to get a job."

"But you're like thirty."

Francesca sat straighter. "Twenty-nine."

A quick jaunt inside her head proved that was a lie. "You're thirty-two." I wasn't in the mood to play this game. "Are you seriously telling me you've never had a job?"

Francesca's eyes flared with something dark. "I'm a party planner."

I scanned her again. "Helping your mother with a fundraiser does not make you a party planner."

Genuine shock filled her eyes. "I've done way more than that." It was a lie.

"Two years ago, you helped your mother plan a benefit for orphans," I replied, my tone neutral even though I wanted to smack her around a little bit. "You spent the whole time complaining about spending money on toys for the kids instead of flowers for centerpieces."

"Flowers are important."

"Gifts for underprivileged kids are more important. Did you think they would take the arrangements home and play with them?"

"I wanted the arrangements for a party I was going to throw later that night." She said it as if I was the one being ridiculous. "Multitasking is important if you're going to be a party planner."

"I'm sure that was helpful to the kids," I said.

"It was."

I didn't like her. Not even a little. Sometimes that made readings more difficult. Sometimes it made things easier. "Do you really think that your father deserves to lose his wife because you don't want to get a job?"

"Yes. My mother agrees that I should be able to embrace my party planner lifestyle."

I didn't have to dive deep inside of Francesca's head. Her thoughts were all on the surface. "Your mother doesn't want to deal with you. Just because she doesn't argue doesn't mean she agrees with you. She thinks you're a lost cause."

"That's what I said."

"She's just too tired to fight with you," I continued.

"She'll still do what I want. My father has decided he's putting his foot down." Her eye roll was cartoonish. "I want that foot to go someplace else. If Mom divorces him, she'll only get half of his money. If he goes to jail, she'll get everything."

Gawd, I hated this woman. "Why should he go to jail?"

Francesca looked momentarily thoughtful. "What have you got? I can say he beats me."

"He doesn't."

"I could say it."

Now it was my turn to roll my eyes. "Your father is a philanthropist. He's not perfect, but he's a good man."

"Says you." Francesca's lip wrinkled into a sneer. "He's terrible."

"Just because he wants you to get a job."

"Hey, this is his fault." Francesca's voice ratcheted up a notch. "He raised me a certain way. Now he wants to treat me differently, and that's not fair."

"Life isn't fair."

"He needs to learn a lesson."

Her father wasn't the one who needed to learn a lesson. "Your father isn't going to jail." She needed some brutal honesty. It wasn't going to change anything, but I was going to enjoy providing it. "In fact, if you mount an offensive against him, you'll end up in jail."

Francesca was taken aback. "Excuse me?"

"You heard me." I had no further patience for this woman. "You're not the shiniest penny in the roll. Your plan will backfire, and you're going to be put in jail for trying to extort money from your father and for lying to the police."

Francesca's eyes went wide. "I have a very high IQ."

I ignored her. "Your mother isn't going to divorce your father. The plan you have to make your mother believe your father is cheating on her will backfire. Your mother already knows that you're plotting. She genuinely loves your father. She won't side with you."

"I know my mother better than you."

"You don't know her better than she knows your father. She's well aware of the type of person you are. Not only will she side with your father, she'll suggest disowning you so that when they do die you won't get an inheritance."

Francesca's eyes looked as if they were going to bug out of her head. "You're lying."

I shook my head. "That's not what I do."

"You're supposed to tell me what I want to hear."

"That's nowhere in my job description. I'm supposed to tell you the truth, and sometimes the truth is brutal."

Anger roiled through Francesca, and she was already wondering if she could get me fired.

"Go ahead and try," I said. "I look forward to the attempt."

She went two shades paler, then growled. "I don't think I like you."

"I'm fine with that."

"I don't want to get a job."

"That's okay," I assured her. "You won't get one. You're far too lazy."

Francesca's smile was instantaneous. "So my father will give in. That's good."

"He's going to give you a deadline to get a job or move out. You really are too old to be living with your parents. He's going to kick you out."

"He can't." Francesca sniffed, which I found altogether irritating. "I have nowhere to go."

"One of your friends will take you in. Tina."

"Tina lives in an even better house than I do." Francesca preened. "That doesn't sound so bad."

"It won't last. You'll sleep with Tina's father in an attempt to break up his marriage."

"He's on marriage number three. That might be a good move. He has a lot of money."

"He'll kick you out the next day," I continued, my voice even. "Once you're out of that house, you'll move in with another friend.

That will last two weeks before you're kicked out again. You'll decide your only move is to marry one of your father's friends."

"If I get a nice house out of it, what's wrong with that?"

"He'll knock you up, make you believe you're in the will, then die and give everything to his kids. You'll be homeless again."

"I don't like that."

"You're really not going to like what happens after," I agreed. "You'll be too old to be a mistress at that point and end up in an apartment complex on Golden Gate Avenue in Tenderloin."

Francesca immediately started shaking her head. "I would never live in that area."

"You won't have a choice. You'll be stuck there the rest of your life ... which won't be long because of the crime in that area, and your inability to take care of yourself."

Francesca's lower lip started to tremble. "I can't live in Tenderloin. That's embarrassing."

"You should be glad you'll still have a roof over your head."

"I don't want any of that," she snapped. "I want to stay where I am."

"Then get a job."

The growl that erupted from her was otherworldly. She almost sounded like a shifter. "I don't like you."

Did she think that hurt my feelings? Why else would she keep saying it? I laughed. "You're in control of your own fate. If you do anything other than put honest effort into getting a job, karma is going to get you."

"Maybe karma will get you instead. You're mean. Karma doesn't like mean people."

"It doesn't like lazy people either."

She stared me down, as if she could bully me into giving her what she wanted. Then she snorted. "I'm going to do this on my own."

I waved her off as she stomped toward the flap. "Enjoy jail."

. . .

I WORKED STEADILY UNTIL lunch. I decided to do one more reading before taking a break. That turned out to be fortuitous—for someone other than me.

Jackson looked as if he was embarrassed to enter my tent. His eyes were wide as he glanced around, taking in the decorations and my peasant blouse and skirt, before smiling as he sat across from me.

"I figured I'd see what all the fuss is about," he said. He didn't look nearly as sure of himself.

I smiled at him, then pointed toward the sign. "Which reading do you want?"

"The standard tarot." He fished in his wallet and came back with some cash. "If that's okay with you."

I took the money and tucked it into the cash box. "I'm fine with whatever you want." I grabbed the tarot deck and started shuffling. "Don't take this the wrong way, but this is the last place I expected to see you."

"I wouldn't have ever imagined myself doing something like this either," he admitted. "It's just ... um..."

"Your sister left her husband," I surmised. "I was right, and you want to know what other tidbits I can show."

"It's not just that," he said hurriedly. "I wanted to thank you. My brother-in-law—my soon-to-be former brother-in-law—was raging last night. She needed me and you knew it. She wouldn't have called me because she was embarrassed, but you saved her."

"She would have eventually saved herself," I countered. "Things would've been much worse for her if she waited, though."

"Still, thank you." Jackson gripped his hands together in front of him, humbled. "I love my sister a great deal. I've always thought it was my responsibility to keep her safe. You helped me do that last night."

"I'm glad she's okay."

"She's with my mother now. Her new apartment isn't ready, but she's safe for now, and that's the important thing." His expression darkened. "Now I need to decide what to do with her husband."

"I already told you, don't do anything," I said. "Just let him be."

"I can't do that. He was going to hurt my sister."

"If you intervene, he'll go to jail. If you do nothing, he'll do something that will make your sister's life much easier. She won't even have to divorce him."

Something sparked in Jackson's eyes. "You're saying..."

"Everything I told you last night still stands," I assured him. "Just let him be. Your sister will be better off for it in a few months. He'll be a jackass during that time, but then he will no longer be a concern."

Jackson looked as if he had questions. To my surprise, he wasn't interested in his brother-in-law's fate. "Just out of curiosity, how often do you see things like you saw last night?"

"Every day that I conduct readings."

"Do you always step in?"

I thought about Oliver and his father, about the tragedy they would've faced if I had done nothing. "I do what I can." I chose my words carefully. "Sometimes, even if there's a tragedy in someone's future, the best thing is for them to go through it.

"I can't always be Superman," I continued. "If I can make things better for someone—and they deserve it—I help as best as I can."

"Do you see your own future?"

I shook my head. "That's not how it works. I've had a few glimpses. For example, I'm in a prophecy that applies to one of my friends. It's her future, but I will be part of it."

He took it in, considering, then nodded. "What do you see about me?"

I handed him the deck. "Cut it three times."

He did as I requested and silently handed them back. His gaze was keen as I started dealing them.

"You're at a crossroads," I said as I studied the cards. "You have a big opportunity for career advancement. The feds want you for a monster-hunting team."

His mouth dropped open. "How...?" Then he asked a different question. "What are you?"

"I have friends who are even more powerful. There really isn't a word for what I am."

His lips quirked. "You might not want to let me in on your secrets but I'm not your enemy."

"I met the enemy last night. Her name is Catalina."

Jackson looked taken aback. "You met her?"

"She followed us to a bar, and we had a conversation."

"You talked with her?"

"Yes."

"Why not kill her?"

"I was hoping that wouldn't be necessary."

"She's evil."

His succinct, two-word response nudged a sigh out of me. "The world is not black and white. That's not how this works. So far, Catalina hasn't tried to kill anyone."

"Then what is she doing?"

"Looking for something."

"What?"

I held out my hands. "She won't tell me, and I can't see what it is."

"But isn't that your job?"

His naïveté made me laugh. "I can't see everything. She's shrouded."

"What did she want from you?"

"She wants us to back off."

He sat straighter. "Because you're a threat to her?"

"Yes, but I don't think that's the only reason. She doesn't want to hurt us. She believes we should remain separate from what she has going. I explained that can't happen—despite her best efforts, she's still a threat—but she wouldn't listen."

He fell silent.

"We have to figure out a way to stop her, and I don't want to kill her in the process," I said.

"What if I kill her?"

I smirked. "You won't."

"You said you couldn't see her future."

"I can see yours. Killing her is not part of the plan."

He grew frustrated. "I can't leave this place, move forward, until this is over. I need to know how to make that happen."

"I don't have an answer for you. I'm trying to figure it out."

"But—"

"Just let it go." I leaned forward and touched his wrist, the oxygen escaping my lungs as a series of images bombarded me. So many skeletons and so many screams. "What are your plans today?" I asked, changing course.

"I'll be hanging around the park." If he thought my question was odd, he didn't say anything. "Why?"

I shrugged. "Just curious."

"Are you worried I'll steal your glory and kill this Catalina?" His smile was smug.

"No, that's not what I'm worried about." *Not even a little,* I added silently.

24
TWENTY-FOUR

I closed my tent the second Jackson left and went looking for Nellie. I found him next to Nixie's booth—her voodoo dolls, which were really evil humans shrunken down and forever trapped in their own karma—were a hot item.

"I'm doing really well." Nixie's eyes sparkled as she met my gaze. "I was worried about having to move all my inventory to Moonstone Bay, but I don't think I'll have much left."

"That's great," I said. I would've meant it under different circumstances, but I didn't really care now. "Nellie, I need you."

He was in one of his favorite costumes, which covered his beefy shoulders but plunged down to his belly button, with wiry hair sticking out in every direction. "I can see that. I always knew that Kade wouldn't be able to push all your buttons."

I gave him a dirty look. "Not for that." I cuffed him. "Why must you always take things to an uncomfortable place?"

His shrug was lackadaisical. "It's what I do."

"Focus." I grabbed him by the back of the neck and stared into his eyes. "I need you to find Detective Jackson."

Nellie balked. "You know how I feel about the fuzz."

There was no give to my tone. "He might be in trouble."

"So? If he gets in trouble, that's on him."

"Nellie." I gritted out his name as if I had a mouthful of rocks. "I'm deadly serious."

His sigh was long and drawn out. "Why am I trying to find him?"

"He was just in my tent. When I touched him, I saw some very freaky images."

"How exactly were you touching him?"

"What is the matter with you? I saw skeletons and heard screams. There was blood. I think there's going to be an attack and he'll try to insert himself into the situation."

Nellie was quiet a beat, then nodded. "Fine, but only because I'm afraid innocent people will get hurt if he sticks his nose where it doesn't belong."

"Great." I shot him a sarcastic thumbs-up. "He was just here. Hopefully, he's still on the circus grounds. If not, find him."

"In a park this big?" Nellie snorted. "I'm good, but not that good."

"Just do it." I gave him a shove. "Text me the second you find him."

"You're so freaking bossy," Nellie complained as he took off.

"Do you want me to go with him?" Nixie asked.

"Nellie has it," I said. "Keep your eyes open here."

"What are you going to do?"

"Get Kade and Cole on the job too. More eyes can't hurt."

I FOUND KADE AND COLE AT the picnic tables by the trailers. Baron was with them. Until laying eyes on the loa, I'd almost forgotten he was here.

"Where have you been?" I demanded.

Baron looked up from his sandwich, mayonnaise on both of his cheeks, and shrugged. "I had a pretty good time last night. Thanks for asking."

"I didn't ask."

"Sure you did." He smiled, showing off his disturbingly white teeth. "San Francisco is a happening town. I like it."

"Great." I shook my head and focused on Kade, who was making his own sandwich. "We have a problem."

"Skeletons?" Kade jerked up his chin. "Where?"

"No skeletons. At least not yet."

Kade looked relieved.

"That doesn't mean they won't come," I said. I told them about my interaction with Jackson. They listened while continuing to assemble their sandwiches. When I got to the part about seeing the flashes when I touched his wrist, they remained calm.

"Let's not get ourselves too worked up," Cole chastised. "You said yourself that you didn't see a clear image. It's possible he wins whatever fight is coming."

"That's not how it felt." I shook my head. "I think he's going to lose."

"But you didn't see that last night when he was here," Kade argued. "You saw something was going to happen to his sister, but he wasn't in any danger."

"Time is not a fixed line," I shot back. "Things change."

"I thought what was meant to be always happened."

Was he trying to irritate me? It almost felt as if this was purposeful at this point. "Kade, I need you to focus." My tone was icy. "Whether you like him or not—and I don't really care if you do—he's a force for good."

"Really?" Cole made a face.

My eyes flashed, and I tugged on enough of Cole's magic that I breathed actual fire for a moment. "You know what? I'll take care of it. You two do whatever it is that you're doing. I hate to interrupt sandwich hour." I stormed away from them.

"Poet," Cole called to my back. "We were just joking."

I stopped long enough to lob a glare over my shoulder. "Nothing about this is funny."

For the first time since I'd approached, Kade looked contrite. "I'm sorry. Jackson should have to take care of himself. He's not a random innocent."

"He could die." I wanted to scream. "I'll find him. I'll fight the skeletons. You guys don't worry about a thing." I couldn't remember ever being this angry with them. I was committed to my plan to track down Jackson, but Cole stopped me.

"I'll find him," he said. "Take a breath."

My eyes narrowed as I swiveled back to face them. "Maybe you should take a breath," I countered.

"Nobody is trying to give you a hard time," Kade assured me. "We just don't know what you want us to do, Poet. We can't insert ourselves into police business."

"I need to know where he is," I replied. "Find that out, and I'll handle the rest."

"You're going to turn this into a thing, aren't you?" Kade whined. "I don't want this to turn into a thing."

"It's far too late for that."

I TRIED TO PUSH MY IRRITATION ASIDE when I reopened my tent. I'd been so frustrated with Kade and Cole that I hadn't even bothered with lunch, and an hour later I was regretting that decision.

Just as Baron let himself into my tent, my phone illuminated with an incoming text. I grabbed it eagerly, then let loose a breath when I read the message.

"Good news?" Baron asked as he handed me a wrapped sandwich.

"Nellie found Jackson. He's appointing a member of the security detail to follow him."

"That's good." Baron sat down in the chair across from me. "You seem calmer than when last we spoke."

"Are you here to drive me crazy?"

"I'm here to explain something to you."

"What's that?"

"I affect people's moods. That's part of who I am."

"I don't know what that means, or why it's important."

"It's important because you're angry with your husband and the other one."

"Cole. Their names are Kade and Cole. You should know that by now."

Baron shrugged. "Neither are as amusing as Luke. And Nellie. I love him."

"I have no idea of what you're trying to get at," I complained.

"I'm a loa. Part of what we do is affect moods. I'm a partier, so sometimes I make people giddy without even realizing what I'm doing. It's not always on purpose."

"I still don't..." I trailed off, the picture becoming clearer. "Are you saying you're the reason Kade and Cole were acting the way they were?"

He nodded, a sad smile taking over his features. "I didn't mean for it to happen. They're serious men. I enjoy when they cut loose. When Nellie and Luke aren't around, occasionally I need a break from all the morose stuff." He held out his hands and shrugged, as if that was supposed to be enough of an apology.

Rather than tell him it was okay—it wasn't—I frowned and grabbed the sandwich. I needed something to do with my hands. Other than wrap them around his neck and squeeze. "I'm a little confused," I admitted. "If you can change moods, why haven't you done it before?"

"What makes you think I haven't?"

"I don't know. Wouldn't I have noticed?"

"I keep waiting for you to notice. Instead, you use your magic to offset mine. You don't even realize what you're doing."

"Are you saying that I affect people's moods?"

"Definitely." He bobbed his head. "How can you have missed the fact that when you're giddy others around you are giddy?"

"I don't often think of myself as giddy."

That made him laugh. "You rarely allow yourself to give in and enjoy the silly side of life," he agreed. "The same is true when you're in a bad mood. If you'd hung around for a few minutes longer at lunch you would've seen that up close and personal."

"Meaning?"

"Your mood took over right after you left. Kade and Cole were no longer happy because I exerted my mood on them. They were annoyed—mostly with themselves—because your mood had taken over."

"I didn't even know that was a thing," I complained. "How could I not know that?"

He held out his hands. "My best guess is that you're still coming into your powers. You haven't set about practicing your new magic. It just pops up when you need it."

"Well, that's nice to know, I guess."

Baron stood. For once, he didn't need to be dismissed. "You're very powerful. You're going to grow more powerful. Your biggest problem is that you insist on doing things the old way. You should embrace new options."

"Just as soon as I get a chance to think about what I'm doing, I'll try that."

He sighed. "So much like your grandmother." He looked sad, but then an impish smile took over. "I like it."

I wanted to be annoyed with him—he was the reason I was irritated with Kade and Cole—but I didn't give in to my baser urges. "Thank you for telling me. I appreciate it."

"You're going to do big things with this magic, Poet. You just have to believe in yourself."

IF MY VISIT WITH FRANCESCA HAD PUT me in touch with the evil side of human nature, my visit with Derek Sloane was an exercise in exasperation for a completely different reason.

"No." I was firm as I shook my head. "I'm not going to help you figure out a way to sell pot in states where it's illegal."

"Hear me out." Derek raised his hand and bobbed his head like an eager little ... actually, I had no idea what to compare him to. He was kind of like a golden retriever with chihuahua energy.

"Nothing you've said has convinced me that this is a good idea."

"People need pot. It's like ... a basic human right." He was such a stoner that he didn't realize he had had no mind defenses in place. Strolling through his brain was as easy as eating my weight in fries at McDonald's.

"I'm of the mind that it should be a basic human right," I said. "I see no reason people can't smoke their pain away. Pot is extremely helpful in certain cases."

Derek beamed at me. "Then help me figure out how to do it."

"Even if I was up for it, why would you think I know how to do something like that?"

"You're a psychic. You know all and see all."

"Not really."

"But it's true." Derek sounded absolutely fried. "Pot is the one thing that can unify everyone in the world. When you smoke pot, nobody cares about Republicans and Democrats, or Catholics and Protestants, or Leos and Libras."

I managed to keep from laughing. This kid—he was twenty but had the intellectual capacity of a fourteen-year-old—was hilarious. He was deadly serious in his own mind, but a complete moron. "That doesn't mean I can help you."

"But why?" Derek turned whiny. "This is the best idea ever."

"I'd say the person who developed penicillin had a better idea," I said. "Oh, and the guy who created those little chocolate-covered donuts that you find in bags at gas stations. That guy was a freaking genius."

"I'll give you that guy," Derek said, "the penicillin is a matter of opinion."

I pursed my lips and simply waited him out.

"Not every state is enlightened," Derek continued. "There are certain states where you can actually go to jail for smoking pot. That's a waste of time and resources."

For Derek to know anything about resources when it came to drug arrests felt like a bit of a miracle. "I'm all for legalized pot," I assured him. "I think it should be regulated and taxed."

He frowned. "Taxes are evil, man."

"The taxes on pot could do a lot of good. But I'm not going to magically enchant you to get away with selling pot in states where it's illegal. That's not what I'm about."

"You want people to suffer?"

He was too much work. "It's not happening, dude. Make another wish."

"Fine." He threw up his hands. I didn't expect him to come in with a new wish right away. "I want my friend Ariel to like me."

I placed my hand on top of his, sighing in relief when I easily found Ariel. "She does like you."

"As a friend. I want her to like me more."

"She does."

Derek's eyes narrowed in suspicion. "How do you know that?"

I pointed to the crystal ball. "I see all and know all."

He bobbed his head, then exhaled heavily. "Wait, are you saying she really does like me?'

"That's exactly what I'm saying." In truth, Ariel thought Derek could do anything. They were both a little flaky—okay, they were a lot flaky—but at their core they were good people. In eight years, they would be married and expecting their first child. They would laugh about their pothead days. By then, the pot would be an indulgence, not a crutch. They weren't bad people. They were just immature.

"But she treats me like a friend."

"That's how you treat her."

"I only treat her that way because I don't want to make things uncomfortable between us."

I raised an eyebrow and waited. It took him longer than it should have to realize what I was insinuating.

He sat straighter. "She's doing the same thing?"

"She wants you in the same way you want her."

"Really?" He took on a dreamy expression. "That's awesome."

"I'm glad you approve."

"It would be more awesome if we could sell pot in Oklahoma together."

I shook my head.

"Fine," he grumbled. "You're killing my dream. I just want you to know that." He rose to his feet.

I could've let him go without saying anything else—he was on his way to a happy ending, although the road would be full of curves—but I couldn't stop myself. "Derek, you don't even know what your real dream is right now," I offered in a soft voice. "You'll figure it out, and eventually, when you look back on this dream, you're going to laugh really hard."

"None of this feels funny," he countered.

"You didn't really think I was going to help you sell pot in all fifty states?"

"Well, no," he replied.

"I helped you toward a future dream. Have a little faith."

"I guess." He didn't look convinced.

"Ariel is a bigger prize than you had in mind when you came in here. Trust me."

"I am excited to see Ariel," he conceded.

"She's going to be happy to see you too."

"Okay." He grinned. "I'm going to find her now."

I stopped him one more time before he exited the tent. "And, Derek, don't drink too much on your first date. You'll regret it."

"Will I throw up on her?" He looked horrified at the thought.

"Worse."

"What's worse than that?"

"Have you heard about the little soldier who refuses to stand up and salute?"

It took him several seconds for it to sink in. "Oh!" He slapped his hand to his cheek. "We can't have that."

"Definitely not."

"Thanks for the tip. Have a good day."

I smiled at his back. "Have a good life."

25
TWENTY-FIVE

Jackson stayed in the park the rest of the day. The security personnel watching him switched out at regular intervals. The plan was to keep an eye on him and wait.

"We should talk," Jackson announced as he appeared at my tent flap. The circus was shutting down for the night and everybody was working to clear the grounds.

Jackson's appearance was a surprise—I hadn't been warned—but when a message popped across my screen, everything became clear: *I lost him.*

That was all I had from the security guard who had been watching him the last two hours. I pursed my lips as I read it twice.

"Who was that?" Jackson demanded. There was fire in his eyes, but he kept his voice neutral. He knew.

He expected me to lie, so I turned his expectations on their head and told the truth. "That was the security guard we had watching you," I replied as I pocketed my phone. "He wanted me to know he lost you."

Jackson opened his mouth—was he about to shout at me?—then caught himself. "You're just going to admit it?" he asked.

"Why not?"

"I thought you would deny it."

"Are you going to deny you've had people watching us?" I didn't really care, I was merely curious about his response.

"I'm a police officer. It's my job to watch suspicious people."

I smirked.

"Are you about to tell me that you find me suspicious?" he challenged when I remained silent.

"No." I shook my head. "Well, yes," I corrected almost immediately. "You have to look at it from our point of view. You swooped in that first night and treated us like crap. Your judgment regarding the circus is obvious, but you don't need to take your narrow misconceptions out on us."

He frowned. "What makes you think I have misconceptions regarding the circus?"

"We've been in this business long enough to recognize someone like you."

He sighed. "I guess I did have attitude about you at first," he acknowledged. "I didn't mean to be rude, but clowns freak me out."

I had to hold back a laugh. "I don't particularly like the clowns either. My husband absolutely loathes them."

"Then why do you have them?"

"People like them."

"I don't believe that."

I shook my head. "Being under suspicion is normal."

"Because you're constantly on the road."

"The people who come to us for an afternoon of fun have nice homes and live by their rules. We don't do that, and it confuses them. Maybe a little too much."

"You said you're moving to a permanent location."

I nodded. "This is our last year on the road. Then we'll build our own community. On Moonstone Bay, an island south of Florida."

He cocked his head. "I've heard of it. It's supposed to be spectacular."

"It fits our needs perfectly. Plus, paranormals are out and proud there. Not having to constantly hide who we are will be a blessing."

"I can see that." Jackson smiled, but it didn't last. "Why are you having me followed?"

I appreciated his bluntness. The conversation had been nice up until this point. "Why don't you walk with me?" I inclined my head toward the big top. "I need to help make sure the grounds are cleared out, and we should talk. I was going to track you down as soon as we were done here anyway. I'll explain how the circus works as we go."

He fell into step with me. "I won't forget the fact that you were having me followed," he said. "I would've expected it before our conversation last night. Now, though…"

"It wasn't meant to be a slight. It was for your protection."

He looked taken aback, and I giggled at his confusion.

"I don't need protection."

"We all need protection from time to time." I gestured toward Nixie's booth. She was closing it on her own, no Dolph in sight. "Those are our voodoo dolls."

Jackson eyed the dolls with a great deal of distaste as we approached. "Creepy."

"They're not really dolls." I moved to the window Nixie hadn't closed yet and pointed to the bottom shelf. "Give me Craig Gray."

Nixie followed my instructions without hesitation.

"This is Craig." I grimaced at the doll. The evil that had coursed through the man was still contained in the doll. "Three years ago, in San Antonio, he was killing teenagers. He fancied himself a Ted Bundy. The police arrested him, but he got off on a technicality and continued to hunt. He wasn't going to face jail time—not before ending another seven lives—so we handled the situation."

Jackson's forehead creased. "That's a man?"

"Yes and no." I shrugged. "He was a man. Nixie used her pixie magic to shrink him after we drew him in with the dreamcatcher."

He jolted at the word. "That's what you call the magical net."

Now I was surprised. "How do you know about that?"

His lips curved at the corners. "We watched you the first night, before you went out for dinner and drinks. We weren't watching you because we thought you were a danger to the community, but..." He turned sheepish.

"You knew we were magical."

He bobbed his head.

"How?"

"There's a network of investigators. Your deeds have been recorded. People are afraid to get too close to you even though you are listed as forces of good."

Well, that was something at least. "Which of our deeds have been recorded?"

"It probably doesn't work like you think it works," he replied. "It's not like we have write-ups for all of your people. There's no entry that says the pixie chick makes voodoo dolls of serial killers."

That made me laugh. "I guess that's good."

"Bad people disappear when you get to town. The thing that happened in New Orleans is described as a demon fight. You took out a demon that was threatening the entire city."

That is not what happened with Marinette. "Not so much," I countered. "That's not it at all."

"Investigators are afraid to get too close." He shrugged. "Your abilities freak people out."

"You weren't afraid to get too close. You knew what we were that first night, and you came right over."

"I figured it might be my only chance to talk to you. I knew you weren't to blame for the skeletons, but I thought you could help us."

"That is our goal," I acknowledged.

He inclined his head toward the voodoo doll. "Why not just kill him?"

"Then he would be free. This way, he's punished forever."

"Are they aware in there?"

"Yes. They can't move. They never sleep. They're always just this."

"Can the spell be reversed?"

"I'm reticent to say it can never happen because I've seen a lot of things that were never supposed to happen. Odds are long, though."

I handed the doll back to Nixie and led Jackson to the big top. Along the way, I smiled at people as they passed. The workers knew what they were doing, and the grounds would be clear in fifteen minutes.

"So this is where the magic happens," Jackson noted as we entered the tent, his eyes dancing around the big space. "This is pretty much what I expected." He sent me a teasing grin. "Do you ever get on the tightrope?"

"Oh, no." I shook my head. "I'm the exact opposite of graceful. Luke is good on the tightrope."

"What does he do with the circus?"

"A little of everything. When we move to Moonstone Bay he'll take over as ringmaster. Our current master is retiring. He doesn't want to make the move. He's not magical and doesn't get the appeal of moving to a magical island."

"How many of your people will make the move?"

"All of those who are magical. The midway workers, the clowns, the janitorial staff and food workers likely won't make the trip. We'll have to hire on the island to fill those positions."

"Why don't they want to go the island?"

That was more difficult to answer. "People don't join the circus on a whim," I said. "Well, I guess some do, but they don't last. It takes a specific personality to want to live on the road as we do."

"But if you joined because you wanted a life on the road, why are you planning to settle down?"

It was a fair question. "I didn't join the circus because I wanted to move around constantly. When Max—the owner of the circus—found me, I was living on the streets of Detroit."

Jackson looked taken aback. "I'm sorry. How old were you?"

"I was an adult, but not by much. I had been on the streets a few years."

"What happened to your parents?"

"They died when I was a kid. I was in the foster care system."

He didn't press.

"I met Max outside a diner and tried to use my magic to pick his pocket." I laughed at the memory.

"Is he magical?"

"That doesn't matter."

"You don't want to out his secret. I respect that."

"Let's just say he recognized me for what I was, and instead of giving me grief, or teaching me a lesson, he offered me the chance of a lifetime."

I led Jackson through the side flap of the tent and to the animal tent. "He said that I would keep getting smaller and smaller if I stayed in Detroit, until I eventually disappeared like all the other lifers who never got the opportunity to escape. It wasn't the city. It was just ... I couldn't become larger than life if I didn't go with him."

"Is that what you wanted? To be larger than life?"

I shrugged. "I wanted a different life. It was hard on the streets. I did my best, but it had become apparent that survival might not be in the cards, or I wouldn't be the person I wanted to be."

I opened the flap to the animal tent, grinning as he looked around and reality set in. "I took a leap of faith and went with Max. He allowed me to see enough of his mind and heart to realize that he didn't want to hurt me. He really did want to offer me a better life."

He waited for me to finish.

"I joined Mystic Caravan and left with them when they finished in Detroit," I explained. "Luke and I became best friends right away. I forged relationships with the others. For the first time since I lost my parents, I began to understand what the word 'family' meant again.

"It didn't happen overnight," I continued. "But now they are my family, and I'm forever grateful."

He blinked. "Why are you telling me this?"

"I had a conversation with Catalina last night," I replied. "That's her name. She tracked me down at a bar and asked me to back off."

"You mentioned that when I was in your tent."

"Not all of it. I declined her request, of course."

"How did she take that?"

"She said she would have to kill us. She almost seemed apologetic. She made a promise to her son eighty years ago and is determined to see it through."

He straightened because I had his full attention now. "What promise?"

"She didn't say. I was hoping you could help us track down that information. You have access to records. Maybe you can find a reference to this Catalina."

"Okay, but is that why you were following me? I gave you my number. All you had to do was call and ask."

I took a deep breath, debating, and then went for it. "When you were in my trailer earlier, I touched your wrist."

His eyebrows knit in confusion

"I'm the fortune teller for a reason. I can see things."

He lifted his chin. "You saw what was going to happen to my sister. I guess that means you saw something bad happening to me."

"I saw flashes," I replied. "I didn't see the whole picture. I saw you fighting in the darkness. There were skeletons and blood. You were surrounded by screams."

He dragged a hand through his hair. "When?"

"I don't know."

"Where?"

"I don't know that either."

"You're saying I'm going to die." Now he managed a smile. "I'm capable of taking care of myself. As you've seen with the skeletons—more than once—they're not that difficult to take out."

"They haven't been until this point," I concurred. "That could've been by design. Catalina doesn't want to kill anyone. She's looking for something, but death and destruction hasn't been on her to-do list. Until now. Maybe she's getting frustrated because she can't find what she's seeking. She sees us as an obstacle. She'll add you to that list. It's likely you'll stumble upon her when she's conducting another search and she'll decide to eradicate the threat you pose."

His eyes flicked to the empty cages. "I guess that makes sense."

"It's a mess," I said. "I sent people to follow you so I'd be aware if you found her, or vice versa."

"It's sweet that you planned to run to my rescue."

"It's not just you." I didn't want to burst his bubble, but he needed some reality sprinkled on his popcorn. "If she decides to ramp up the skeleton outings, everyone who already believes they're not that dangerous will be in trouble. We need to end this."

"How?"

"If I knew, this would already be over. In fact—"

My words were cut off by a loud keening, magical lights flashing above our heads. I jerked my gaze to the tent flap.

"What the hell is that?" he demanded, his hands clenching into fists at his sides as he prepared for an onslaught.

"The dreamcatcher," I replied. "She brought the fight to us."

26
TWENTY-SIX

I took the lead leaving the tent. I didn't bother to see if Jackson followed. There was no question he would.

Things were eerily silent outside. The dreamcatcher was illuminated with magic beneath my feet, but only those with supernatural abilities could see it. I risked a look at Jackson and saw him staring at the pulsing lines.

"This is amazing," he said. "Can it kill your enemies?"

"That's not how it works." I thought about it—the second he heard the dreamcatcher, I should've realized—then growled. "You're magical."

"What?" He jerked up his chin. "I ... no ... I..."

Well, that answered *that* question. He knew he was magical. "If you weren't one of us, you couldn't see or hear it. That's the way it's designed."

He snapped out of his surprised state quickly. "Is this really what we should be wasting our time on?"

"Tell me what you are."

"You haven't told me what you are," he reminded me.

"I'm the new breed of loa."

"What the hell is a loa?"

Before I could answer, Baron appeared in front of us, his coat rippling in the wind.

"What are you doing?" I snapped.

When he turned, his skull mask was in place. Not the paint he used hanging around and enthralling his fans in the French Quarter. He actually had his game face on.

"He's one of them." Jackson reached for his service revolver, but I stopped him. "Don't," I warned. "He's not one of them."

"What is he?"

"A loa," I replied.

"*The* loa," Baron clarified. "If there were a list of loas, I would be at the top."

All I could do was roll my eyes. "Nobody cares about that right now." I strode forward. "What's happening? Have you seen what crossed the line?"

"Skeletons," he replied. "A lot of them."

I stared between the tents, searching for movement. I found what I was looking for near the empty ticket booth. Two skeletons were skulking about.

"I can kill them," he said.

"We can all kill them," I said.

"I can do more than that."

I waited for him to expand.

"I am the loa of the dead," Baron reminded me.

My already busy brain turned into a whirlwind. "You can control them."

He nodded, as if I'd just given him the compliment to end all compliments.

"Freeze them in place."

He lifted his hand and snapped his fingers. The only skeletons I could see had frozen in place.

"Well, this might not be so bad," I said as I scampered in their direction. When I got to them, I punched each through the ribcage and they disintegrated into dust.

"Can't you just blow them all up like you did on the bridge?" Jackson demanded. He'd followed me, but he was giving Baron a wide berth. I couldn't blame him. Baron was off putting even when he was serious.

"I knew you were aware," I grumbled. "Why didn't you say something?"

"I mentioned the bridge. Heck, I mentioned you on the bridge."

"You didn't mention the magical show we put on," I countered.

He didn't look bothered by my change in demeanor. "Why didn't you say something?" he fired back.

"I don't usually go around volunteering that information. Why would I out myself that way?"

"I know you," Baron said, adopting a tone I'd never heard from him before. His eyes were fixed on Jackson. "You're one of the duende tribe."

I glanced at Baron, then back at Jackson. "What's that?"

"I have no idea." Jackson's response was too quick for my comfort level.

"What's a duende?" I asked Baron.

His smirk told me that he found the situation amusing. Around the circus grounds, I heard my friends and co-workers taking out skeletons.

"In Spanish folklore, they're demons," Baron replied. "They're real. They had territory on the Iberian Peninsula and then took over areas in Latin America as well."

"Demons is such a generic word at this point."

"In Spanish legends they were essentially the equivalent of dwarves and gnomes." He considered it a moment. "And leprechauns. I always feel disappointed that I haven't seen a leprechaun in the wild in at least a century. Have you ever seen one?"

I shot him an incredulous look. "This is not the time to lament the population decline of leprechauns."

Baron bobbed his head. He hadn't taken his eyes from Jackson since he'd dropped that word. *Duende*. I didn't know it, but it felt important. "Duendes are tricksters," he explained. "They like to get up to mischief and misdirect others. They never come at you from the front. Instead, they distract you and then slip a knife between your shoulder blades."

He sounded as if he was speaking from experience. "Have you ever come into contact with one?"

He turned grim. "About a hundred years ago they were prevalent in New Orleans. The town does like to party, and so do duendes. There was a fight with some witches—it always turns into a fight with witches—and they decided to go south. I assumed they'd taken over part of Latin America and were thriving. And yet this one is here."

I looked at Jackson. "You're a demon?"

"I have magic in my blood," he replied, "but I'm not a demon. Demons are evil." His nostrils flared to prove his annoyance at the question.

"That's not entirely true," I countered. "Demons are basically fire elementals."

"They can be other types," Baron corrected.

I ignored him. "They're not all bad or good," I continued. "It comes to choice."

"I'm not a demon," Jackson insisted. "I can do a few things."

"Like what?"

"I can sense things. When I'm hunting suspects, I almost always find them. If there's a choice to make, left or right, I always make the correct choice."

"That's just an inherent ability," Baron mused. He cocked his head. "He's not strong. Everything he has is latent. If pressed enough, the magic would likely come out to protect him, but he doesn't embrace what he is."

"Your magic is the reason you got interested in hunting paranormals," I said.

"I'm not a demon! I'm a man."

"There's nothing to fear from your heritage," I said.

"I'm not a demon!" he shouted.

I lifted my hands in surrender. "Okay. You're not a demon. We get it." I cast a quick look to Baron and found him grinning. "Why do you find this funny?"

"He doesn't understand what he is," Baron replied. "He's oblivious." He paused a beat. "Actually, he's afraid. He found the magic exciting as a child but then he grew to fear it. Now that he's seen actual evil on the job, he fears people will assume he's part of that evil."

"You're not evil," I said to the fretting detective. "You're just different."

"Where have you been?" Jackson snapped. "Do you even live in the same country I do? Look what is happening to people. Anyone deemed different is persecuted."

"If you hide from it, you're proving that people have something to fear," I argued.

"We can't all live in an insulated bubble where everyone is crazy and no one cares about the crazy," Jackson shot back. "You're taking refuge on a magical island. There's a reason for that." He didn't wait for me to respond. "You know you'll never be accepted in a normal community."

"James." I used his first name for the first time. "Do you really think San Francisco is normal? This city is filled with self-proclaimed freaks. That is the normal here."

Jackson didn't respond.

"If you live in fear you can never truly embrace the light. It's better to be yourself—even if you alienate some people—because you won't figure out where you belong unless you live an authentic life."

Baron beamed at me. "You get that part of your personality from me. You are willing to try different things, and that makes you strong. Your grandmother keeps insisting that rules are more important than feelings."

"Or is she trying to keep you from drinking and smoking so much?" I countered.

"Same thing."

I rolled my eyes until they landed on Jackson. "I can't tell you what to do with your abilities. I can't even tell you what will happen, because you're wound so tight you could explode at any moment. I will tell you this, though."

I took a deep breath before continuing. "If you keep going down this road in which you believe all paranormals are evil, you're going to turn into someone you don't even recognize." Something occurred to me. "You're already more than you realize. I tried to see if I could find anything paranormal in you but couldn't."

"He hides it," Baron said. "He doesn't even realize he's doing it."

Jackson looked shaken. "I don't want to have this conversation."

"Fine." I held up my hands. "We need to focus on the here and now anyway. That includes dealing with Catalina." I fully intended to have this conversation with Jackson at some point. "Now, can you swear to me that you don't know anything about her?"

"I didn't even know she existed until I saw the footage from the bridge," he fired back. "I thought it was just the skeletons. Your interaction with her—and your continued interaction with her—is the only thing I have to go on."

"What about you?" I asked Baron.

"I didn't pay that much attention to her last night," he replied. "She doesn't ... shine ... as brightly as she should. She has magic, but whatever is fueling her is consuming her. She's on a crash course with her own destruction."

"Is there a way to hasten that?"

He lifted one shoulder. "Not off the top of my head, but we could ask her."

"Great. Why don't you get her over here and we'll ask."

Baron wrinkled his nose. His face was back to normal, the skull gone. "She's here now. You can ask her yourself."

My mouth fell open as I watched him turn on his heel and walk toward the House of Mirrors. Confused, I gave chase. His legs were longer than mine so it was difficult to keep pace with him. Once he was through the door, however, I caught up, but only because he'd stopped in the middle of the room and I was moving so fast that I smacked into his back.

"Give a girl a warning," I complained as I rubbed my nose. "You're a walking calamity sometimes I swear."

That was all I got out before Raven—who I didn't realize was present—spoke.

"Poet," she said in a low voice. "Now probably isn't the time."

It was rare to hear her so subdued, so when I turned what I saw was enough to steal my breath.

Raven stood near the archway that led to her office. She was paler than normal, but otherwise unharmed. Next to her, Nixie leaned against the wall. The pixie looked as if she'd been through an ordeal. Despite how rough Nixie looked, she wasn't the point of interest. That was Catalina.

The skull woman stood in the center. All around her, the mirrors reflected back a decrepit, stooped woman. She looked nothing like the glamour she'd shown the previous night. She didn't resemble the skull creature that I could see with my own eyes.

"What's up?" I said. I sounded like an idiot, but I needed a moment to gather myself.

"The dreamcatcher went off," Raven replied. Her eyes were trained on Catalina.

"The skeletons are under control," I said. "If you wanted to visit, Catalina, all you had to do was ask."

Slowly, the creature—she wasn't a woman, and I didn't know what else to call her—tracked her eyes to me. "I'm not here for you."

Out of the corner of my eye, I saw Jackson reaching for his weapon again. I gave him an almost imperceptible shake of my head. He needed to realize that bullets were rarely effective in a magic fight. "What are you here for?"

"Her." Catalina pointed at Nixie.

A bruise was forming on Nixie's arm. She was out of breath and so pale she was almost transparent. She was magically drained.

"What's going on?" I demanded.

"I'm not certain," Raven replied. "I heard Nixie scream and thought it was a skeleton. I saw her run in here with that ... thing ... chasing her." She gestured to Catalina. "Of course, I decided to handle things myself rather than bother anybody for help."

"Of course," I agreed dryly.

"This is what I found when I arrived. It seems Catalina wants to take Nixie."

"Oh, really?" My voice was faux chipper, but inside I was seething. "We're going to have to respectfully decline." I flashed a smile for Catalina's benefit. "You can go."

"Go?" Jackson was incredulous. "She's the reason we're in this mess. We need to kill her."

I didn't necessarily disagree. Catalina had stepped up her attack. But we still didn't know what she wanted, and it felt dangerous to take her on when we didn't have all of our questions answered. "For now, it's best Catalina calls it a night. Your army has been taken care of outside," I told her. "You may go now."

"I came for the pixie," Catalina replied in her deadened voice. "I won't leave without her. She has what I need. She can open the door."

Did she mean a plane door? Nixie could open plane doors, but only to her world.

"What door do you want her to open?" I asked, buying time.

Catalina was disinterested in me. "It's time to go, little fairy."

"I'm not a fairy," Nixie, furious, shot back. "Why does everyone think pixies are fairies?"

"You're coming with me," Catalina said. "I know what I have to do now." Her eyes finally moved to me. "And there's no one who can stand in my way."

I forced a smile I didn't feel. "Just back off and we'll call it a draw for tonight."

"I'm done waiting." Catalina started toward Nixie.

I summoned magic, but Catalina was ready. She deflected what I threw at her toward a mirror. When our magic collided, a swirling vortex opened directly in front of me.

"Oh, crap!" I flapped my arms to get away and Baron reached out to steady me.

Catalina registered him for the first time. "Oh, no." She shook her head. "This won't do." She swirled her hand and increased the size of the vortex.

It was too late to get away. I fell forward, Baron with me.

The last thing I heard was Nixie scream at the same time Raven swore and Jackson fired his gun. Then the vortex closed.

27
TWENTY-SEVEN

My first assumption—that it was a plane door—was wrong. Catalina had opened a door to the past, not a different world.

"Geez," Raven complained as she rubbed her elbow and looked around. We'd hit hard and it had taken more than a few seconds to get our bearings. One glance and we knew we were in Alcatraz.

"What's the point of sending us here?" I demanded.

"Perhaps there's something she wants us to see," Baron, intrigued, suggested.

"Or perhaps this is a byproduct of her losing her temper," Raven fired back, agitated. "She didn't mean to trap us here. She was angry and wanted to send us away and we got caught in the center of that anger."

Well, that was an interesting possibility. "Huh," I said.

"Yeah, 'huh.'" Raven mocked. Her eyebrows moved toward one another as she looked around. "Where is Jackson?"

It was only then that I realized the detective hadn't made the trip with us. "Maybe he managed to escape the spell," I volunteered.

"Or maybe she kept him because he was important to her,"

Raven countered. "Nothing in this town is what it's supposed to be." Her voice ratcheted up a notch. "I hate to be the bearer of bad news, but he's not what he's been pretending to be."

"He didn't know that," I argued.

"Didn't he?"

"He's magical but it never occurred to him that he had demon in his blood. He was appalled at the thought."

"Wait, demon?" Raven turned and faced me, her hands planted on her hips. "I think I missed something."

She hadn't been with us when the truth about Jackson came out.

"He's a duende?" she said on a wrinkled nose when I caught her up. "Seriously?"

"Seriously," I confirmed.

"Well, that is just all types of ridiculous." She shook her head. "Duendes are little imps. I've run into more than my fair share. They never try to do good by any community."

"That just proves nurture is more important than nature," I replied, checking my joints after the hard landing." We were trapped in Catalina's mind.

"How does that prove that?" she snapped.

"If he'd been raised in a duende household, he likely wouldn't be a police officer," I replied. "As it stands, he is appalled at the idea of being anything other than a hero, which would put him on the outs with his own people."

She shook her head. "Only you would turn something like this into a philosophical discussion."

"Right?" Baron's eyes went wide. "It's ridiculous. She gets that from her grandmother. I would never do anything like that."

Raven gave him a dirty look. "You're a pain too," she complained.

"Nixie is in trouble," I reminded them.

Raven's smile disappeared. "That thing wants to drain her."

"We still don't know what that thing is." I turned to Baron. "You saw her. You know how to read creatures like that."

"I'm very good at reading people," Baron agreed.

"Then what is she?"

"She's more than one thing," Baron replied. "I didn't get a lot of time to study her but she's more than the sum of her parts. It's not as easy as you'd like to give her a name. You know how I said she was like a wendigo but not really a wendigo?"

I nodded.

"Well, there's some legit wendigo in there. There's also some ghost ... and maybe a little demon ... and certainly a side of figment."

Raven was shaking her head before he finished. "There is no single creature that contains all that."

Baron leveled a "well, duh" look at her. "Why do you think I just said what I said?"

"But that means she can't exist," Raven insisted. "If it's impossible for her to be what you just said she is, she shouldn't be here."

"And yet she's here," Baron fired back.

Raven blinked, then turned to me. "I don't like this."

"Nixie is in trouble, and we're the only ones who know. We have to find a way out of here and get to her."

A muscle worked in Raven's jaw, and she nodded. "Okay, how do we do that?"

"We figure out what this is." I looked around. "If Catalina is responsible for everything in here, why are we trapped in the Alcatraz of her mind?"

"Because it's a prison," Raven replied without hesitation. "She wants us removed from the situation and the only prison that came to mind was Alcatraz."

It was as good of an explanation as anything and yet it didn't fit. "I don't think she meant to put us here." I looked to Baron for confirmation.

He nodded. "She was trying to send us elsewhere. She thought she was opening a plane door. She was so frustrated and so confused, that she screwed up her own spell. I see how the chalice is inflating her magic now."

Raven made an exaggerated face. "None of that helps us."

"Actually, it does," Baron countered. "If my guess is correct—and I'm rarely wrong—right now she's panicking because she has no idea where she sent us."

"I don't think she's afraid of us." Raven shook her head. "That wasn't fear she was throwing out when I faced off with her."

"She doesn't fear you because individually your magic can't hurt her," Baron replied.

"Thanks for the mood boost." She shot him a sarcastic thumbs-up.

"She wasn't afraid of me either," Baron added.

"Could you take her out if we were in front of her again?" I asked him.

He hesitated, then did the one thing I didn't want him to do and held out his hands. "Maybe. Her powers are very odd."

"That explains why we kept getting so many suggestions about her origins," Raven noted. "We thought she was a figment or a wendigo. The stories about other folklore figures got us wondering." She shook her head. "She's new and unique. That's why we couldn't nail her down."

"What do we do?" I gritted out.

"You said it already." She gestured to the cell block. "We look around. There must be something important here."

I glanced at Baron. "Have you been here before?"

"I visited Alcatraz in 1942 I believe." He took on a far-off expression. "It was an interesting trip, to say the least."

He had my full attention. "Why did you come here?"

Raven made a face. "Oh, don't ask him that. The only reason he's dragging it out is because he wants to torture us with some ridiculous story."

Baron flicked Raven's ear. "You've always been a spoilsport, Raven. I've known you longer than I've known my own granddaughter. You put the sour in sourpuss."

She glared at him as he walked to the middle of the room and stared up at the tiers of cells, then flipped him the bird when she was certain he wasn't looking. Even if he had been focused on her, it wouldn't have hurt his feelings. It was just a way for her to soothe herself. "I'm fine with that."

"You would be." He was quiet as he looked around. For once, he didn't seem as if he was about to make a joke or suggest going for a drink. He was deadly serious. "Alcatraz was even more famous than you realize," he started in a low voice. "It was supposed to be a place of retribution but there were glimpses of rehabilitation. You can't have a place like this and allow hope to shine through. Except that there is always hope. That's why Alcatraz failed."

"The escape attempts were proof of hope," I said.

"Or proof there was no hope, that people were willing to die to get out of here," Raven countered. She pointed to the second tier. "Not all the cells are empty."

I moved closer to her. Sure enough, on the second level, through an open cell door, a man sat on a bunk writing in a notebook. "Who the hell is that?"

"Maybe he's who we're here to find," Raven suggested.

"We should at least check it out," Baron said.

We found our way to the cell. Raven and I argued about who would do the talking without saying a word until Baron shoved between us and strode into the cell as if he owned it.

"Hello." He smiled at the man on the bunk.

Up close, he had dark hair and eyes. He was young, but dark circles under his eyes and a bruise on his cheek aged him. A quick glance at his arms showed bruises there too.

"What are you doing here?" the man asked.

"We were about to ask you that." Baron looked around the cell and made a face. "This is depressing."

"It is," the man agreed. "I've been depressed since I got here."

"How long ago was that?" I asked.

"Time has no meaning here. I'm not real."

How could he know that? If we were in Catalina's mind—or a memory pocket she'd created to trap us—this man in her memory shouldn't be able to mark time. "You're Catalina's son." I hadn't meant to say it out loud. Once the realization hit me, however, the words bubbled forth.

"You know my mother?" The man brightened. "Is she coming today? She hasn't been to visit in so long. I miss her."

I glanced at Raven.

"What's your name?" Raven asked.

"Antonio, but everybody calls me Tony."

"How did you end up in this place, Tony?"

Shame colored the man's cheeks. "I stole from a grocery store. My mother was struggling to keep food on the table when my father left us, and I was trying to help. We needed food."

"They put you in Alcatraz for that?" I challenged.

"No. I went to a different prison, but I got into fights. That's the only way to survive sometimes." He was rueful. "I made all the wrong choices, and that's how I ended up here."

Something told me he'd never left. "Did your mother visit a lot?" I asked.

He nodded. "She moved here to be close to me. She blamed herself."

Guilt like that would be a powerful motivator. There was just one more thing—okay, maybe two—that I needed from him. "Did you die here?" I asked.

Raven sent me a sharp look. I could hear her mind working.

"I died May 2, 1946. It's burned into my brain."

I ran the date through everything I'd learned about Alcatraz's history. "In the Battle of Alcatraz," I said. "Were you killed by an inmate or a guard?"

"A guard. I hid in my cell, but there was a lot of crossfire."

"I'm guessing the report said you died at the hands of another inmate," Raven muttered.

He nodded.

"Your mother already felt guilty because you went to prison

trying to help her," I said. "When you were sent here, she blamed herself even more."

"I was all she had," he added. He looked so sad I felt sorry for him.

"Tony." I said his name in a soft voice, slowly drawing his attention to me. "Was your mother a witch?"

"Bruja," he corrected. "It ran in the family. My grandmother tried to get her to sell potions to make money, but she was always against it. She said preying on the hopes of others when she couldn't really help them was wrong."

"There's karma attached to magic," I whispered.

He didn't shy from the topic. "The last thing she told me, on her final visit, was that she wished she'd embraced her magic. That was her plan. She was going to use her magic to get me out."

"How?"

"I don't know." He looked sad. "But she promised."

I made a promise to my son. I swore to him that I would get this done eighty years ago, and I will.

"I know what happened." I wasn't saying it to him. He wasn't real. He was a manifestation of his mother's guilt. She blamed herself for what happened to him, and that fueled her now.

"What happened?" Baron asked, his expression quizzical.

"You were right about her being a wendigo of sorts. It wasn't flesh that she fed on but guilt."

"She's like a guilt demon," Raven said.

"She was a bruja, and her guilt turned her into something else. Now she's trying to keep her promise to her son."

"But he's dead." Raven shook her head. "She can't free her son if he's dead."

"Can't she?" I lifted my chin. "She wants Nixie because she knows Nixie can trap souls. What if Tony's soul is trapped?"

"But what has she been doing all this time? She hasn't been searching Alcatraz for Tony's soul. She's been searching other areas."

"For someone to help her. She was looking for another bruja, or a necromancer. Someone who could free Tony's soul."

"Because it's still at Alcatraz," Raven realized, her eyes briefly closing. "She realizes that he was never laid to rest."

"Because he was killed in a time of strife," Baron added. "He's trapped out there. She's been looking for help to free him."

"But why now?" Raven argued. "Why didn't this happen right after Tony died?"

I held out my hands. "It's likely that her guilt didn't allow her to die. She transformed into a wendigo of sorts, or a hybrid demon. Slowly, throughout the years, she gained strength."

"Then she started resurrecting skeletons with the power that kept growing," Baron surmised. "She sent them searching. All she wanted was to rest, but she couldn't because Tony wasn't at rest."

"She wants to rest with her son," I agreed. "She really wasn't trying to hurt anyone. She was looking for a magical being in those neighborhoods, someone who could help her."

"And then she got a power boost from the chalice and decided to go whole hog," Raven said.

"And she finally found what she's looking for in Nixie," I added. "In her mind, someone who can trap souls can also free them."

"Okay." Raven licked her lips. "That explains most of it. What about Jackson? Why didn't she trap him with us?"

"He has demon magic she may need."

"Or she may need him to kill her," Baron said. "She might see him as evil. If she frees Tony and Jackson frees her, she'll be able to move on with a clear conscience."

It was all coming together. Except for one thing.

"We have to get out of here." I looked around. "This is all happening in a memory pocket she created."

"She was trying to trap us so we wouldn't get in her way," Raven said. "Even now she doesn't want to hurt us. At her core, she just wants peace."

"We're going to give it to her." I raised my hand. "This is all in our minds." I allowed my magic to spread, and slowly the walls of the memory bubble began to fall. Within seconds, we were back in the House of Mirrors. We'd never left.

"We have to get the others," I said. "We know where she's going. We need to get to Alcatraz Island. We're going to help her. We're also going to make sure that she doesn't trigger Jackson's demon side. We can't lose him."

28
TWENTY-EIGHT

I could teleport, so getting to Alcatraz Island wasn't difficult. Once we arrived, however, I was at a loss.

"Where?" Dolph demanded. Nixie being taken had turned him into a force to be reckoned with.

"I don't know," I replied as Luke and Nellie crowded in at the big man's sides. We were on the walkway outside the main cell building.

"You do know," Raven hissed. "We were there an hour ago."

That's when it hit me. She was in Tony's cell. "How do you think she knows which cell was his?" I started for the big door that led inside. "I very much doubt she was allowed to visit him in his cell."

"Definitely not," she agreed. "He could've told her, though." Raven's eyes darted left and right as she looked around. "He could've told her in a letter. She could've cast a spell. Something tells me she's been here more than once looking for some remnant of him in the eighty years since he died."

"How does that work?" Cole asked. He, Kade, and Luke had spread out on either side of our group. We were expecting a skeleton attack. It was inevitable. It wouldn't come while we were outside of the building, however, only when we were inside.

"How does what work?" I asked as I grabbed the door handle and tugged. It was locked tight. I pulsed magic into the door and tugged again. It was loud when it opened, announcing our presence to everyone inside.

"What is she?" Cole asked. "Is she La Ciguapa?"

The question almost made me laugh. "No. I think it was the hair. The woman who saw her in the bar was probably a witch, a lower level one. She recognized Catalina was magical. She likely heard the legend growing up and made the association. She's not a ciguapa."

"What is she?" Cole repeated.

"She started as a witch." The lights were on inside the building. Were they always on? Probably not. Given the size of the facility, it would cost a lot to keep it lit when nobody was present. Auxiliary lights—which didn't take as much money to keep on—were likely left on at night.

Catalina was definitely here. I wasn't surprised—this was the only place she could feel close to Tony—but it filled me with sadness.

"I don't think there's a word for what she is," I replied as I centered myself. We were barely over the threshold, and my internal warning alarms were dinging at a fantastic rate. "She was a witch. Then she was consumed by grief. Baron was right. She's like a wendigo now. It was the guilt she felt about her son."

"What magic does she have?" Cole couldn't let it go. He needed answers before things finally fit into the appropriate place in his busy brain.

"She has some witch magic," I replied, forcing myself to be patient. "Some necromancer. I think that's how she's raising the skeletons. She has some telekinesis."

"What I want to know is how she got across the dreamcatcher," Kade growled. "We should have been alerted."

I gave him an odd look. "We were alerted."

"No, we weren't. The dreamcatcher went off because of the skeletons."

I waited for him to get it.

"Oh," he said, realization finally dawning.

"If it had been just the skeletons, the dreamcatcher wouldn't have alerted at all," I replied. "They don't have intent. She's been using them as bloodhounds essentially. She needs a specific type of magic to get what she wants. The dreamcatcher alerted for her."

"Because she wanted Nixie," Dolph muttered. "She didn't hesitate when she crossed. She went straight for her."

"I think she's been watching us," I added. "She saw magic in us and thought one of us could give her what she wanted. She settled on Nixie because of her soul magic. Catalina probably thinks she can release souls as well."

"I just want her dead." Dolph was grim. "I'll rip her head from her body."

I slowed my pace. "That's not how this is going to go down."

Dolph shot me a defiant look. "You don't dictate how I save her."

This wasn't a fight I wanted to have and yet there was no choice. "Catalina doesn't want to kill Nixie."

"She took her!" Dolph exploded. "You may have a soft heart on matters like this, but I don't. She *will* die."

He couldn't see beyond his fear. If our roles were reversed and Kade had been taken, I'd want to kill Catalina too. Love made people do crazy things, and Dolph clearly loved Nixie. Their relationship was no longer a joke, but I couldn't let this go sideways.

"Listen to me." I grabbed the front of his shirt and held tight so he couldn't look anywhere but directly at me. "I get that you're worried about Nixie. I'm worried too. I'm afraid Catalina might force her to use too much magic, and you know what happens when Naida and Nixie go full pixie.

"However," I continued, using my most reasonable tone, "Catalina wants to die, but first she wants her son's soul freed from this place." I took a breath. "She wants to be forgiven. We're going to make sure she gets what she needs."

"Speak for yourself," he groused, turning his eyes away. "I want her to feel the same pain she's caused us."

"Suck it up, big guy," Raven drawled. "She hasn't caused us that much pain. In fact, it's been like a military exercise more than anything else. She doesn't want us dead. Let Poet take the lead on this one."

Dolph averted his eyes and muttered something I couldn't make out.

"Just keep a level head," I ordered. "This is going to be quick and painless."

The words were barely out of my mouth before the hallway in front of us began to fill with skeletons. It was as if someone had decided to push the "sense of humor" button.

"You were saying," Luke drawled.

"Geez," I muttered, pulling back from Dolph.

"I've got this." Nellie had insisted on bringing his ax this time. There would've been no explaining it on the tour, but there was no reason for him to be without his favorite weapon this go-around.

"We've all got this," Cole countered. "Stick close to one another." He sent Naida—who had been silent since her sister was taken—a pointed look. "Nobody can be isolated. That's how we win this."

Naida could control the weather, and given the amount of water surrounding Alcatraz Island she could do a lot of damage, including a tsunami. She glanced at Cole, then at me, then back at Cole.

She was worried about her sister, but she was also practical. She understood this wasn't going to be a normal fight. This was about making sure everyone got what they wanted.

"Here we go," I said, moving forward. "*Glacio*," I hissed, allowing my magic to explode out of me. The skeletons froze as I started picking my way around them. "Don't miss any of them," I ordered. "I don't want anyone finding bones here when we're done."

Behind me, my friends started working. They mowed through the skeletons as if they were pesky mosquitos. Whenever one exploded, the familiar poof became apparent. I kept my attention forward, and when I walked into the main cell block, I found Jackson sitting in the middle of the floor, his hands bound behind him and fear in his eyes.

"You're alive," he said in dumbfounded disbelief when he registered my presence.

"Of course I'm alive," I replied as I dropped down to untie him with my magic. Once he started rubbing his wrists, I looked him up and down. Other than a bruise on his cheek, he looked none the worse for wear. "Nixie?" I asked.

"She took her. She said she was keeping me just in case. That if Nixie couldn't do what she wanted, she would make me do it. I told her I didn't have that power—something about untethering a soul—but she refused to believe me."

"She probably senses the magic inside you," I replied. "You bury it well."

I didn't have time to fully explain. At least not in a way he would understand. "You're more powerful than you realize. You can hide that power. I can, too. So can a lot of paranormals. When you hid who you were from us, it was instinctive. You started to trust us, though, and you dropped your shield. That was probably a bad move because Catalina was watching us, and she saw what you were."

"But I didn't set off your dreamcatcher," he said.

"Because intent matters." I smiled as I remembered my conversation with Baron. "You might not have trusted us, but you never wanted to hurt us. I can explain it to you later."

Jackson didn't look thrilled at the prospect, but he nodded. "She's upstairs. Both of them are upstairs." He pointed to a cell I already recognized from the memory hole. "I don't think she wants to hurt anyone."

"She doesn't," I replied. "She's hurting enough for everyone. I'm going to take care of that." I moved away so Cole could drop down next to him. "I'll take it from here," I said as I started toward the stairs.

"You're not going alone," Kade argued as he began to follow.

"It'll be okay, Kade. Trust me."

"I trust you more than anyone, but I'm going with you."

I didn't argue further. It was a waste of time. I took the stairs two at a time and made my way to Tony's cell. It looked exactly as it had in the memory, other than the fact that he wasn't in the cell and none of his items were strewn about on the bed. That's where Catalina sat, looking defeated.

Nixie stood in front of her, a bit bruised and irritated.

"It doesn't work that way," Nixie argued. "I don't displace souls. It's not just the soul I'm trapping in the doll, I'm shrinking down the humans and turning them into dolls. I don't do anything with the soul."

"I want him freed!" Catalina insisted. "It's been too long ... for both of us. Untether him from this place so I can go with him. That's all I want."

Nixie threw up her hands. "I don't know how else to explain this to you." Her tone was icy. "I can't do what you're asking." She turned to me, as if sensing they were no longer alone. "Tell her."

I looked her over again, just to be on the safe side, then moved out of the doorway. "Go downstairs," I ordered the pixie. "Naida and Dolph will lose their minds if they don't see you with their own eyes."

Nixie looked torn. "I want to help her. She's so sad, and I really do want to help, but what she's asking isn't reasonable."

"I know," I assured her. "I'm going to help her."

"I'm glad to hear that, but how?"

"I brought a loa with me," I said. "He's downstairs with Nellie. He finds the dress and the ax amusing. Tell him I need him."

Confusion had Nixie knitting her eyebrows, and then my plan became clear, and her eyes widened. "Loas rule the crossroads between life and death."

"And they can free souls," I added.

Catalina jerked up her head at my words. "You can fix this?" She almost sounded as if she was begging.

I sat on what had once been her son's bunk. "I don't think anyone can fix what happened. Tony didn't deserve the turn his life took."

She was suddenly suspicious. "How do you know his name?"

"I don't know what you were trying to do in the House of Mirrors, but you trapped us in a memory hole. We met Tony. He explained."

"But..." She swallowed hard.

"Not his ghost," I replied to her unasked questioned. "We met the Tony of your memory."

"I promised to get him out of here," she said. "That was the last thing I said to him. I swore I would do it ... and then the next call I got informed me he was dead."

"I'm sorry." I meant it. "Tony told us how you struggled."

"I failed him."

"Life failed him," I corrected. "Life failed you, too. You managed to sustain your life, but only because you recognized Tony's soul was trapped here. You were hanging on until you could free him."

"I don't care about me," she said, "but I made a promise."

"We're going to help you keep it," I said.

"How?" Her eyes were clearer than I remembered. "What are you going to do?"

"There's a loa downstairs. He can straddle two worlds. With that power, he'll be able to free Tony from his torment and send him over."

Catalina looked as if she wanted to believe me and yet she held back her excitement. "Why should I believe you?"

"Because, much like you, we don't want to cause any harm. We try to do good in this world. What's best for this world right now is to help you cross over, but you won't do that until Tony is at peace."

"He was a good boy." Catalina's throat clogged with sadness. "I should've been a better mother."

"You did the best you could with the hand that you were dealt," I countered. "Tony knows that."

"You didn't meet the real Tony," she said. "You met the Tony of my memory."

"You wouldn't have dedicated yourself to this purpose if he wasn't a good boy," I offered. "Let us help you."

"All I want to do is sleep," she admitted. "He needs to be at rest first."

"We're going to make sure you get your rest. We're going to make sure that Tony does the same. You need to trust me. You also need to stop kidnapping my friends."

"I already apologized to the pixie," Catalina murmured. "She accepted that apology."

"And Jackson?"

"The police detective? What did I do to him?"

"He didn't know what he was."

"A demon?"

Someone out on the main floor choked. "I'm not a demon! Why do people keep saying that?"

I smirked as Catalina's eyes went wide.

"Oh," she said. "He really didn't know."

"Nope, and he's a black-and-white guy. He can't reconcile the word 'demon' and being a force of good in this world. He's going to have an adjustment period."

"I'm almost sorry I won't be here to see it."

"Are you though?" I didn't believe her.

She shook her head. "I want my Tony. Then I want to go away."

I stood. "Let me get Baron in here. He'll fix things so you get exactly what you want."

"Finally." She smiled, and it wasn't even a bit terrifying. "I never thought to tap a loa, but it makes sense."

"Quite a few things are starting to make sense."

29
TWENTY-NINE

"You're going to do it."

Baron said it as if it had never been in question, as if I was the ludicrous one for acting surprised by his reaction.

"Me?" My eyebrows migrated toward my hairline. "How do you figure that?"

"I just said so." Baron was matter of fact.

"If this is about me volunteering your services without asking..." I trailed off, unsure how to continue.

He shook his head. "I'm used to bossy women. Why do you think I'm still besotted with Brigitte even though she set my underwear on fire a month ago? And a year ago ... and ten years ago." He grinned, showing off his ridiculously white teeth. "It's not fun to love someone who is easy. That's how you get bored." He leaned closer, as if he was about to grace me with a pearl of wisdom only a loa could love. "I've never been bored. No one will ever be bored with you either."

It was possibly the nicest thing he'd ever said to me, but I remained confused. "I've never done anything like this," I reminded him.

"I'll be here. I don't want her to keep hurting, and there's no reason for the boy to haunt this place the way he does. Can't you feel his sadness?"

I swallowed hard, glancing around. "This place is home to more than one type of sadness."

"We'll end some of it today. The rest will be here for someone else to end down the road. Every little bit helps."

I rubbed my cheek, uncertain. "I don't know how to do it."

"Of course you do." He sent me an odd look. "You're the new breed of loa. You have the same abilities I have, but you're even better. You can move forward with your abilities while we've all been stuck in the past for a very long time. Not only will you give birth to a new generation of loa, you'll force us along for the ride."

On a sigh, I nodded. "I'll do it. If I screw up, I expect you to clean up my mess for a change."

His smile was back, lightning quick. "Won't that be a fun change of pace?"

TWO HOURS LATER, WE WERE BACK AT the circus grounds. After two initial missteps the unfathomable had happened and my instincts kicked in. Finding Tony hadn't been nearly as difficult as I anticipated. Severing his ties to this world had been even easier. The last glimpse I'd seen of Catalina and her beloved son had involved a bright light and what I swore was the faint hum of music.

Then they were gone, and Alcatraz did feel lighter. It wasn't a happy place. I couldn't imagine any circumstances in which it would be. But the shadows weren't as dark, and the silence wasn't as deafening.

Nellie's first order of business upon our return was to crack some beers. Luke cranked up the music. Nixie tossed magic above our heads to illuminate the sky. And Mystic Caravan partied like we were back in New Orleans with Baron behind the bar.

He played with us, of course, laughing as Luke did something funny and readily accepting Nellie's drinking challenge as if it was a scene from the extended cut of *Lord of the Rings*. Several times, however, I caught him looking at me. He wasn't disappointed that I wasn't drinking enough. It was pride.

I'd done what he wanted, and I was stronger for it. Catalina was gone and the city was safe. In another week, the story of the skeletons would be skewed to the point there was very little reality in the tale. In ten years, people would swear that fifty people died and the skeletons were led by a woman in white.

I shifted on Kade's lap as I considered it, resting my head against his shoulder.

"What are you thinking?" he asked, brushing his lips against my forehead.

"I was thinking that maybe—and I'm just spitballing here, so don't get too excited—that maybe we could have two kids."

"Oh, really? What changed your mind?"

"It hasn't been changed yet," I warned him. "I'm just ... considering the possibilities."

He waited for me to finish.

"There's always more room to love," I said.

"There is," he agreed, taking a pull on his beer before returning it to the holder in the canvas chair we shared. "Two kids sounds nice."

"I'm not agreeing until after we've had the first one for at least a year," I cautioned. "We might find out that we're not geared to being parents to multiple kids."

He didn't look worried. He inclined his chin toward a chair on the other side of the fire pit. There, Nixie sat on Dolph's lap and excitedly ran through her adventure. Dolph listened with rapt attention, never looking away from her face.

"Love always finds a way," Kade said.

I watched Nixie and Dolph a moment longer, then glanced at Luke and Cole, who were showing Baron how to line dance. "I know I'm supposed to be nostalgic because this is our last few months on the road, but I'm so excited to actually build a home with you that I think I might burst."

"You can have whatever home you want to have," he said. "That's what I want for you."

"I want us to make those decisions together."

"I'm looking forward to that."

"It won't be long," I said. "We have Portland next."

"Then Kansas," he added. "Are you going to try to see Melissa there?"

Melissa was my former assistant. She'd been gung-ho when joining the circus, and a beaten down shell of herself when leaving. I'd given her a potion to forget the horrors she'd seen, and reports suggested that she'd used it.

"She won't remember us," I pointed out.

"You can still see her with your own eyes and make sure she's okay. I know you feel a lot of guilt where she's concerned, and the one thing we all learned from this trip is that guilt can ruin everything."

"Do you think I should?"

He shrugged. "You don't have to interact with her. Seeing her will probably be enough."

I closed my eyes. "Michigan won't be far behind Kansas. We're skipping the Eastern swing this year. Michigan is our last stop before heading to Florida for Christmas."

"And then on to happily ever after," Kade said.

"I think we're already at happily ever after."

"Is that so? Since when are you such an optimist?"

"I think, deep down, I've always been one. There were times I was too afraid to dream, but that's in the past."

"What do you want to dream about tonight?"

I whispered my suggestion so only he could hear.

He stood, swinging me into his arms as if he was a firefighter—or a fairytale prince—and did a half curtsey for the others. "We're heading to bed," he called out. "See you in the morning."

Baron looked over. "See," he said to me. "I told you that you weren't boring." He toasted us with a tilt of his beer bottle. "Have fun. We'll be living it up out here."

I would sleep well knowing they were safe and having fun. Not everyone got happy endings, but we were well on our way to ours, and that was all I needed tonight.

Made in United States
Troutdale, OR
08/21/2025

33866479R00152